POLLUTO

Polluto is published twice a year by Dog Horn Publishing. Visit polluto.com or doghorn.com to subscribe or for submission details.

Contents © the contributors.
Selection © the editors
All rights reserved, 2010.

Editor-in-Chief: Adam Lowe
General Editor: Victoria Hooper
Creative Director: Michael Dark
Designer: John Eckert

Dog Horn Publishing
6 Athlone Terrace
Armley
Leeds
LS12 1UA
United Kingdom

A copyright record for this title exists with Nielsen BookData/Bowker and the British Library.

If you enjoyed this title, please share it with your friends.

POLLUTO

EDITORS LETTER

Polluto 7 is here, and this time we tried something a little different – an open theme! With all restrictions lifted and the doors thrown open, we asked for worlds and characters without limits, for stories and poems that would amaze, excite and awe. We weren't disappointed. Gathering the best of the bizarre, the thoughtful and the shocking, we've put together an exciting issue, oozing with dark humour, zany satire, surreal horrors and subversive ideas.

Turn to page 9 for our first Editor's Choice winner – congratulations to Deb Hoag for her dark, delicious and larger-than-life story, for which she was awarded £200.

From bone-crushing lovers to a cross-dressing hitman, the night-soil man of the gods and sex-conditioning on squids, the lusts of the shadow-men and the dangerous desires of the diabolically large and seductively small, body-swapping, gender-swapping, exploration, transcendence and re-incarnation, machines that are gods and machines that are cats… some of the strangest and scariest authors are gathered here. Enter if you dare!   -Vicky

CONTENTS

Title	Author	Page
Molting Season	Aaron Polson	p.4
Phat is a Four-Letter Word	Deb Hoag	p.9
August Porman	Glen Krisch	p.20
The Feast of the Night-Soil Man	Jason Heller	p.31
Personification	Rhys Hughes	p.37
Mercy Park	J. Michael Shell	p.40
Eed and Yolk	Scott Morris	p.48
Mascara	Mark Wagstaff	p.55
Science Fiction Story	J.S. Watts	p.70
The Fragging of Captain Yorke	Jay Macleod	p.72
Web 3.0	Jay Macleod	p.74
Mechagnosis	Douglas Thompson	p.75
The Zoo	Kurt Newton	p.86
Infected	R.C. Edrington	p.89
Flesh Wound	R.C. Edrington	p.89
Scarred and Twisted	R.C. Edrington	p.90
So Alone	R.C. Edrington	p.91
Ensenada	R.C. Edrington	p.91
Monarch Butterfly	Claire T. Feild	p.92
Uncertainty	Claire T. Feild	p.92

POLLUTO

Reserved	Claire T. Feild	p.93
Rev. Thomas	Claire T. Feild	p.93
Merlot	Claire T. Feild	p.94
Loup-Garou	Claire T. Feild	p.94
The Envious Are Grateful Lovers	Colin James	p.95
Lust Enlightened	Matt Chase	p.96
This Mother's Son	Mark Brandon Allen	p.98
The Never-Ending War	Jonathan Greenhause	p.99
A Tale of Geophagy	Jonathan Greenhause	p.100
Submersion	Jonathan Greenhause	p.101
A Small Song Sprung From Inside	Jonathan Greenhause	p.102
Sebastian and the Stationary Sun	Jonathan Greenhause	p.103
My Doppelgänger's Most Recent Dream	J.J. Steinfeld	p.104
This Elaborate Plan	J.J. Steinfeld	p.105
It Isn't Relevant	J.J. Steinfeld	p.106
An Existentially Tottering Writer Confesses	J.J. Steinfeld	p.107
Out of His League	Bruce Golden	p.108
Now It Can Be Told	Fred Russell	p.111
Pavlovian Transitioning	Andrew Rivas	p.119
My Life as a Fish	Brian Edwards	p.127
Cat-H@ck	Alexander Hay	p.133
How Daphne Lost Her Hero	Sharon Reamer	p.148
Thug	Steve Mathes	p.152
The Making of True Confessional #7	Kek-W	p.160
Lemmings	Cris O' Connor	p.166
Blind Light	J.S. Watts	p.168
Lash Back Puritanical	Dave Migman	p.171

MOLTING SEASON

AARON POLSON

Ben began to molt on a Saturday evening after having 'the talk' with Traci. He cut most of his extra faces off with a folding utility knife he used as a stock boy in high school. The extra faces slipped neatly into gallon freezer bags– the premium kind with zippers. Ben stashed them in an old Amazon box, hidden under a stack of frozen pizzas in the deep freeze he inherited after his parents died in the car crash on vacation in Mexico. He kept the knife in his sock drawer.

For three days in a row, Ben cut and peeled off the extra faces. He missed work and refused to answer his phone.

When Traci rang his doorbell on Tuesday night, the knife was laying on his dresser. Ben was halfway up the stairs when he heard the clanging 'ding-dong' sound from the foyer. Fingertips explored his new face. His heart stuttered.

'Gimme a second!'

Ben hurried to his bedroom, folded the knife, and tucked it behind a pair of black dress socks. He glanced at the bathroom mirror and brushed off a small line of blood. If he waited until the skin was loose enough, until his face was ready to peel neatly, the knife was relatively useless. Removing the old faces became a rather quick and painless affair.

'Hey Ben,' Traci said when he opened the door. With her auburn hair pulled into a ponytail, Ben could easily trace the edge of her face– the line where chin met neck.

'Traci.' Ben smiled, working out the stiff dryness that sometimes lingered on a new face. 'I didn't expect you tonight. Don't you have work?'

She put a hand on his chest and looked into his brown eyes with her own. 'Not tonight. It's Tuesday. I'm off on Tuesdays, silly.' Traci paused, expecting that he would move, and squeezed past him into the living room when he didn't.

POLLUTO

Ben felt his face flush with blood. 'You could have called– I would have been ready…' He waved a hand to the living room.

'I wanted to do this face to face. We need to talk, Ben. I'm not worried about a few empty bags and magazines.' She collected a small pile and tossed them on his couch. 'Sit down, please?'

Ben scratched the corner of his chin. Something was wrong. His new face itched too much. He moved to the corner of the couch and sat. 'What's up?'

'I've got an offer. A job offer.' Traci rested her elbows on her knees and leaned forward, twisting her hands together in front of her.

'You have a job.'

'In Memphis.'

Ben felt the frown, but his face didn't move. He was afraid of cracking the fresh skin. 'Memphis?'

'I didn't really expect this one– I didn't go out looking for it. I've only known that it was a possibility for the past week.' She turned to him, raising her eyebrows. 'I would have told you earlier, but…'

'But?'

'We've not been…talking much lately.'

Ben unconsciously tugged at the edge of his face, pinching a bit of flesh between his forefinger and thumb. The face wasn't going to budge.

She continued, 'I wouldn't even think about moving if, well, if things between us were still passionate…still engaging. After the talk the other night…well, I guess I expected something from you.'

'Memphis…' Ben's eyes were unfocused, floating in his skull.

'Look. I love you, Ben. Really.' Traci pressed her hands together and leaned forward on the couch. 'But lately…you've been distant. We haven't talked in days. I tried to call– '

'I've been busy.' He rubbed the palm of his hand across his cheek.

'Right.' Traci's eyes swept slowly across the room, taking in the debris, the disordered piles of half-folded laundry, the stack of dirty plates on top of the TV. 'I talked to Sean. You haven't been to work in a couple of days.'

The faces, he thought, she knows I've been molting. 'I've been sick.'

She looked at him, her brown eyes like two drill bits trying to penetrate the bedrock of his face. Nothing. Traci's shoulders rose and fell with a deep, near-shuddering breath. 'I'm going to go.' She stood.

An involuntary twitch shuddered across his face. 'Please don't.' Ben tugged at the skin under his chin.

'I wish I didn't have to.' Traci moved to the front door and wrapped her fingers around the knob. 'Goodbye.'

POLLUTO

Ben's face tingled, burned. The new lips wanted to press against Traci's. He lunged from the couch and caught her arm. 'Please don't go.' His voice wavered, almost broke. He thought of the freezer bags stashed in the basement. The mouth holes flapped open and shut in his imagination like bits of cloth snapping in the wind. He shivered. 'I don't want to be alone.'

She turned. 'Ben...'

He kissed her. His new lips pressed against hers as his tongue explored her mouth. The new face was good– aggressive. Traci relaxed in his grip.

Ben's bedroom was drowned in dark blue when he woke hours later. In bed next to him, the sheets rose and fell with Traci's breath. He stared at the ceiling, imagining faces in the mix of shadows tossed there. The stubble on his chin felt surprisingly coarse under his fingertips. Ben rolled on his side and tugged the sheet from Traci's body.

Her skin shimmered like blue mercury in the twilight. She was naked since they made love. With one index finger he followed the curve of her hips past her breasts, across her collarbone, and to the slender nape of her neck. He turned his hand over and touched her chin with the back of his fingers. Traci shivered slightly at the touch. Ben paused for a moment, but she didn't wake.

Her face looked pale and unresponsive, slack and lifeless like those faces in the basement. He imagined peeling the skin back and finding a new face underneath. The edge of her jawbone looked frayed. Loose.

Traci, too?

After pulling the sheet back over her body, Ben slipped from the edge of the bed, pulled on his boxers, and crept from the room. In the kitchen, he poured a glass of water, and drank quickly, swallowing in large gulps. The house was warm, not hot by any means, but warm enough that Ben's mouth felt like a rough wad of cotton.

He had seen it, hadn't he? Traci was starting to molt, too. Would she understand? How could he make her understand?

At the top of the basement stairs, Ben flicked on the light switch. A single bulb hung in the center of a semi-finished basement room, and it sputtered to life. He started down the stairs. The cooler air crawled up his legs, across his stomach and chest, and wrapped around his neck as he descended, step by step, toward the sprawling concrete floor below.

The freezer, a white sarcophagus with silver-chrome Frigidaire in raised letters along the side, sat against the wall to Ben's right. It hummed with a deep, thrumming voice. It waited. He touched his own face again, another involuntary check. The skin was taut but no longer smooth– a fine layer of stubble coated his entire jaw now. With a click and a slight shudder, the freezer snapped off, entering energy saving mode.

Ben sucked in a deep breath through his nose. A damp, earthy odor lingered in his nostrils– a smell that spoke of the dirt pressing against all sides of his basement. He ran his tongue across his lips and stepped to the freezer. His hand rested against the lid with the thumb rubbing against the white rubber seal.

He waited, lost in the silence of the basement.

With a sudden push, Ben opened the freezer. Nearly invisible puffs of frosty air spilled out. He shoved aside the frozen pizzas, and pulled out the Amazon box. The lightness of the box surprised him. Too light for anything but a few thin layers of skin. With a whoosh-thump, the freezer lid fell back into place.

Ben placed the box on the floor and then sat with his back against the cool metal walls of the appliance.

After a minute's meditation, Ben unfolded the flaps of the box, lifted each bag one at a time, and laid them in a semi circle in front of him. The faces were iced over– stiff and white with empty eyes and mouth. Soundless, empty mouths. Each had a wrinkle of extra skin where the nose would protrude but was now forced flat. Two tiny nostrils poked though under the nose flap, echoing the larger eye gaps. There were eight in all. Eight old faces that Ben shed in a period of three days.

He couldn't even tell which one was first, and regretted his negligence in labeling them.

As they were, flattened and covered with a thin later of ice crystals, the faces looked the same, each a clone of the next. *Not quite clones.* Ben knew each had a flaw, a scar, maybe a slight wrinkle around the edge where the skin didn't quite meet flush with his neck. *Each imperfect.* His fingers walked along his jaw from left ear to right, feeling for such a defect.

The new face was fine, wasn't it?

He closed his eyes, rubbed his fingers together and remembered the loose flesh at the edge of Traci's face.

Yes, Traci too. Maybe, after she molted, they would stay together. They would be right together.

Ben carefully stacked the frozen packages back into the box, placed the box in the freezer, replaced the frozen pizzas, and dropped the lid in place. He ran a hand across the smooth cover of the freezer, thinking of the silver edge of his utility knife.

Retracing his steps, Ben quietly entered the bedroom, pulled open his sock drawer, and found the handle of his utility blade. He pushed the thumb action up and down a few times, watching the razor sprout from the handle and vanish again. A magic trick. Almost like trading one face for another, one Ben for another.

Traci sighed and shifted on the bed.

He moved closer and stood between her prone body and the wall. With his left hand, Ben gently tilted her face toward him, revealing the curved line where her chin met her neck to the moonlight filtering through the window. His fingers scrambled over the jawbone, searching. The knife trembled in his other hand.

Traci's eyes flickered open.

Ben yanked his hand away.

'Ben?'

He dropped the knife to the floor, and it hit the carpet with a whisper.

'Yes…here.'

'Come to bed, okay?' She reached into the dark bedroom, her lithe fingers searching for his hand like antenna.

Ben's stomach burned. He tried to smile, but the skin felt loose again.

'I can change…I've changed.'

'Come to bed, babe,' Traci said again. Her voice still sweet and quiet, but with more force. 'We can talk in the morning.'

Ben stooped and picked up the knife. Both hands shook now. The new face wasn't right. Sure, he kissed her, they made love, but…he wasn't ready to talk in the morning. 'Just…a minute. I have to go to the bathroom,' he muttered.

Traci murmured something low and indistinct and rolled toward the far wall.

In the bathroom mirror, a strange face stared back at Ben. He touched the skin of the face, but felt nothing. With trembling hand, he brought the knife to his jaw line and pressed into the flesh. A line of blood appeared immediately, and the pain shot to his fingertips, but Ben pushed the blade to the bone.

How many times would be enough? He thought as crimson drops stained the sink basin.

THE END

POLLUTO

PHAT IS A FOUR-LETTER WORD

DEB HOAG

Our 'Editor's Choice' Story

Sandy Dennis was a hell of a woman. She had flaming red hair, great waving cascades of it, nearly down to her waist. She stood six-foot, five-inches tall, and weighed in at a voluptuous, steamy 410 pounds.

She was the Reference Queen at the local library, rising from her specially designed steel-reinforced rolling chair to assist the student, the researcher, the occasional bon vivant by virtue of her vast knowledge and succulent laugh.

The head librarian had tried to shush her, early in Sandy's career of service, education, and enlightenment for the masses, and had the rare opportunity to witness the other side of the jolly fat woman. Sandy had fixed her with a haughty and poisonous glare. "You're telling me to shut up? Is that what you're telling me? You know I could squash you like a bug?" Sandy rose to her feet and advanced on her pitiful prey like a rutting walrus, until there was nothing left in the world but Sandy and her flaming hair. Sandy raised her hands, framing the other woman's graying head between them, making little pumping motions as if she meant to squash the older woman's cranium right on the spot.

Wise woman that she was, Sandy's supervisor fled in terror, pursued by Sandy's laughter. Sandy's good humor had been restored. The head librarian developed an anxiety disorder, and ended up taking an early retirement for an undisclosed medical condition. Her replacement was both wiser and more easy-going. He left Sandy alone except for an occasional offering of chocolate.

So, all in all, Sandy was happy - more than happy - delighted in her lubricious, porcine size, her thick armor against the slings and arrows of everyday life. She could give a shit about airplane seating and big-and-tall shops. She wore her hair teased and curled into a Byzantine bouffant

9

that added at least a foot to her height. She made up her face every day with the same care Botticelli had used for the pouting fleshy angels that rolled across his canvasses. She wore eyelashes made of mink and rhinestone.

Sandy also sewed, and made her own clothes, a rainbow of electric hues and shocking spandex creations that thrust her bulk directly in everyone's face. Fuck the polyester and the oversize tee-shirts with teddy bears and flowers. Sandy decked herself out in sequined cat suits and leather body stockings adorned with ribbons and feathers and chains and fringe.

For amusement, she viewed TV and ate. She watched the stock market and invested wisely. She took classes online and stretched her stunning intellect to its full potential. She wrote penetrating articles on a variety of obscure subjects for even more obscure journals of science and art.

Once in a while, she watched the weight shows and the exercise shows, and snorted with laughter or wept with pity, depending on her mood. She pitied their hosts and their targets - pitied their skinniness, their earnest weaselly faces, their weightless, powerless pomp and pump and prostitution of their desire for love and admiration, male and female both. What lies they told! What magnificent drivel! They knew nothing of true power, true sweaty, beaming, glowing, weighty, rosy beauty, and never would.

She would hoist a cake in a sad homage to their impoverished hips and scraggly buttocks and lumpy triceps. Their twiggy penises and hollow, chilly, dried-up vaginas. How much better her own fleshy folds, hot, wet, secret scents, acres of milk-white, rounded rolling flesh! Standing up, she would strip off her clothes and pirouette naked in front of the dozens of mirrors that adorned her apartment, reveling in her own curves, running pudgy hands over those floating, jouncing, jiggling rolls of fat, bouncing a little to make them dance under her fingers. Was ever a woman more beautiful than she?

She had followers, worshipers at the alter of her zaftig corpulent beauty, mostly skinny young men who would drive for miles just to gawk and mumble, blushing if she looked at or spoke directly to them. Often, one or two of them would wait till the library closed, and then trail wispily behind her, as mesmerized as if she had been the Pied Piper rather than the local reference librarian.

She thought of them as her Shadow men, and the most dedicated of these she called "Shadow King," not caring enough to learn his real name, but admiring his perseverance - and his excellent taste in women. When the mood struck her, she would hold court in a local club, where one Shadow man would text another to spread the word of her appearance, and soon the facility would be stuffed to the gills with her lackeys.

Occasionally, one of the lesser Shadow men would forget himself in public and get arrested for pounding his pud under a library table as he worshiped her, or even while shadowing her on the street or outside her apartment window. But for the most part the Shadow King was quick to quash any inappropriate expression of their adoration. Her reward for their devotion was a thin shade and a bright table lamp. And mostly, they were well-behaved, her admirers. The Shadow King especially. So she tolerated them, accepting the gifts they left her - tributes, really - outside the door of her first-floor apartment, on the long counter where she worked at the library.

The gifts told her something about how they saw her - chocolate, flowers, perfume, poetry from the Shadow King, jewelry, exotic body oils, the occasional whip or set of restraints, redolent of submission and desire. More occasionally, a ball gag or a vibrator, a gift begging to be used on the giver.

She kept the gifts in her sewing room, the most fetching displayed like trophies. It was amusing, and rather flattering, but left her largely unimpressed - Sandy was and always had been a loner, content in her own company, and not much needing or wanting that intimate connection with others which most humans seemed to crave. Still, she allowed them, in an absent way, to continue their worship, entertained by their blushes and their adoration and their clammy masturbating palms, their gifts and their sighs and their skinny, toothpick thighs and meager asses wiggling as they trailed her to her apartment, to the market, to the fabric store, to the library.

And the super of her charming apartment, she came to realize, viewed her much the same way, not making a peep at these odd young men who came and went and cluttered up the bushes, as long as she let him enter her precious apartment once a month to collect the rent, chat for a few moments, and get the barest glimpse of the gifts that lined her sewing room walls. It made his breath catch, those glimpses, and his face go a strange mottled red that amused her. She pictured him leaving her apartment and racing back upstairs to his own, to lock himself in the bathroom and fist his cock in his Vaseline-coated hands wishing it was Sandy's jiggling flesh he was pummeling until he came hard enough to spot the ceiling and the walls.

When she heard he got married, and she saw the skinny, pathetic wench who had claimed him, she laughed outright, immune to the younger, slimmer woman's glare. From the miserable look that bloomed on the super's face as his wedded status took root, she deduced he felt the same. It pleased her, knowing that he was laid so low by his miserable choice of brides. Surely he would have been better off to remain single and worship her from afar, groveling and moping for the briefest glimpse of her smile, her curves, her fair, fair skin and glorious bright copper hair.

It was her due, after all, was it not? She was the best, the most beautiful and fearless of women. A treasure totally unique, a glorious Goddess deserving of worship and reverence. A Goddess sadly in need of a garment that fully revealed and embraced her divinity. Grabbing a pad of paper and a pencil, Sandy got busy designing an outfit that would once and for all proclaim her transcendent, nascent perfection for all to see.

While she sewed, she ate. And ate. As shimmering material wound through her fingers and her sewing machine, her breasts, pendulous gardens of earthly delight, grew and expanded. Her thighs quivered and splayed and thickened, her rolling belly and jellied ass, those huge dimpled calves, those amply padded toes and fingers got larger and larger and larger.

She kept her minions busy fetching ribbon and thread and sequins and fancy silver buttons, and monitored her steadily increasing bulk with satisfaction as she sewed. Some of it she did by hand, as the work was too delicate and precise to be left to the vagaries of a machine, even a Singer 6000 with super-surge.

Finally, it was ready. She donned her garb, her Goddess-wear, her superhero gown of light and power, and stepped out of her apartment, out of her building, pausing on the steps to test her outfit on the group of Shadows crouched on the pavement waiting. Around her ankles and wrists coiled links of platinum and glittering stones that would have served as necklaces on lesser women. Her fingers were adorned with rings, gems glittered at her ears.

The first of the Shadow men to spot her shot to his feet, made a brief, gurgling noise, and swooned on the spot, the Shadow King barely catching him before he cracked his head on the pavement. Sandy smiled, satisfied. Then she rolled down the sidewalk, juggernaut of passion and purpose, and headed to the nearby club she sometimes graced with her presence.

All along the way, pedestrians cleared her path in awe and astonishment. Shimmering, translucent fabric clung to every curve and dimple of her 450 pound frame. In the street-lighted evening, nipples the size of a man's fist, dark as cherries, thrust defiantly against the soft breeze. The outline of her flaming pubic hair, barely escaping the deep and brooding cavern that delved between thighs and belly, was clearly visible. The Shadow King ran up to catch the waterfall train of her garment, and followed proudly, holding up the flimsy fabric with all the honor of a flag of state, lest it get soiled or snagged on Sandy's journey.

For the entire two blocks they walked, Sandy nodded graciously to those who, having scrambled out of her way, gawked and stared in her wake. She could feel the sidewalk tremble as she passed, quivering at the beat of her lovely feet, encased in butter-soft, size-eleven silver slippers.

By the time she arrived, a vast crowd of her followers had materialized, waiting at the door, and oohed and ahhed as she passed. The evening was a smashing success, and Sandy arrived home gratified and beloved, beneficent Goddess who turned on the steps to wave queen-like to her hordes in dismissal.

There was a note pinned to her door.

She took it down, even as she flipped the key in the lock. It was from the super of her darling, rent-controlled apartment, and she read between the lines as easily as she read the words on the paper. It was the Goddess outfit, she realized. He must have seen her leaving from his window, and had finally been driven around the bend.

Ms. Dennis *My Goddess, my Love*
The gawkers and rabble that hang around outside of your apartment can no longer be tolerated. *I am jealous to the point of rending my own flesh with your pinking shears, my darling, my heart, my love, and can no longer bear the agony. I would rather stab your sewing needles repeatedly into my eyes than go without you another moment.*

I must speak with you regarding this matter at once. Please come up to my apartment when you return home. *My jealous wife has been sent away. I must be alone with you, no matter what the cost.*

If we cannot reach an equitable solution to this problem, I am afraid I will have to ask you to seek housing elsewhere. *My lust knows no bounds, it cannot be contained! You must, you must be mine!*

Sincerely, Your Super
R. Kadaship

Sneering to herself at his boldness, Sandy closed her apartment door and went to the elevator. The super lived on the second floor, and she had no intention of compromising any of her hard-won poundage to a jog up the stairs.

She knocked on the door and when the super opened it, she was rewarded by the look on his face as he took in the vision of her complete loveliness and reeled back, gripping the door handle for support. He didn't actually swoon, but it was a near thing. "You've actually come! I do not believe my fortune! Please, please come in, gorgeous one!"

She accepted this as an invitation and swaggered through the door into an apartment redolent of curry and Lysol. "Where is your wife?"

The super swallowed and hurried forward, eyes clamped to her nipples with all the force of a greedy mouth. "She's gone out. Lydia had some errands to run, and will be several hours."

"Did she know we were meeting? Did you tell her you left me a note requesting that I come up?" asked Sandy, almost coyly. She trailed a finger across the corner of a cluttered table and looked at the super from under a thick fringe of midnight-blue eyelashes.

"No, no," he said, breath catching. "This is business. I told her nothing."

"Oh, good," replied Sandy, stepping closer. "I'm so glad you're a discreet man, Mr. Kadaship. This could be so . . . awkward . . . otherwise."

She could see his Adam's apple bobbing as she got close enough to touch, and as if helpless to stop himself, his hands flapped at the end of his scrawny arms and he reached, up, up to stroke her silk-clad nipples, and she marveled at his daring.

"A man could drown in your garden, and never question the cost," he said breathlessly.

She moved slightly, allowing his skinny penis to ride up and down against her thigh, and watched his eyes glaze with pleasure. She felt as if she were a St. Bernard, all bulk and muscle, being humped by a Chihuahua.

"There's something I've always wanted to do with you, Mr. Kadaship," she said, as the lust built and flooded his eyes.

He never took his eyes from her huge, taut nipples as he responded with a sound that was less than a word, a simple humming note of inquiry.

She took half a step back, removing her nipples from his reach, her thigh from his dick, and he blinked, eyes finally refocusing on her face. "What is that, my princess?"

"Sit with you," she said.

He blinked some more. "Ah. Sit. Yes, of course. Please, what was I thinking, not to offer a seat to the most lovely, the most riveting woman in this universe?" He gestured toward the ugly plaid couch that took up much of the living room.

"Oh, perhaps I misstated myself," Sandy said, staying where she was.

"I beg your pardon?"

"I said sit with you. I should have said, sit on you." And that was exactly what Sandy did. She noted with both satisfaction and surprise that as he hit the floor, her on top, as his ribs cracked and shattered, puncturing heart and lungs, as blood welled and trickled from his ears and the corner of his mouth, his lips curled up in soft smile and his body jerked in orgasm - the last he would ever know.

As she considered what to do next, Sandy rocked back and forth on the increasingly boneless meat-sack beneath her pantiless buttocks. Just to see what it would feel like, she gave a little bounce, feeling more bones break and grind as she did so. She climaxed, a flash of blistering heat that bent her double and made her teeth snap together in shock, and her mouth formed a small, soft 'o' of surprise and delight.

Finally, Sandy stood, looking down at his flattened frame, the stain of jism on his cotton trousers, with fondness. She leaned over to give a final stroke to his engorged and bulging face. "I'm so glad we were able to have this talk and come to an understanding, Mr. Kadaship. I'm so glad you've decided to let me stay in my apartment and not make any more fuss about my lovely Shadow men. Thank you."

And Sandy sauntered back down to her own quarters, to await the sounds of the wife returning, the screams of horror and denial, the flashing lights and thrilling sirens of the police. Maybe she wouldn't watch TV tonight at all. Life itself was sometimes entertaining enough.

◊

It didn't take long for the police to come knocking on her door. Sandy had changed clothes and stripped off her makeup, hair slicked back in an unflattering, lifeless tail when she opened the door.

The cop's eyes widened slightly as he took in her mountainous body, and she could see the dismissal in his eyes. He asked her a few questions nonetheless, but they were by rote - how long had she been home, what had she seen, or heard that might pertain to a death upstairs. He had already forgotten her, except possibly as a joke to repeat to his friends and co-workers, she saw, by the time he'd turned away.

Good karma for her divine nature, she supposed, she had drawn an idiot right out of the box.

Nearly two weeks went by before there was another knock at the door, and this cop was no idiot. His eyes also widened at the sight of her, but it was appreciation, not dismissal, and he stepped inside without an invitation.

"I was on my way out," said Sandy, with a carefully chosen hint of annoyance. "What can I help you with, officer?"

"Detective. I'd like to talk to you about the death of your super."

He walked further into the apartment, caught sight of the trophies displayed in her sewing room, and whistled. In his sharp eyes she saw swiftly dawning comprehension. Now she was annoyed.

She stepped around him to close the door before he could enter her inner sanctum. Regret on his face, he turned to her.

"We've turned up some additional evidence in the case."

"What's that?"

He extracted a small plastic bag from a pocket and held it up for her to see. Inside, curled a single white thread.

She squinted and shook her head. "I don't get it."

"It's a very modest thing, actually. Plain white cotton. From a pair of woman's panties."

Uneasy, she shifted, remembering the resounding orgasm she'd had riding the squashed body of her super, and a blush of guilt crossed her ample cheeks. Then she shook her head. She didn't wear panties, Goddamn it. What was he up to?

He'd watched her expression go from alarmed to irritated to wary. He stepped closer, dangerously so. "Let me see your panties, Ms. Dennis. The ones you're wearing right now."

She stared back at him, alarmed again. "I'm not wearing any. White cotton, I mean."

"In that case, I've brought some that you can use." He reached into yet another pocket to pull out a pristine pair of women's white cotton panties, still in the package. As she watched, he opened the plastic and pulled them out. They were as big as a pillowcase.

The truth flashed through her. He too was a Shadow man, although bolder than most, and she smiled, knowing, even as she considered her options. "You live dangerously, Detective."

"Not that dangerously. I've got a gun. And, I'll stay on top."

"How did you know?"

"My mother was a big woman."

Slowly, she reached out to take the panties from him, and began to take off her clothes.

◊

It wasn't so bad, as sex went, she supposed, except that it wasn't her idea. She felt a stunning slap of arousal at being his object - his toy. It was as humiliating as it was stirring to be a helpless victim of his lust. He insisted on making use of the various toys and appliances she had on display in her sewing room, in order to make sure the event would be consummated to his liking, rather than hers. Like the super, the detective had underestimated her. While he'd lusted after her phenomenal beauty, he had discounted her lethality, her deadly focus. He had no idea of the magnificent brain that whirled behind her smooth white forehead.

In shame, she put away her magnificent new Goddess gown. Could she deserve to wear it when she allowed herself to be so subjugated? Her mortification, ever new and endlessly nuanced, kept her tranced and docile for a good two weeks. She lost five pounds.

But it didn't take her long to shake off the initial shock of her violation, and realize that, like the cotton thread he'd tried to trick her with, his threat was illusion. He couldn't tell anyone about their illicit, garish, humiliating encounters, about how she looked with a ball gag in her wide, furious mouth, on hands and knees as he rode her from behind and still claim her as a suspect. He knew it, long before she did. Even entering her building was an event he handled with surreptitious skill; he came in through the alley, a basement entrance that was all but forgotten since the time of daily coal deliveries had passed. She doubted even her awed minions realized he was in her apartment, subjecting her to every depraved whim his debauched brain could come up with.

And he had not wanted anyone to suspect her, to threaten the fleshy Nirvana he had found. His report to his superiors suggested that the death had been the result of a Bananastani turf war, the super crushed by the ancient torture technique of placing a plank of wood on a man's body and piling rocks on it until the victim was crushed. It was an impressive theory. No one asked where the rocks had come from. Or gone.

No one but the detective ever considered that the object used to crush the super to hamburger was a human body.

He never relaxed his guard when pleasuring himself on her; but eventually he relaxed his mind, and Sandy was a patient woman. He began to tell her about his cases, criminals caught, puzzles solved. She listened as he talked, her fascination not a feigned thing, because she knew her salvation lay in there somewhere.

Finally, the opportunity presented itself.

A series of stakeouts, involving drug dealers, multiple murder suspects and the same Bananastani gang he'd blamed for the super's murder. He blathered on so endlessly about how boring it was to be on stakeout that she decided to give him a little excitement.

She probably could have sprung the trap with a simple phone call to one of the gangsters involved, but she really felt like she owed him a more personal touch. So late one evening she got up, carefully making up her face, her hair, donning her Goddess-wear, her jewelry, her best ermine lashes, and sauntered out her front door. The worshipers gathered there scrambled to their feet, watching as she walked down the steps, across the street, down the sidewalk.

When her adoring minions made to follow her, she turned and raised a hand, nails painted a sultry plum. They came to a halt, all piling up together line a gang of Larrys, Curlys and Moes, and she smiled, loving them. "I vant to be left alone," Sandy said, thinking fondly of Garbo and the many delightful hours they had spent together late at night in the flickering television light.

"But what about your train?" asked the Shadow King, in a plaintive voice.

She frowned, her lovely brow creased ever so slightly. "Very well. You may come. You alone," she said, holding up a hand to stop the onrush of eager would-be train carriers. "But you must wear a blindfold. I want my privacy tonight." She thought of the weapon she had packed in her bag, and smiled, taking it out, wrapping it around his flushed face, tying it so that he was blinded indeed. When she was done, she leaned forward and whispered in his ear, so that no one else could hear, "If you do not survive this night, will you die a happy man, to know you have my love and gratitude?"

The Shadow King's bottom lip quivered, then firmed. "Yes, light of my life."

"Very well, then. Come." And they set off in search of the detective, he carefully holding her train off the ground and she using it like a leash to turn and steer him in the direction she wished to go.

Finally, they arrived in the vicinity of the dingy warehouse the gang used for headquarters. It was nowhere near as well illuminated as the streets around her own darling sanctuary. She took her train, and her weapon, back from the Shadow King, instructing him to wait on his knees, eyes closed until her return. Happily, he complied. Strolling down the dark street, she made out the detective's dingy sedan, and swaggered over to stick her head in the window. He jumped a foot when she did, so focused on the buildings and its inhabitants that he hadn't noticed her approach. Foolish man, poor detective. Her lip curled in contempt.

"What are you doing here?" he said, scowling.

"Why, darling, I brought you something to help pass the time," she replied, and knotted her weapon in both hands. Before he could ask what she had brought him, she whipped her arms around his head and pulled tight, jerking the plain white cotton with such force that it nearly garrotted his rattling throat. She pulled tighter and tighter, as his feet and hands shook in a death dance, and his eyes bulged wildly. When she was sure he was dead, and then some, she calmly removed the cloth from around his throat and placed it back in her bag. She returned to the Shadow King, waiting giddily for her return, and rewarded his patience with a soft kiss on the mouth that nearly undid him.

"I rather think I like you, darling. I may be able to find a place for you on the mat outside my door, rather than amongst my bushes. Would you like that?"

She stroked his delicate cheek and watched his eyes fill with tears of gratitude. It was enough. She would let him live. She picked up her train and twitched it back into his waiting hands, then covered his eyes as before and headed home.

◆

It was another two weeks before a new super was assigned to her apartment building, but a building can't be expected to run itself, and personally, she felt it was rather overdue. Soon enough, he made his way to her door, and when the Shadow King came to let her know they had company, she emerged from her sewing room in a cheery outfit of scarlet leopard-print and faux-fur trim.

He was already frowning as she stepped into view, but she didn't miss the flash of lust that crossed his face when his eyes rose to her massive breasts. The world, she was discovering, was filled with small men. Small men who yearned for big, big women. "Ms. Dennis. I'm here to talk to you about that crowd of perverts that follows you around everywhere and crowds the bushes at night. Not to mention the one who sleeps on your doorstep."

She bounced, oh-so-slightly on her toes, making her breasts jiggle, and underneath the scarlet leopard print, she could feel the plain white cotton panties she wore caress her like loving hands. She batted the thick ruby eyelashes that fringed her eyes.

"Why, Super. Have my boys been annoying you? I'm sure we can work something out that . . . satisfies . . . us both. Why don't you come in, so we can discuss the matter?"

She shut the door on the Shadow King's wary face, giving him an absent as she did so, then turned her attention back on the man standing before her. "I was just about to have a cup of tea. Would you like to have a seat in my sewing room?"

THE END

AUGUST PORMAN

GLEN R KRISCH

A story from Glen Krisch's collection Through the Eyes of Strays: Misanthropes and Misfits, *due out in 2011 from Dog Horn Publishing*

August sat behind his desk in his cubical at the Regional Department of Inanimate Object Placement. File folders for cases-pending stood in unstable towers in front of him. He stared at a thin folder, trying to stay focused. The words "personal and confidential" were stamped across the folder. He thought of the rest of the office: the bare walls, the lack of windows, the central processor humming in the center of the office. Who else would see the enclosed information? No one. If someone did happen across the file, chances are that person would be illiterate.

Punies were everywhere and without the Punies, the economy would collapse. Punies didn't work; almost no one worked anymore. Not in the traditional sense of the word. Nanotech took care of the mundane 9-5. Punies spent their days searching for easy money to sustain their own lives, by suing people who might have done them wrong. The slightest wrong meant money, money in the form of punitive damages, mostly. Illiteracy was the surest way for a Puny to make a living, an insurance policy against the possibility of a court judge assuming the Puny "victim" had any understanding of the most common life tasks.

Inanimate object placement was a hot new revenue stream for the Punies to troll. Litigation involving inanimate object placement had quadrupled over the last five years. August was the lone human working cases in his regional office. The rest of the work was up to the machines. It wasn't a difficult job, and August rarely felt challenged intellectually or otherwise, but he went home every night with a sense of pride and accomplishment. Most people didn't understand August or his eccentric ways.

August opened the file folder in front of him. He skimmed through the legalese to raise the facts to the surface. It was his job to mediate the civil suit. If he could settle the differences between the two litigants, no court would have to get involved. He read cases like this every day. In this particular case, Mr. Stuben was suing his neighbors, Mr. and Mrs. Van Pelt, over several pieces of gravel that had somehow left the Van Pelt's driveway and had somehow obscured the road. Mr. Stuben was suing because he felt the Van Pelts were endangering the lives of the Stuben family, their dog George, and any other unwitting citizen who might:

...slip on the above-mentioned obstruction, or come into some dangerous contact with the obstruction through unknowingly falling on said obstruction, being struck with said obstruction, or through unwittingly swallowing said obstruction.

August glanced at a handful of snapshots attached to the file. Six pieces of gravel of medium size sat near the edge of the road in front of the Van Pelts's property. Each picture was from a different angle to document the inherent danger. A video presentation directed by an up and coming film auteur also accompanied the file, but August pushed it aside.

August knew Mr. Stuben and how he worked. The Van Pelts had just won a case in which they had sued a national super market chain. The smell of the household cleaner's aisle at one of the chain's stores had offended them. After three months of intense argument the Van Pelts won a settlement that included a small monthly stipend, an unlimited supply of household cleaners (the unscented variety), and an undisclosed amount of company stock. So now, Mr. Stuben probably needed household cleaners for his own use. He figured he would get a piece of Van Pelts' pie by suing over the gravel. August felt like crying.

Even though he was the only worker at the Regional Department of Inanimate Object Placement, he still fought back his frustration. The only other worker was the central processor that continued to hum rhythmically. His name was Herbert. His ceaseless simmering noise caused August to contemplate the stacks of file folders with droopy eyes.

"August, what are you thinking about?" Herbert asked from the next cubicle.

"Did you say something?"

"I asked what you were thinking about."

"Nothing in particular."

"Why aren't you being honest with me, August? Did I offend you?" Herbert had become somewhat nosey since his latest software upgrade. It brought his Human Interaction Efficiency Quotient up to national standards.

"No, you didn't offend me."

"Then what were you thinking about?"

"Nothing."

"It had to be something. During the last four minutes, the temperature in your cubical has risen by almost four tenths of a degree. Such a sudden increase in temperature, considering the environmental controls that the R.D.I.O.P employs would have to be linked to some frustration or other stress on your part. So which is it...?"

"Hmm?" August tried to ignore Herbert's annoying mechanical voice.

"So which is it...? So which is it...?"

August turned on the power to his brand-new Apple Evolu-tunes player. The newest musical composition, which he started a couple days prior, fell upon his ears like a deep feather pillow drowning out the droning Herbert. When he began the tune, it had started with a generic accompaniment of subtle strings, a placid flute and the undulations of a stoic guitar. From there, the Evolu-tunes player keyed in on August's chemical response to the song, and began a near subliminal rendering of the music to his personal tastes. It was a feedback loop fed by endorphin levels, blood acid levels, heart rate, eye dilation, synapse firing sequences, follicle reaction, glandular production, metabolic fluctuation and intestinal absorption. After two days, and the increasing stress that had weighed on August during that time, the music had morphed into a thundering brass calamity with undertones of manic crashing and climatic operatic singing.

Herbert had control over his own volume.

"Now how can you concentrate with such a ruckus?" Herbert would have screamed if that were an option in his new software upgrade. His voice coil echoed with faint static from his increased volume.

August glared at the cubical partition separating him from his co-worker, mashing his fingers against his temples as he tried to fight off an oncoming headache. He considered the open file in front of him, and then slammed it shut.

"August...?"

The Apple player rose through varied scale sequences, searching for a happy medium August's body chemistry would approve. Chanting opera singers sang in Italian about the tragedy of loss and miserable loneliness.

"August, please respond to my inquiries. I need to know if you're listening to me."

"Can't you see that I'm listening to my new song? If I wanted to talk to you, then I would respond to you. Got it!"

"Well, first of all, I technically can't see you--you're in your cubicle and I in mine. I just wanted to inform you of the fact that your lady friend is on her way up the elevator as we speak. Wait, she's not in the elevator any longer..."

There was a knock at the office door, loud enough for August to realize that his music was blaring through the office. He felt somewhat guilty, but then realized there were no other people in the building to disturb. Since he really didn't want to see Jolena, he considered turning the volume up. Instead, he turned off the Evolu-tunes player and made his way to the door.

"Jolena, love." August patted a dry kiss against her cheek as she entered the office. Their son, Conroy, followed behind, carrying his new toy steam gun. He entered the room in a methodical military amble, checking nooks and shadows for enemies to vanquish.

"Conroy, how're you? Having a good day?"

With an anger-furrowed brow, Conroy shushed his father, his index finger extending vertically across his lips.

"Jolena, we have to do something about him! When I was his age, I would've been grounded from the Net for that kind of attitude!"

"Calm down. You shouldn't talk about stuff like that. Just because your parents abused you, doesn't mean you have to take it out on Conroy."

"Okay, okay. I guess I just over-reacted." August ran his fingers through his rapidly graying hair. He refused to have any of his genes tampered with, so he showed all thirty-eight of his years on his face. Jolena was actually older than he was by almost three years, but she looked as fresh as she did at twenty.

"Well, even so, I think you should talk to Dr. Marchant again about your hostility."

"Jolena!"

"Not another word, August."

From Herbert's cubicle, his tinny voice joined in, "I agree wholeheartedly, Jolena. It sounds like August needs a change in his sedation routine."

"I don't have a sedation routine and I don't need a sedation routine, for your information. Mind your own business. Don't you have any work to do?"

"Not at the moment. I've been idling for the last hour and a half. The regulation litigation that recently sided in favor of the Regional Computer Workers Union #29101-03, allows me to work without speed regulation. Through multiple double-blind case studies, it was found that controlling the speed at which the RCWs work is detrimental--"

"I don't really care about your work speed! Just shut up!"

"August, I've never heard you speak like this before. You must be under a lot of stress," Herbert said.

"Herbert, I'm sorry about August's behavior. He has been under a strain lately," Jolena said, peeking her head over the partition.

"Jolena, merely having the joy of your presence is more than adequate for me to withstand such torment." Somehow, Herbert's voice carried a snide tone.

August didn't hear Herbert finish speaking. He had already rushed out the office door, waving his hands wildly about his head in frustration. When Jolena finally tracked him down in the vacant 79th floor worker's lounge, August was slowly tapping his forehead against a cool cinderblock wall.

"Honey, I think we need to hire a Search Agent," Jolena mentioned as tactfully as possible.

"Is that all you can talk about? Nothing else up there troubling you?" He pointed at her grayless head.

"Be nice. I'm just thinking of what's best for us. Our future."

"I'm not going that route. I'm a Porman, and Pormans work for a living. Don't you understand?" He turned from the cinderblock, his bloodshot eyes full of desperation.

"But a Search Agent would free up your time. You could spend more time with your family. We need you. No more working thirty hours a week. I was at the Procreation Enclave today, and all the women were shocked that you work so much. No one knew of anyone working more than ten hours a week. And no one *didn't* have a Search Agent."

"Then what's the point?" his voice was weak, a mile away.

"What point?" Her face was taut with concern.

"My point exactly."

"I'll never understand you, August Porman."

An explosion broke through their conversation as Conroy shattered a flowerpot near the window ledge with his steam gun. His parents both looked in his direction.

"Conroy! You are in big trouble, young man!"

"August!" Jolena stood with her fists perched on her hips.

"Yes... Urghhhh... I... I'm sorry. Conroy, I didn't mean..."

◊

August sat on a bed in a room barely bigger than the queen-size mattress beneath him. The wall in front of the bed was a video wall, but he had not turned it on. He didn't feel like watching pornography, and didn't feel like asking Raney (or was it Linda?) who sat next to him on the bed if she wanted to, either. He was fully clothed, but Raney--yes it was Raney, Linda was her twin and fuller through the hips--was half bare. Her dark skin contrasted with the white lingerie she wore. She twirled a curl of hair over her finger. Over and over.

They both stared at the black screen in front of them, having not spoken a word since they entered the room together. August didn't like the Procreation Enclave anymore. Sure, when he was younger it filled his desire to sleep with different partners, but his current mental state didn't veer too often in that direction.

His only reason for bringing Raney to the procreation room was to bother Jolena. At one point or another since joining the Procreation Enclave, August had slept with all of the woman members, but Jolena didn't like Raney, or Linda for that matter. They were more attractive than Jolena, their eyes deeper, their legs longer, and so in Jolena's eyes, they were off limits for August.

When Jolena had seen August grab Raney, she probably went off with the nearest man to the nearest procreation room. Lately, Jolena stripped August's nerves raw, and because of that, he hoped she picked an unattractive mate. Then maybe she'd get pregnant again and have an unattractive baby. They both shared the common bond of raising Conroy, but maybe someone else would want to share the burden of having a child with Jolena. If someone else could get Jolena pregnant, August would be a happy man.

Infertility had increased over the last couple of centuries to its current near-perfection. Since some studies had proven that increased sexual partners had a tendency to boost fertility, people formed Procreation Enclaves. Approved members congregated in bedroom-centric buildings, watching pornography, trying to make babies, regardless of parentage. The Procreation Enclave was August's country club.

"Raney?"

"Huh?"

"Do you have a Search Agent?"

"Actually, Marcus and I have two. We thought with the addition of little Jimmy to our family we needed more than one. They work part-time so they can cover more ground. We also don't have to provide them with benefits and insurance."

"They just get their commissions?"

"Yeah." She sounded surprised that he was actually trying to start a conversation.

"Hmm," he rolled over to her and slid a hand into her brassiere. She reacted to his touch, and inched closer to him. She was nice in every possible way, but he was still unmoved. He pulled away and twined his hands together behind his head.

She seemed frustrated that he pulled away. "Are you thinking about adding another? If you are, I highly recommend it."

"We don't have any."

Raney sat up, looking at him fully for the first time since they entered the room. "How can you not have a Search Agent?"

"I work in an office."

"And that's it?"

"Yeah, that's it."

"But... but don't you have bills or lawsuits to pay off?"

"Sure, but you know, I've been working at R.D.I.O.P. for fifteen years now. Government workers get the best compensation and benefits. It's not that bad, all things considered."

"Does your insurance at least cover sedation routines?" She was beginning to sound interested.

"I'm not sedated."

"You're... not sedated?"

"Never been, never will."

She started to push away from him, to reach for her clothes. "I can't believe I'm in a procreation room with a non-sedated worker!" she nearly screamed. "For God's sake, we've slept with each other before. You should have told me. Isn't there something in the Enclave's charter about this?"

August could tell even with her back to him that she wore a suggestive smile and she was actually toying with him. Maybe she realized August was someone a little different from anyone else she was using to get her pregnant. Maybe that uniqueness would make his genes more viable.

That's what brought August out of his funk. Her slight unwillingness, but with heated curiosity just below the surface. He gently ran the tips of his fingers across her neck, down the length of her spine, then back up again. She stopped grabbing for her clothes and arched her back at his touch. August unfastened the catch of her brassiere and found the will to try to procreate.

◊

August brushed the hair away from Conroy's eyes as he tucked him in from the night.

"Daddy?" His dark, sunken eyes seemed to plead with August. He always got upset when August readied to leave for the night.

"Yes?"

"I'm sorry I broke that plant with my gun today."

"It's okay. I'm sorry I yelled at you. It's not like anyone ever went to the employee lounge to enjoy that plant."

"Am I going to be okay?"

"Don't worry about it. Everything's going to be fine. Back to normal in no time." August leaned over and kissed his son's forehead, then turned away and left the room. Tears weighed down his eyelids as he closed the door behind him.

Jolena met him on his way down the hallway.

"Trudy, you know, from the Enclave, she gave me a couple of names--"

"Why do you always bring this up?" August cut her off.

"How do you expect us to survive without a Search Agent?"

"We're doing fine. You have this nice house that's paid for. Conroy goes to the best schools. What else is there?"

"We didn't even have Conroy sequenced!"

"That was not a money issue, but a moral one. I didn't want him tampered with. It's not natural."

"You mean, like me? So *I'm* not natural? Well, I was good enough for you to have sex with!"

"You're missing the point. I want to support us. Just me. We don't need someone searching for lawsuits to spring on others."

"But with no one looking out for us, we're missing out on so many opportunities."

"Don't you find it slightly odd that most people make it through life preying on the weakness of others?"

POLLUTO

"That's just the way it is. That's the way it's always been."

"Whatever. I have to go. I have to be up early tomorrow. Herbert's processor is being upgraded and I have to be there."

August put on his coat. He wanted to slam the door when he left, but knew Conroy needed his rest.

◊

August was back at the R.D.I.O.P., the towers of cases-pending files worked back down to a reasonable level. Somber ancient rock 'n roll seeped from the Evolu-tunes player. Over the last few weeks, he had spent most of his time in the office. Herbert's efforts at trying to hold down a conversation with him grew more seldom with each passing day.

"Herbert?"

"Uh... yeah..." Herbert said after actually pausing. August hadn't initiated a conversation with his coworker in over a month.

"How much can a man handle...?" August said, his voice weak.

"Um... August, what do you mean?"

"What are the tolerance levels for the everyday human male? What I'm talking about is kind of like metal fatigue. When do humans suffer from metal fatigue? When do we become brittle under the weight of repeated stress?"

"I don't think I understand... Hmm... The structural integrity of the human anatomy differs greatly from one example to the next."

"So the result of repeated stress is hard to predict?"

"We can assume so."

"Herbert?"

"Yes, August?"

"Thanks."

"You're welcome."

August got up from his chair and tidied up his work area.

"Going someplace?"

"Yeah. I need to talk to someone."

◊

The chair at the doctor's desk pinched August's back and would have been downright intolerable, but August barely knew where he was anymore. He sat in a room the size of an airport hanger with one doctor's desk following another in neat, symmetrical rows. Most of the hard plastic chairs were filled.

"I'm sorry, but I can't help you, Mr. Porman," Dr. Marchant said. He was a computer terminal with a human face with which patients interacted. August could see a ridge of white collar that surrounded the computer-projected doctor-head. Dr. Marchant wore a white lab coat to dress the part, to make his patients feel more at ease.

"Why not? You're my doctor, right? I've brought my family to see you for the past fifteen years. Now you say you can't help me?" August leaned forward in the chair, hiding his

27

facial expression behind the small dividers that separated one patient from the next.

"Euthanasia is illegal. My Hippocratic Oath binds me. Now, I know you've been suffering from tremendous stress, especially for someone without a sedation routine, but there are alternatives. There's an Emotive Suppressor that's new to the market, maybe I can prescribe--"

"No. No other drugs. Unless you give me a fatal dose," August said, nearly pleading.

"I think you're being melodramatic, Mr. Porman."

"Melodramatic? How can you say I'm being melodramatic? Under the circumstances, I think I'm more than adequately level headed. Jesus Christ, my son has leukemia!" August stood abruptly, pushing the chair away from him with the backs of his legs.

"And we could have fixed that when we sequenced him, but at the time you said you didn't want us to. Now, I'm afraid, it's too late."

"Damn it, this should have never gotten this far! Leukemia! My son is dying from an extinct disease. How the hell is that possible?"

"Since you haven't been sequenced either, there was obviously the risk of passing something on to your children." The pixilated Dr. Marchant nodded to an observation window high on the wall next to him. "Now, Mr. Porman, let's discuss this rationally."

"I will not be rational! Not until you tell me you can save my son!" August pressed his palms into the desk and brought his face within inches of Dr. Marchant's computer screen. As August spoke his volume lowered, but his intensity grew, "Tell me Dr. Marchant, where did you get your medical license? And another thing, why am I talking to a computer and not a human being? Where is everyone anymore? We live in a world where anyone can do anything they want, there are no limitations of time or resources, and yet as we speak, my six-year old is in bed dying of a disease that has been extinct for a hundred years! He's withered away to half his weight. You know how hard it is to even look into his face and not break down and start mourning for him right now? Do you know how that feels, Dr. Marchant?" August paused, catching his breath. He looked around and he had an audience. He found it odd that the dozens of patients surrounding him simply looked bored, not sick. Not a single sick person amongst the whole lot of them.

"Of course you can't know what that feels like. No one knows what to do for him, and all you can say is that it's my fault for not having him sequenced." August fell back into the plastic chair and buried his face in his hands. Sweat rings soaked his shirt and tears began to fall from between his fingers.

"August, maybe we can run some more tests."

He looked up from his hands. Three large men dressed in white starched suits entered from a side door and approached Dr. Marchant's cubicle. The only sounds in the hanger-sized room were August's voice and the clicking of the orderlies' shoes on the gleaming white tile.

"Whoa, you're getting so advanced. Now you call me by my first name. Your bedside manner is unbeatable! I feel so much better! Thank you so very much!" August said. He stood, glaring at the doctor. He walked past the orderlies before they felt too needed.

Dr. Marchant spoke as August walked away. "Hmm... Well, August, anytime you need anything... something to make you feel more even-keeled, something to take the edge off, you just let me know! Say hello to Jolena for me!" Dr. Marchant hadn't received the latest human interactive upgrade concerning sarcasm.

◈

Conroy gripped August's neck as he carried his son down the street, but his arms lacked the strength to stay there. August held him tightly against his chest, trying to make up for all the times he had felt too uncomfortable to show his affection for his son over the years.

"Where we going, Daddy?" Conroy said with a raspy-weak voice.

"We're going to go live like people used to live."

"Oh." Conroy rested his head on his father's shoulder and began to doze lightly.

August bumped into a woman as she exited a clothing store. Her Search Agent immediately began speaking detailed notes into a recorder before taking an official statement from his traumatized employer.

August paid no mind and continued down the sidewalk. Punies were everywhere, on the prowl, their Search Agents clogging the city streets, acting as guides and translators for their employers. For the most part people maintained the integrity of everyone else's personal space, but when someone made the mistake of making contact with another, a lawsuit was inevitable.

"People used to hunt their food, people used to make their clothes, people used to build their homes..." August spoke into Conroy's ear, even though he was asleep. "People used to build fires and knew how to use them: they cooked with it, they kept warm with it, they gilded nighttime skies with it..."

Conroy pulled in closer. August felt like he was carrying a bundle of twigs wearing a light brown wig.

"People used to have actual families and didn't have to rely on a Procreation Enclave," August continued speaking, his voice getting softer. A passerby seemed curious that August was carrying an unconscious child, but she quickly averted her eyes as to not offend. August made his way to the downtown arboretum. Trees from various parts of the world lined the well-manicured path. Not a single piece of gravel was out of place.

"People were named after namesakes, people were born with birthrights, people were given nicknames." August crested a steep hill without Conroy stirring. Under a sprawling oak tree, August eased himself down to the lush carpet of grass.

"I'm sorry, Conroy, but this is the most natural area I could think of."

August held his son on his lap. His eyes were still closed. August didn't want to find out if he still had a pulse or not.

"People knew how to care. People knew when not to, also. People knew how to love and people knew they had little control over it..."

Until long after the sun went down, along with the passing of nightly citywide curfew, August sat with his son, occasionally brushing the hair from his brow, teaching him about how to live.

THE END

POLLUTO

THE FEAST OF THE NIGHT -SOIL MAN

JASON HELLER

No writ, no scripture, no testament nor scroll will tell you.

But I will.

The Gods shit in their sleep. And through this incontinence, they send suffering and desolation to the lives of those who hold them most high.

I have come to this blasphemous truth because I am Xihu, and for many years I was their Night-Soil Man. Why the Gods chose me, I do not know. One day I shoveled corpses and manure into the brown, poisonous Swollen River for anyone in my plague-stricken village that would pay me a bowl of rice; the next, I collected the sleep-shit of Those who dwelled on the distant mountaintop, Their long, oily slicks of discharge staining the snows on which They slept.

Together They were known as Yu-in, and Each manifested Its face and form on the surface of a single gigantic and rumbling body at different times each day. First was fair Ith, His slim cheeks and single, dream-caked eye greeting me each morning as I cleaned up after my night's dark toil.

I was forbidden to gaze upon Yu-in in the full light of the day, so it was only Ith I came to know. Sometimes at dawn in Yu-in's cavernous chamber He mistook me for some long-dead lover, reaching toward my manhood with languid, clanking fingers. He smelled of iron and vanilla – that is, after I had finished my work with Him. With rag and shovel I scrubbed and scraped at the thick slime and barnacle-like shingles that collected around His vast and nautiloid anus. After flushing the waste down the cracks of the mountain's glacier as I had been instructed, I would return to anoint Him with a perfume of ambergris and afterbirth, spices and sperm, that Yu-in deposited in a bedside urn daily for this purpose.

But earlier – that is, when I would climb to the slumbering, snowbound Gods in the hours just after star-rise – the smell was far less ambrosial. Like a tomb cracked open and left to fester, Yu-in leaked a black and brackish feculence that stunk of rot and waste. They wallowed in their filth, tossing and turning until even Their single, blank face – for Yu-in seemed to be possessed by none of its constituent deities as it slept – was slathered in that rank muck.

To this day I shudder to think of the dreams Yu-in must have had. Ith told me once; it was morning, and I was still wiping away the last festoons of stool that clung to Yu-in's massive hindquarters. Ith awoke in a panic and told me of a nightmare He and the Others had been having.

In it, the fathers of the mothers of man left their graves and lifted their fists to the heavens. A war between God and servant tore the sky asunder, poisoned the seas, and forced Ith and his brethren into exile – leaving the men in the valley below to reap fields of disease and watch their pale, mortal shadows lengthen in the glare of the pagan sun.

I had to stifle a laugh. "Ith," I said, my insolence no doubt fueled by lingering contact with His most intimate discharges, "that is no mere dream. That is Your own Gospel, handed down eons ago. Every schoolchild in my village knows it. Before I shoveled waste and stricken flesh into the Swollen River to earn my keep – before I shaved my head in shame, became too tainted to trust with faith – I even gathered the little ones at my feet and taught them myself."

As I laughed, though, my blood ran cold – not just at the abrupt and melancholic recollection of the loss of my former calling, which pained me more than I could have ever expected, but at the final and terrifying realization that the Gods were as unclean, if not more so, than men.

◆

That day – for I slept during those bright hours Yu-in was conscious – I had a dream of my own. In my village, infants crawled forth with an uncanny grace and began consuming their mothers. Their pink gums bruised breast and bone as they burrowed into the nourishing flesh of their procreators, each mewling babe hungrily seeking the womb from whence it had been expelled.

I tried to warn my neighbors of this horror, but my tongue leapt from my gaping mouth of its own will and began inching across the dust. As I tried to pick it up, the dry earth turned to blood and surged up my forearms in foaming torrents.

Suddenly those torrents became the familiar shit of Yu-in – and I found myself no longer in my village but drenched and wretched at the edge of the glacier atop His mountain.

I bathed in the slow drip of the melting waters and watched the corruption swirl off of my body and across the ice before plunging into a river that flowed away from the mountain, down into the valley.

The river. The Swollen River.

When I awoke – writhing on the mat of straw in the modest hut Yu-in had seen fit to grant me in exchange for the execution of my duties – the sun was high in the sky. The images from my dream felt burned onto my brain.

It was then that a notion came to me.

I had once sternly warned the children of my village against acts and even thoughts of unholiness, of uncleanliness. The suffering you know at the hands of plague and famine, I had taught them, is nothing compared to the punishment Yu-in justly bestows on the impudent and sinful.

But that had been long ago. I was now a damned creature – damned by the perverse ordainment of the Gods Themselves.

And so, with my heart boiling and my soul reshaped in the flame of sacrilege, I took my ritual rag and shovel and crept toward the sunlit lair of Yu-in. To see Him as no man ever had.

◊

As I crept near to Yu-in and hid behind a large stone near His urn of ritual unguent, He appeared no differently. He lay in his bed of snow and quartz, both substances blackened beyond my ability to clean them. Soon, though, He turned to face the place where I hid. The planes and angles of His body were folded into an almost crystalline configuration, a geometry at once sublime and grotesque. His broad face blinked and flickered as many images in passing possessed it, a feverish parade of shifting visages. Ith was but one; Others came and went, some of which I swear I recognized as the pagan idols of the ancients.

Fear scorched my throat, but I doubted Yu-in could see me where I hid. Ith's eyesight – a faculty I had never previously considered prone to atrophy in the Gods – had always been poor, and I assumed the same could be said of Yu-in as a whole. His unfocused gaze passed over my shadowed perch.

Then He began to speak.

The voices crashed into me like a physical thing, a blow like the wind driving a tree before it. Ith's whisper, lisping and sleepy, was buried within, but it was overpowered by a deafening babble of screeches, grumbles, cackles, and howls that seemed to violate all laws of harmony. Still I clung to my hiding place, an insect riding out a tornado.

Impossibly, Yu-in's monstrous voice was drowned out by a sudden and even larger noise that seemed to split my skull along with the very air. I was blinded for a moment; by pain or noise or light I could not tell. When I was able to see again, there was flooding into Yu-in's chamber, one stone wall cleft in twain by the energies that had been hurled against it.

Through that vast crack, the sky leaked in. Clouds drifted by, and a fresh breeze stirred the clots of filth that had congregated around the corners of the Gods' great nest.

Below, the valley sat. Cradled within its green slopes was my village. From this high vantage, the Swollen River--tainted, I now realized, by the waste that I myself had leaked into the glacier all these years – ran black and stinking into the village.

We the villagers had always assumed it safe to shovel our shit and disease, the rancid dung and postulant corpses of our fellows, into the Swollen River, so long as it would be swept downstream and away. I myself had long been an instrument of this disposal.

It seems Gods and men were more alike than either of us thought.

My head awash in confusion and aching with the strain of the vision before me, I turned to flee. With one last glance I saw Yu-in's mighty abdomen open and reach out into the air, a massive bladder twisted inside out and snapping at the air like a starving frog at a swarm of flies. Some kind of mist arose from the valley, from the village itself, a haunted fog that Yu-in's inverted guts sucked at with a greedy lust.

Within that mist were faces. Howling faces, ravaged by buboes and etched with pain, sculpted from the dung-scented gasses Yu-in gulped out of the sky. A stray tendril wafted to where I stood frozen, ready to scuttle away from the site of this repulsive gluttony.

It was then that I knew what Yu-in feasted upon. Not the damned ghosts of the villagers, nor their eternal souls. Despite our broad interpretations of the Gospels, there were no such things.

There was only pain. Pain that Yu-in ate. And shat. And that shit in turn desecrated the waters of the Swollen River, the suffering returning to its source to cause suffering again. An insidious wheel, of which I had been a willing if ignorant spoke.

Stunned and too sickened to run, I didn't feel the hot breath of Yu-in on my scalp until it was too late.

◊

Drunk on agony, Yu-in snatched me up and held me before Him, the screams of villagers staining its teeth like wine. It seemed not to recognize me at first, and its multitude of mask-like faces blurred by faster than a hummingbird's wings. At last it settled on the incarnation that knew me best. Ith.

"Adored servant," Ith said, "why are you here? You know it is against our commandment for you to loiter in our chamber after the sun climbs into the heavens. We ask not much of you. Why do you disobey?"

Ith's voice was tender, even bruised, as if I had delivered unto him a personal affront. But even as his tone was almost childlike, the fist he held me in grew tighter. I felt my breath wane and my ribs creak at the force.

"Ith," I bellowed with the last lungful I could muster. I had only one chance, even though I knew it might mean the end of my life. "Listen to me. I am sorry for my sin. I… I must confess, I have long been lured by your beauty. I disobeyed you and snuck to your bed in hopes… in hopes of sharing it with you. I know you are lonely, Ith. Lonely and alone, as am I."

There was half truth to what I said, and the loneliness I had felt for many years--even before I had been chosen as the Night-Soil Man--welled up in me like infected humors. Weeping, Ith became overcome at my own show of emotion. His blubbering sounded louder than thunder as sobs began to shake his body. He let his fist go limp.

In that second I drew a sharp breath, threw my rag over his eye, and plunged my shovel into it.

Ith screeched, his own gross vanity as wounded as his face. A font of ichor bathed me, and I slipped from His grasp. I landed heavily, my ankle twisted, and I crawled toward the safety of the rocks as Ith thrashed and cried. Before I could escape, he let loose one last great sob and fell into a hill-sized heap before me.

He was not dead. I know I could not kill the Gods, and that I had little time before Ith and his brethren awoke.

It was then that I knew what I must do.

And so, that evening, as I prepared once more for my nocturnal trek back up the stinking cliffs and across the shit-marbled glacier to the nest where Yu-in lie dormant, I gathered more than just my ritual rag and shovel.

I took a spoon.

It has been centuries now since I felled Ith. Centuries that I have sat in the nest of the Gods, spoon in hand, consuming Yu-in's discharge before it can seep into the ground or flow into the Swollen River. Centuries since the village – cut off from the source of its corruption and blight – has grown virile and prosperous again.

But as the village has become pure, I have become corpulent, bloated by my sacrificial feast. My face is as broad as the cliff face, gray as a corpse. Worms tunnel into my flesh, ravenous for the rich waste it senses just beyond the thin membrane of my skin. The stench is unholy.

I once called out to the villages, the descendants of my former neighbors, from my faraway perch. I bellowed at them, begged for help, explained what I did and why. I told them of their true role in the

Gods' circle of filth, anguish, and gluttonous lust.

But the villagers know only their own Gospel, that of their many-faced God, Yu-in, handed down to them long ago. They call me Demon and curse me for trying to lead them astray from the path of the righteous. They credit their convalescence to the purity of their own souls, the sanctity of their own acts. The defile me in effigy – shitting into burlap sacks one day a year, drawing my face crudely in charcoal thereupon, and striking them with sticks until they burst. Then they shave their heads and feast on the fruits of their fields, forcing themselves to vomit upon the green earth, laughing, mocking.

That is their Holy Day. The Feast of Xihu, the Night-Soil Man. Their own way of purging.

Still, I know I cannot cease my loathsome repast. Even now Yu-in stirs in his deep sleep, his night-soil a thin and watery trickle from his rusted bowel now that the villagers provide Him little suffering to gorge upon. And so I sit, spoon to mouth, the fetid tang of undernourished dung my only sustenance. I grow ever larger, ever more horrible, to the point where my own bulk and stench threaten to drive me mad.

But as I gaze out the shriven wall of Yu-in's chamber, the Swollen River plunges sweetly and cleanly down the cliffs and over blanched rocks and into the valley, where mills spin swiftly in its churning currents and children now bathe in its clear waters without fear of pain or plague.

I gaze at that, empty yet full, and I am content.

THE END

POLLUTO

PERSONIFICATION

RHYS HUGHES

I sat with Hannah in the park and a man on a bicycle passed us at high speed. We were smoking a joint, encouraging the colours of the blossom to shimmer, and the velocity of the rider seemed incongruous. We watched him descend the grassy slope towards the distant sea. Then Hannah exhaled slowly and said:

"He's not a real man but the personification of the North Wind. That explains his haste."

Although the sun was shining, it was chilly on the bench and her statement made sense. Then it occurred to her that perhaps we were all personifications of something, every man and woman on the surface of the globe, rather than authentic human beings.

"What are you the personification of?" she asked.

I pondered for a minute. "Procrastination."

She blinked at me. "Are you really?"

"One day I will be," I announced.

"And what of myself? What do I personify?"

Again I considered the question carefully. "The Spirit of Marijuana," I finally concluded.

"It's getting cold. Shall we go now?"

I made no effort to move. "Soon."

Hannah had smoked her joint down to the roach. She wanted to roll another but somewhere warmer. To distract herself she continued developing her theory. "Not so long ago we were real people, all of us, but there was a change. Some force entered the world and converted us into walking symbols. I can't believe the change was a natural process. It has been imposed."

"Do you imagine that if we find the force responsible and neutralise it we will return to our former condition? Or is the change permanent?"

"I think we should look for it and make the attempt. But how will we know where to search?"

I scratched my nose. "Maybe it will come to us of its own accord now it has been rumbled!"

She nodded. "We can only wait and see. Do you remember that really bad poet, Martin White? We saw him perform at those amateur poetry nights. You know, the slimy one with the oddly shaped head. What on earth do you think he personifies?"

His image glooped into my mind's eye. "The mushroom cloud that rose above the detonation of the first atom bomb. That's my guess."

"Let's go home. I'm really cold."

With a gigantic effort I rose and followed her. "I want to pick some plants on the way back."

◊

I sat on her sofa and stretched my legs. I had just paid my rent and so I felt less guilty for sprawling and slobbing. Crumbs dusted my lap. Hannah was upstairs in the bath. There was a knock on the front door. I waited five minutes and then went to answer it.

"May I come in?" asked the figure who stood there.

I called up the stairs. "Hannah! May I invite a friend in for a cup of tea?"

"Of course!" came the muffled reply.

"Hannah, do you mind if we smoke some of your weed?"

"Go right ahead. Roll one for me while you're at it. I'll be down when I'm ready."

The stranger entered and I led him into the lounge. He was formally polite but his eyes sparkled with a mirth that was primitive and malicious. I am extremely bad at rolling joints. They tend to be lopsided in the wrong way, with the fat end near the roach, but I did my best and rolled one for my guest and one for Hannah. The stranger took a long drag and offered the joint to me.

I shook my head. "I smoked enough earlier."

He continued to puff and then cast me a suspicious glance. "I insist you join me."

"Very well," I said and I picked up Hannah's joint. "Keep that one and I'll take this."

"That's not very sociable!" he protested.

"I'm not the personification of Sociability," I pointed out, "but the personification of Procrastination."

His eyes still glittered. "How did you work it out?"

I shrugged. "Just one of those things."

"When an individual learns the truth I always pay a visit and make them forget. My assistant, the personification of Forgetfulness, will be along shortly."

"He has gone to the wrong address," I smirked.

He puffed angrily on his joint. "What do you mean?"

"Well how will he remember the name of this street or the number of this house?"

"There are ways and means. I left a trail of sweets right up to your front door. He's fond of sweets."

"That must be very expensive."

"Indeed so. He keeps forgetting he's on a diet."

I couldn't delay him with small talk any longer. Hannah was out of the bath and would soon be down for her joint. I needed to roll her another but I kept putting it off. I waited for my guest to finish his own joint and then I leaned forward and said:

"I've actually had an inkling of the truth for a long time but I couldn't be bothered to gather my thoughts properly until now. How do you feel?"

"Dizzy. Stoned but in a bad way."

He slumped back with an open mouth that resembled an ashtray. But I had nothing to flick into it and even if I had it would take more energy than I cared to expend.

◊

Hannah frowned at the prone figure on her sofa. "Where's my joint? And what's wrong with him?"

"Coming," I answered, "and neutralised."

"Kindly explain," she demanded.

"That man is the force that changed humans into personifications. It required a constant effort from him. He has now been put out of action and every man and woman has reverted back to their original condition."

"But who exactly is he?"

"The personification of Personification. He embodied the concept of personification itself. Without his malign influence, personification simply can't exist!"

"So you got him utterly stoned? But what happens when he recovers and wakes up?"

"He won't. I spiked his joint with the belladonna I picked in the park earlier. He's a goner."

There was a knock on the door. Hannah went to answer it. "Who's there?" I called.

"A very forgetful man," she answered. "He can't remember why he's here, but he's real enough."

"He has probably come to pick up the body," I said.

"I'll tell him to get a move on," she replied.

As the body was carried out I thought again about rolling Hannah a new joint. It was past midnight before I did so.

THE END

MERCY PARK

J. MICHAEL SHELL

She appeared to him with dark, faun-set eyes. Even in the dimly lit atmosphere of *The Cavern Pub*, those eyes caught wisps of light that sparked gold flecks in their deep brown irises. It was those sparks that somehow caught him from across the room – those little lights dancing beneath her wild black bangs that shined like coal, that hinted the iridescence of crow feathers.

As his feet began their shuffle toward her, he noticed, as he drew nearer, how tiny she was – how gorgeously tiny. So perfect was she in this miniaturization that his teeth clenched with the desire to have this toy girl – to play with her in ways that flashed like heat through his mind and then his body. Though he believed in spells and the magic that can create them, these things never broached their subject in his thoughts. And perhaps that, too, was part of this spell.

◊

Her smile grew slowly, first from one corner of her mouth, then from the other. It was drawn on lips the color of crushed blackberries, with hints of red plum toward their outer edges. Her skin was milk white and seemed almost luminous. "Hi," he breathed at her, and then wondered if he'd actually spoken.

"Hello," she said softly, looking up at him through the notches in her bangs. "I saw you coming."

Somehow her words, spoken in that high yet throaty, songbird voice, seemed edged in double entendre – seemed erotic in tone if not substance. This was another spell that intensified the first. "How could I not?" he whispered, and then, again, he was unsure if he'd spoken.

"The roses are blooming in Mercy Park," she told him, her smile growing to reveal teeth so perfect they seemed like glazed china – delicate and sharp. "I'm afraid of thorns," she continued. "Will you pick a rose for me?"

At that moment, for her, he would have embraced and uprooted a stand of roses. The urge to take her into his arms and squeeze threatened to overwhelm him. Then she held out her hand and he took it. She led him toward *The Cavern's* exit.

◊

Mercy Park stood just across from the pub. Though the road was lined with street lamps, there was no illumination, other than from the thin Moon, deeper into the lightly wooded areas. When the cooler, fresher night air embraced Malcolm, he seemed to come awake. "What's your name?" he asked, as she drew him across the empty street.

"I'm Jasmine," she told him, and he noticed a scent of Carolina jasmine on the air. "My friends call me Jaz,"

"I'm Mal," he said, smiling. "It's short for Malcolm."

"Mal is a *beautiful* name," she said with a sigh. "It means 'bad' in so many languages."

When Malcolm and Jaz came to the rose garden, he asked her, "What color rose would you like?"

"Black, of course, but there aren't any so make it red. Find me a good one," she said, squeezing his hand before letting it go.

The smell of the roses, mixed with that night jasmine, was heady – almost intoxicating. Malcolm waded into that little lake of flowers and found an enormous, blood red bloom. Carefully, he maneuvered his fingers onto the stem and snapped it off cleanly. Only when he handed it to Jasmine did he notice the thorn in his finger. "Let me take it out for you," she told him.

After plucking the offending sticker from the pad of his forefinger, she squeezed out a little bead of blood. Then she put his finger to her lips. "Mmm, your blood tastes sweet. What other sweets do you have for me?"

When she dropped to her knees, Malcolm laced his fingers into her midnight hair. Just moments later, the orgasm that shook him was like a seismic event of great magnitude. So intense was the phenomenon that his knees weakened and he fell to them. As soon as he did, Jasmine crushed her lips onto his, producing such an erotic kiss that he immediately felt himself becoming aroused again.

When, finally, she turned him loose, she said, "Come with me to my house. I want you all night. I know some tricks that you might enjoy."

Malcolm never answered, but he let her lead him out of Mercy Park.

◊

Jasmine walked Malcolm to a bus stop with a little, black bench. "We could take my car," he told her. "It's parked down the street from the pub."

"This bus goes right to my house," she told him. "Look, here it comes."

Though this tiny city had just purchased new buses, the one that arrived was very old. The lighting inside was dim, and Malcolm and Jaz were the only riders. For such an old vehicle, the bus seemed to make no noise at all. Only the clinking of the coins Jasmine dropped into the box sounded inside the carriage.

"I love the old buses," Jaz said to Malcolm, as they made their way to the seats farthest back. "Those new ones look like cracker boxes with windows. They send this one out to my neck of the woods because so few people ride it."

"Where do you live?" Mal asked her.

"Just outside the city. The house I live in is older than this bus, much older. There are magnolia trees in the yard twice as old as you are – *more* than twice as old! And there's an ancient willow out in the back who watches over me. If anyone would think to do me harm, he'd form his branches into a noose and hang them. Don't worry, though. I'll tell him you won't hurt me."

"What about *you*?" Malcolm asked with a mischievous grin. "You don't intent to hurt *me*, do you?"

"If I did, he wouldn't protect you. He loves me, you know."

"I can certainly see why," Malcolm said, bending in to give her a kiss.

But Jasmine eased him away and said, "Wait! Wait till we're home and can have it *all*. Can you wait that long?" she teased.

"I can, but it's hard," he said, and Jasmine giggled at his choice of words.

Before long, all traces of the city were behind them and the bus made its way through a tunnel of overhanging trees. Then it stopped, and Jasmine said, "This is it, let's go."

As they exited the bus, Mal turned to the driver and said, "Thanks for the ride."

Though the driver was deep in shadow, Malcolm could see that he didn't move at all – nor did he speak. "He doesn't like young people, I think," Jaz told him, as they hopped off the last step.

"I guess not," Mal agreed, turning to watch the driver reach over and pull the long handle that closed the door.

"C'mon," Jaz told him, taking him by the hand and beginning to run. "My house is through these trees."

◆

Laughing as she led him between the old oaks and sycamores of this little wood, Jasmine brought them into a clearing on which stood a huge, old monument-of-a-house. Under the thin Moon, it was barely illuminated, and seemed like a great, hulking shadow on the night. "Isn't it lovely?" she said to Malcolm.

"Yes," he told her, "but you should be taller and named Morticia."

Jasmine produced a mock scowl and punched him on the arm.

"I was kidding," he told her.

POLLUTO

"Were not," she pouted. "But that would make your name Gomez, wouldn't it? Or are you Uncle Fester?"

"Maybe I'm Pugsly," he smiled.

"Then I'll be Wednesday, and we'll be incestuous."

"I always thought Wednesday was cute," Malcolm told her.

"Do you think I'm cute?" Jaz asked him, cocking her head and squinting her eyes.

"I think you're beautiful," he told her, that spell removing the smile from his face. "I think you're glamorous."

"That's probably closer to true," she said. "And *you* are so handsome that you're pretty."

"Men aren't pretty," he said, the smile reappearing on his face.

"Oh yes they are," Jaz said with certainty. "And *you* are *very* pretty."

◊

Malcolm and Jasmine entered the house through a massive oak door with stained glass windows and sidelights. From a stand just inside, Jaz retrieved and lit a hurricane lamp. "Don't you have electricity?" Malcolm asked.

"Of course I do, but do you want that kind of light intruding on our mood? Do you want to see every little blemish on my face? And when I'm naked, wouldn't you rather see my soft lit softly?"

From somewhere deep inside Malcolm came a sound like a lion's purr. Then the purr turned into a, "Yessss," coming up through his throat and into his mouth.

"Mmmm, you sounded like you meant that," Jasmine said.

"I *mean* that," he confirmed.

"Then follow me. I keep two bedrooms up these stairs– one for sleeping and the other for...*not* sleeping."

"What's the difference?" Malcolm asked.

"The difference? Well, you can't do what I have in mind while you're sleeping."

"I *mean*," he clarified, "what's the difference between the two rooms?"

"One is *much* darker."

◊

Even lit by her lantern, Jasmine's special room was dark. In fact, it had no windows, and the only door, other than the one through which they'd entered, led to a little bathroom, which also had no windows. The huge bed was shrouded by a canopy, and dark blue, crushed velvet drapes. "Wow!" Malcolm exclaimed as she pulled back the drapes. Behind them, an eider down mattress was swathed in satin and covered with satin cased pillows. "Now *that's* a bed!" he said enthusiastically.

"I hope you can live up to the potential of this bed," Jasmine told him, looking up through those bangs again.

"I will! I promise!" he told her.

Lowering the flame on her lamp to a flicker, Jasmine asked, "Then why am I still standing here?"

◊

Jasmine's body was the perfect miniature Malcolm had imagined it to be. Other than her size, there was nothing childlike about her. She was full grown and curvaceous. At one point, while he was down there, Malcolm noticed that her toenails were painted a shiny black. He'd noticed earlier that her fingernails were a deep, ultraviolet blue.

After what seemed like hours of intense play, Malcolm finally lay quiet with Jasmine in his arms. Though the room was warm, their sweat cooled them. After a while, Jasmine brought her lips to his ear and whispered, "Would you like to go further? Would you like to go somewhere you've never been?"

"What makes you think I've never done that?" Mal asked her, smiling because he'd been thinking along the lines of what she seemed to be suggesting.

"Not that," she whispered. "Not yet. What I *mean* is, how would you like to trade places?"

"I think we already..."

"Stop thinking so mundanely," she admonished. "How would you like to trade bodies for a while? Think about it, Malcolm, a whole new passion to add to what we've already known."

Malcolm smiled and squeezed her tighter. "If it were possible, I'd gladly climb inside your magnificent little body."

"And let me in yours?"

"Could you love me as well as I've loved you?" he teased.

"Better!" she said adamantly.

"Oh, you think so," he mock-scolded. "Well, I wish we could."

"Say it again."

"What?"

"Say what you wish."

"I wish we could, I wish we could, I wish we could," he said with his eyes locked to hers.

Jasmine reached down beneath the sheets and took him into her hand. When he'd grown a bit, she dug a fingernail in and slid it sideways, making a little scratch. "Ow!" Malcolm protested. "What did you do that for?"

Then he saw her wince as she took that finger to herself. "Take me now!" she insisted. "Lubricated with both our blood! *Do* it, Malcolm! Remember the promise you made earlier? Can you match my bed's potential?"

Perhaps with just a twinge of anger for the pain she'd inflicted, and perhaps with a touch of bravado, Malcolm threw her onto her back and pushed himself in– deep and hard. Relentlessly he drove her, pounding till he heard her bumping into the headboard. Harder still, until he could feel that bumping on the top of his head. No, *her* head, and he was staring up into his own wide-eyed and grinning face. "Does it feel good?" she asked with his mouth.

"Yessss," he said, tentatively. Then he closed her eyes and succumbed to this strange ecstasy.

"There was something you had in mind earlier," his voice spoke. "Are you ready?"

"Yes."

With that permission, Jasmine reached down and rolled her body onto her stomach. Then she clutched her hips and pulled Malcolm up onto her knees. With his left leg, she maneuvered her legs apart. "Is this what you wanted to do?" she asked, pushing him in from behind.

"Yes," he moaned. "It hurts."

"But it's good, isn't it? Relax and see how fine that pain can be."

"Oh, please..."

"Please what?"

"I don't know. It hurts, but..."

"But you want to feel me come, don't you?"

"Yes."

"I will."

"Hurry."

"I will."

As Malcolm's body gave up its seed, Jasmine reached around with his hand and massaged that delicate pea in its pod. Then she listened as her own voice cried out with the pleasure of something the crier had never known. "Do you love me, Mal?" he said, easing her legs out straight again.

"Yes."

"Will you always love me?"

"I love you," he heard her say.

◊

Though it was morning, the room was buried in darkness. Someone had extinguished the lamp. Malcolm could feel himself nestled into Jasmine's arms. "I can't see you," he heard her say, though he was certain he'd said it.

"Hush," his voice whispered into his ear. "I'll light the lamp, just a bit, but you need to remember what we did last night. Are you sore today?"

"Yes," her voice whispered. "But it's not really pain. It makes me feel...I don't know."

"Is it *longing*?"

"I don't know."

"Do you know who you are?"

"I'm Malcolm," she said, but he knew it wasn't his voice.

"You're *Mal*," he told her. "And I'm Jaz. We traded, remember? And I love you as much as I love myself," he giggled.

Then her little body began to shake, and she curled in tight on herself. She could feel his arms release her, and then a small flame came up from the lamp. "Look," he said, running his hand down her smooth, naked body. "See how beautiful you are – how pretty!"

"I feel so weak," she said.

"You haven't the wherewithal to animate that body. Soon you'll get a little stronger, but you'll always be weak. I had my body shrunk down on a lonely island in the South Pacific. I compacted its size to consolidate certain powers of suggestion I'd cultivated there. Powers that would work well with the magic I'd learned. And I also loved the result for aesthetic reasons. Remember how enticing you found it? Well, I'm similarly enticed. And now I've placed someone pretty as that body inside it, and I will always love you."

"I want to trade back," she whimpered.

"This would be the last day that's possible, but I won't permit it. Should the sun, before it sets today, or even just a reflected glimmer, enter your eye, we'd go instantly back to where we were. But once the sun sets this evening, it can never be reversed."

"Please let me see the sun," she sobbed.

"Tomorrow. Tomorrow I'll take you out and buy you presents, if you're strong enough. But today you must stay in your room and rest – gather your will so you can carry the burden of that shell. Now come. I'll help you to the bathroom. I have things to do and may be gone a while. It'll be very hard for you to walk today. Tomorrow it will be easier."

Jaz lifted Mal, still naked, and carried her into the bathroom. When, after a while, he carried her back toward the bed, he stopped halfway and set her onto her pretty feet. "See if you can walk the rest of the way."

Mal tried to take a step, but faltered. Jaz quickly swept her up into his arms and carried her the rest of the way. "I wanted to see if I needed to tie you, but I'm sure now that I don't. Even if you could make it to the door, that lock is formidable. I'm glad, little darling, because I didn't want to tie you. I really do love you. Soon you'll be happy and grateful for this change. And I promise to match this bed's potential every time we lie together. Now tell me you love me."

"I love you," she sobbed.

"Then why are you crying? I don't like to see you cry, but it makes me want you in the worst way. Why do you suppose that is?" he asked. Then he gently kissed her, and made a tender love that drained her and put her back to sleep.

When Mal awoke, she was alone, and the room was totally dark again. The only sounds were her own labored breaths. Gathering her wits, she remembered that the door was to her left. Could she make it there? Could she find a way to catch a glimpse of sunlight?

She was weak – so weak. It took all her strength to move herself to the edge of the bed, but there was no climbing down. Trying the only way she knew how, Mal shimmied herself till she tottered and fell. It was a longer fall than she'd expected. She could feel a bump beginning to rise on her forehead.

The floor was clean and smooth – polished hardwood. But the door was at least ten feet away, and her strength was nearly gone. Still she tried, pulling with her hands pressed flat against the floor –pushing with her knees and her toes. At one point, exhaustion made her stop, and then she fainted for a time. But finally she made it to the door. She could feel the tiny space between the bottom and the floor. She tried to press her eye there, but it was too tiny, too far down. The spaces between the door and the jams were also tight, and no light passed between. There was no keyhole. Then she felt something with her foot. It was Jasmine's shoe, a little Lucite pump, abandoned in passion the night before. Somehow Mal managed to scoot it up to her hand, and with its heel she began to dig at the bottom of the door.

For hours she clawed with the heel of that shoe, until finally she could feel a little hole– a little widened out place where she might look under and catch the light of day. Then she heard someone coming up the stairs. Quickly she put her head to the door and managed to peek through that tiny space. Light! There! She could see it! "It's the sun!" she called out with her weak little voice.

As Jaz gently pushed on the door, Mal managed to roll out of the way. Still she waited for the change he'd told her would come. Then she looked up and saw the lamp in his hand. "My poor little darling," he said. "I didn't mean to be gone so long. It's very late. Come now, let me help you back to bed. I've had a long day, but I'll never be so tired that I can't make love to you."

◊

With Jaz's help and loving care, Mal grew stronger. As he'd promised, Jaz took her out on short shopping trips, and bought her clothes and jewelry and perfume. Then, one night, he took her to Mercy Park. As they stood by the roses, he asked, "What color?"

"White," she told him. Then she watched as he retrieved her rose.

Once he'd handed it to her, he gently pressed his hands on her shoulders till she went to her knees. Then he wove his fingers into her raven hair, and told her how much he loved her.

THE END

EED AND YOLK

SCOTT MORRIS

Oedipus takes his mother to dinner. Their feet collide beneath the table while the animated conversation above pretends not to notice. Eed offers her more wine. They are drinking a chardonnay, "nutty... refined... a subtle yeast complexity." It is exceptionally dry. As they pull the glasses away from their mouths, their lips smack like badly-judged kisses. They are conscious of the sounds they make and exchange embarrassed smiles. So, "Tell me about yourself." She wonders where on earth she should begin, he shrugs his shoulders in encouragement. He knows the story inside-out already, could probably tell it much better himself. But he's interested to hear her edited version. What she chooses to leave out, her carefully selected omissions, how obviously these omissions nonetheless shape and shadow her tame, rambling tale. How much does she recall? Does she even recognise her young, dashing date? Eed suspects not, but then, who can tell? They are playing some kind of game; they cut their asparagus cautiously, as they might deploy plastic troops. Eed is thinking very dirty thoughts.

"Ladies first."

This date has been a long time in the making. It has taken a while for him to catch up with her, not least because the universe's soul redistribution scheme is unpredictable at the best of times. The few thousand years dividing the roasted antelope of the Theban court from the plates of creamed venison in front of them now have been spent as subterranean polyps, as segmented, hermaphroditic creatures, almost certainly as an antlered being for one lifetime. For the best part of his first millennium, Eed found himself either in the armpits of unmappable caves or clutching the banks of deep-sea brine pools. Troglobite and extremophile, he has enjoyed the routine of both. He has wallowed in these consistently sightless existences and been grateful for the security of their pre-nervous systems. Of course, this does not sound like the concept of reincarnation that we have all come to hope for. How might Oedipus feel grateful for the eyelessness of the cave dweller, how can he appreciate the layered irony of life as a blind cavefish while living the life of a blind cavefish? This is surely reincarnation's primary appeal – a complete biological metamorphosis, swapping the miseries of one bag of cells for the freedom of another. A complete start afresh. If we wish to remake contact with our defunct selves, why, we must add ourselves to various waiting lists, we must pay specially trained therapists to do the job for us, to chip away like palaeontologists week after week and recover these fossilised psyches. We cannot hope to – and in most cases, would not want to – do this ourselves. Oedipus as pitcher plant should be Oedipus no longer. But the extremity of the violence committed by the king, all that ghastly eye-tearing on top of the bitter pill of anagnorisis, is not the kind of thing to be so easily shaken off by a change of body, a shift from skin to scales. Remember, Eed spells his tragedy with a capital T. His sockets – when this capricious soul-allocation system decided to grant him any – maintained a steady itch throughout. This itch was mnemonic, obliging him to constantly remember what had happened. But in spite of this, he was glad to be blind, still. Memory was past, a nightmare rectified.

"Where to begin?"

No surprise that Jocasta-Louise Griffiths (Yolk to friends) had never known her father. Her mother refused to discuss him, to offer even a farfetched excuse for his absence. Her first experience of a clearly focused male face – a half-memory, loitering in some formative lacuna of her consciousness – was that of her stepfather-to-be. Blotched, stubbled skin, a perpetual rash, this became Yolk's automatic template for the male form. Even now, the polished and aftershaved jaw lines of men like Eed manage to disturb her on an unexplained, unexplored psychic level. Once in power, the stepfather revealed his clumsy fists and temper to both women but there was little that could be done besides suffering in peace. We can draw arrows from childhood to her sixth form days and the glamour of single sex education, to those fumbled attempts at recreating the documentary footage of bra-burnings someone said they had seen, footage that made only half-sense to her and her friends. Her mother would scream at the ingratitude, incinerating her Christmas gifts so thoughtlessly. Yolk would roll her eyes and tell her she just didn't understand, but she didn't either, really. The girls balanced their time between sit-ins and university applications, between declaring boycotts on testosterone and losing their virginities. Yolk watched her friends as they grew armpit hair and started to wear their boyfriends' clothes. Feeling pressured, she experimented with football and lesbianism, but found she had the calf muscles for neither. Her biology teacher, Mr Kendal, (a man obsessed with rods and cones) began to take a shine to her. He complimented the colour of her scatter diagrams, wrote kisses in the margins of her lab reports. One afternoon, she cornered him in a chemical cupboard and threatened to dissect his penis with a compass. For this, she was thrown out of college, three weeks before her A-Levels. She could have turned the tables on the deciding committee, shown them his academic love-notes and filed a complaint. Something prevented her from going so far, some form of perverse dignity, mixed with a genuine flattery at his attention. Even so, she could have waited until next year, done her exams at a different college maybe, but her mum saw it as an omen and forced her into getting a job.

"Not that this makes respectable dinner table conversation, sorry."

Eventually, Eed began to notice the daylight. He transmigrated outside. A world of currents, breezes, ripples. Back into the thick of things, gradually. He grew legs, fur, a backbone. Retinas. His sockets lost their itch as they become functional once more, but the itch moved elsewhere: between the ears, between the legs. Guilt bristled into a kind of appetite. He was looking for something, someone, but could not work out what, who. Twice, Eed found himself human again - three times, counting the current dinner table charmer. First, as a sixteenth-century Maori girl, a life worth writing about, had it not been cut short at the age of four in the jaws of a great white. Second, cycles and cycles later, he found himself a Parisian carpenter by the name of Marcel. He was an albino, a metempsychotic flashback to his cave-water days no doubt. His career began with bookshelves, progressed to the construction of timber guillotine frames for the Revolution, and ended beneath the wheels of an unseen carriage. His widow, Sofia, reflected, with mournful wit, that he had approached death in much the same way as he had approached life – never looking where he was going. But she knew nothing. Only when human – these short, inappropriate segments of his continually renewed being – only then was Eed able to identify what it was he was actually looking for. What he needed, in fact, because only then, with a human's grasp of metaphor, did it become clear that his was an itch that needed scratching at all costs. Only with the human imagination could he picture the fingernails best suited to that task: chewed, filthy, a few rope fibres trapped beneath them. Fingers as long and tapered as his own. He had sucked these fingers as a boy, surrogate nipples when his mother had been too exhausted to feed; he had sucked these fingers as a man, pulled from his wife's pudendum in the tangles of foreplay. But where could they be? Even as Eed (as Hupai and Marcel) considered them, fantasised over them, they knew it was ridiculous to assume they still existed as such. They would be the mandibles, the tentacles, the clawless petals that Eed had himself lived with. Impossible that Oedipus as human and Jocasta as human could ever again coincide, and even if they could, that they could ever coincide in the same neighbourhood, in the same social circles. And even if their trajectories could coincide, impossible that their bodies would follow suit, impossible that she would ever want to set eyes on him one more time. Bodies, gender, species may change, but some things don't. This is, we mustn't ever forget, a tragedy spelt with a capital T.

"OK well forget that bit, the beginning."

Yolk moved to the city. Her journey was made with dreams of bohemian attic existences, Saturday night Sambuca orgies and bit parts in ITV Drama Premieres. As things turned out, she essentially settled for the commute. The London Underground offered her employment, manning faulty barriers and advising passenger safety over the tannoy. She took to it without complaint, quickly and quietly earning enough to rent a small flat in Walthamstow. Her friends, she was surprised to find, were in full support. They saw it as a woman's valiant struggle against type, refusing to take up her sewing kit and Fairy liquid, preferring instead to insert herself into that most hyper-masculine of professions, that of the tunneller, a modern day miner ("Why Yolky, you're an underminer," Jayne guffawed, "of everything this conservative patriarchy expects of you!") servicing the foundations of society, oiling the hub of civilisation, all the while confronting the ubiquitous roots of manhood's evil. Their language grew more excited, elaborate and nonsensical. She chose not to admit her actual logic, that of the Pretty Woman scanning the escalators for her pitying Richard. Richard turned out to be called Vic. He was bald, heavy and married. He worked with computers. He gave her a son, Anthony, and then gave her the shove. She suddenly found herself distraught, weeping at inopportune moments and eating far too much. This, she told herself, was being grown up. She secretly enjoyed turning up to work of a morning red-eyed and pale, drawing comments of concern upon her, the magnetism of misery. "No, I'm ok, honest," she would smile, "just going through a lot right now." Nobody dared to clarify or measure "a lot", not wanting to be the one to provoke an obviously upset young mother to tears. Instead, they gave her sensible shifts and moved her upstairs, away from the density of desolate faces that collected along the tunnels, into a booth at Clapham North Station, digesting these faces into individual cases, serving them to her one by one rather than en masse, diluting the desolation and putting a window between her and them. And there she sat, it had already been a couple of months, issuing tickets, negotiating refunds, happier maybe, content at least, when who should appear before her ticket office but -

"And that brings us up to date."

Eed, re-formed as an advertising mogul, his scales now authentic Armani, had gone to the ticket office to make a complaint – about what he can no longer remember, perhaps could not remember at the time. It was as the girl with an unpleasant face behind the glass pushed the relevant feedback forms into the tray between them that he noticed – with a lump in his throat and in his trousers – her fingernails: jagged from biting, black filthy and with small fibres jutting out from under them. He gripped them tightly, stared into her bewildered, blotched features and asked if she might like to go to dinner some time. With him. Together. Of course she did, so that was that.

"And here we are. And what about you? Tell me about yourself."

Eed lies, even about the innocuous stuff. He can tell, from the simple arrangement of her smiling lips, that she doesn't suspect a thing – about her own mythology, let alone his. Whatever would her feminist comrades make of the Queen of Thebes? What would her mother make of Yolk's maternal conduct? Does this sheep-eyed ignorance turn Eed on even more? He's not sure, but by this point, as two servings of panna cotta are laid before them, he's thinking some very dirty thoughts indeed. She tells a forgettable anecdote and he exploits it, grabs her hand in paraded disbelief. It is damp with sweat. He can guess her own thoughts accurately enough: her mind is on the bill, the hoped display of chivalry from an all-earning, all-paying knight in dry-cleaned armour (her purse is, he assumes, awkwardly empty), a bus journey made hand-in-hand and a goodbye kiss outside her garden gate. She probably doesn't have a garden, let alone a gate, but still. Eed's already practising a thoroughly transparent request for coffee. Inside, she will ask if he takes milk and he will make some fantastic joke about how milk and semen can be so readily substituted in conversation to comic effect, and how "to take" something can also mean to utilise sexually and with force, before tearing down her skirt and fucking her against the dishwasher. He will dangle her consenting body from a ceiling light, wrap her legs around his head and plunge his tongue inside her. Maybe they can begin by stripping each other in Anthony's room, using only their teeth, before he sodomises her against the bars of the boy's cot.

"Sorry, I am very interested, but I do need to pop to the loo. This wine..."

All these acts of debauchery and more have been practised, perfected and surpassed countless times before by the royal couple. Oedipus and Jocasta had quite a reputation in Thebes before that reputation eclipsed it. And that's the point, that's halfway towards scratching the itch. Eed has been doing his research. He studied himself at school. He cried with laughter at the play's ending, found he couldn't help himself. His teacher said he had to think himself back to those times, people did things differently then. Oedipus and Jocasta: they're a Penguin Classic now, for Christ's sake. They're an excuse for theatre students to march around in togas. Even better – if only you knew, Yolk – they're now trendsetters. He has read his Hamlet, and he has read his Freud. He's come to love the latter, this new adoptive father, quite considerably. As a couple, Eed and Yolk are the governing principle of the modern condition. They're spokespeople for the united fate of a troubled humanity. They're the dream, the ultimate pin-ups of the collective unconscious. Little boys all over the world are growing up with dreams to usurp their daddies and sleep with their mummies; little girls spend their childhoods gaping at their brothers' cocks in green-blooded jealousy. Some learn to deal with it; others don't. Those that don't, they say, go mad, turn kiddyfiddler, lock themselves in a daddy-fucking closet. And others, a few, maybe only the two of them – some actually manage the act itself. And at what cost? Eyeballs and windpipes perhaps, but how temporary, a small price to pay when set against the cost of the chardonnay, the cut of Eed's outfit, the figure of eight his toes dare to trace over hers under the table. Some people manage it...

"Well. That's me all done. I think. Heh. What next?"

Next. What next? Eed conducts his new life through the grammar of the boardroom. The momentum of advertising cannot be content with billboards and commercial breaks, it must force itself into every unexploited cultural crevice, and just as the product-messages of his clients must thus be inserted onto the bottoms of pint glasses, backmasked onto self-help CDs or scratched into the contact lenses of an increasingly myopic species, so he cannot live without expanding. He must power his way into every opening he can find or rip for himself. To breathe, his lungs must surely, every minute, threaten to pull themselves apart, his clenched ribs must feel themselves on the verge of flinging open before crumbling inwards on the exhale. So what next, she asks, he asks? The sex is beyond question, as good as perpetrated. He will infiltrate his mother tonight, love her once again. Almost certainly, as spent lover, cigarette in hand, he will reveal his secret identity. There will be tears but they will be the tears of an overworked actor, too tired to pretend she genuinely suspected otherwise. This is nothing to get excited about, the final chorus of an overplayed, overlong pop song – this is not what he has waited epochs for, this is not what happens "next". Next, they go at it again. No fuss. But things will be different, that time around. No more hesitant soundings of half-explored bodies. Because Eed has been reading into himself. Executive logic maintains that this is an opportunity not to be missed. And Sigmund's logic is in agreement too. Why should he have to spend another infancy eating his way out of a surrogate mother, or suffer another hundred lifetimes fertilising his own segmented self? Why should he, when a way out of this tedious cycle is now metres away, threading her way through the restaurant, returning from the toilet. It was a way out that would be visible, and tempting, each time he stuck his head between her legs; in some ways, his exit sign, in other ways, the stage door out into the

POLLUTO

real realness of things. This is what Sigmund means by the death drive, the compulsion felt by all human beings to reunite themselves with the bliss of oblivion, the inorganic world they can hardly remember having been a part of until their parents cheated them out of it by getting them conceived. Surely it is Eed's duty to set yet another example to the species and embark on this psychodynamic voyage. That, that is what he needs, that will put a stop to this prolonged itch. Yes, they will go at it again. She will open for him, open the pipe that drove him out into the world and which he has filled many times since. Tonight, he will fill it again, though not with the withering clumsiness of an erect penis. Tonight, he will drive himself into her, all of him. Her body will crunch with the force of him, parental bonding at its most extreme. He will trample himself into her placenta, pull down her ileum for a new umbilical cord, awash with nostalgia. As he came into being, so will he go behind it.

"Sorry I took so long, you know what the Ladies is like."

THE END

POLLUTO

MASCARA

MARK WAGSTAFF

An extract from Mark Wagstaff's novella Mascara

If I'm ever glad I do what I do, it's when I'm in shitholes like this. The old man, he was out of step with the world. Had a mind - for want of a better word - for the bygone days of family; of your turf, your place: the ground you stood forever. Your right - for want of a better word - to own some thin scrap of town. He'd see all this: these blocks of flats, this yard: he'd think it was the promised land; he'd build walls of hate around it. I got no feel for tradition; I got no respect.

Now these lads, kicking ball, they're giving me a good looking-at. My whole life I've been watched. I'm glamorous; here, in bargain bin city, I always got the boys restless. I swish my arse for their greedy, jealous eyes. I got nothing to prove.

The elevator's broke. Stairs are good for the calves anyway. I got no ill feelings for shitholes like this. When people wanna piss their lives away, let 'em. But I couldn't live in this grease, this bones and phlegm. Couldn't live where it's okay, pissing the stairs. Don't get me wrong: I've seen lords and ladies with shocking habits. But I got values: never mind you got nothing, you still got your pride. Maybe the old man's fist landed a punch after all.

This flat is fucking rank. Just seeing the net curtains I feel dirty. He lives alone, you bet: he got left here and never unpacked. He thinks he's it: dealing for bigger arseholes than he is. Well I'm the biggest arsehole. And I'm back in town.

He's nervous: hear that? Keeps the door double locked in daytime. He ain't liked: see those cracks there? Someone's tried to kick a way in.

"What...?"
"Come for me drill, 'a'n I?"
"Get in."

Can't move in here for crap. Fuck: this kitchen's a toilet; everything bust and rotten. Can't sit here. Can't put my bag down. Everything's running, betcha, with little paws come lights out. I can feel my beautiful, soft skin getting stained off the air.

"Where you been?"

"I'm here now."

He's a fat bloke got stains for clothes, poisoned on junk in a craphole flat. In a craphole life. I get twitchy sometimes when I think my best has gone. When I have to paint on slap for what soap used to do; when my arse don't fit a mini. But then I see states like him, and I feel gorgeous. I'm itchy, not just with his scabies. He'd better have the goods, not kid crap. A little toy's okay to rob drink shops. But I want men jealous, before I close their eyes.

"Here."

Not bad: smooth shape. Good lines. Not top of the range: a Monday gun. But new. Nothing worse than having to lift a gun out of bad habits. He's staring. I'm getting irritable with his staring.

"You a bloke?"

"*What?*"

"You're a bloke."

'Course I'm a fucking bloke. "*Yeah?*"

"Fucking hell."

He's having some kind of fit: his flabby cheeks got twitching.

"You seen?"

"What?"

"Getting here. Were you *seen?*"

There's a strangled urgency to his voice I recognise as fear. That sound pisses me off like no other. "Yeah: there was a crowd all wanting their cocks signed."

"I gotta *live* round here." His eyes are popping like targets.

"No you ain't." Run a clip. Feels good.

"What you doing?"

"Checking the goods, dipshit."

"I gotta be *careful*. Round here…"

He can stop fucking being scared. I got lines on my eyes from the anger that fear's caused me. Weak or strong, you get dead just the same. "Then *be* careful. Got a bathroom?"

"Bog's…"

"*Bathroom*. I wouldn't piss in your bog. I want a mirror."

"Mirror?"

"To do my fucking eyes. Don't fret," I chuck him, swishing by. "It ain't catching."

I can't say I like this mascara. Just a flash label. What you pay for, innit? Shit: got a lump. Have to re-do. Eyes are key. Vicente, of the lilac days, he was mad for my eyes. Used to call me the beautiful one, eyes to get lost in, lips for endless kisses. Spanish he was, *obviously*. I'm fucking soft for all that: guys spinning me moonbeams. Siesta time I'd lay on the couch, my head in his lap, do nothing. Sometimes for days my trigger finger wouldn't itch. Holiday romance, innit: over when you hit the airport.

"You done?"

"Well I ain't getting comfy."

"I got other *calls*."

"Listen…" Anger: bad for the skin. "I don't give a *shit*, get me? You get the goods, do as you're told, watch cable with a pizza. That's all you do. But if I go out with smudged eyes that's murders, understand me?" Barge by: think always what I look like from behind. There's more in my handbag now than lippy and tissues. More than that stupid phone thing that bleeps and flashes missed calls. I can make a difference now; I'm sweetheart of the block.

Feel girlish, running downstairs, little boots ringing on the concrete. I'm tall but ain't got freak feet. Proper sixes for kittens and courts. But today I got these little boots for walking. I got nice hands, too. Petite. Just a bit veined from the trigger. Gotta get my tone back, though. I want *skimpy*, now it's summer.

The lads stop their kickabout to watch me. I'm a well-travelled girl; I can swear in foreign ways. But *body* language, that's my mother tongue. Now their body language says mischief. Sling my bag on my shoulder and *swing*. When you front-up a gang, you always fix on the toughest: latch yourself to the real trouble-starter, 'cos you bet the rest are just fists and grievance.

"*Oi*."

What an English sound. *Ethnic*.

"*Oi*."

Seven boneheads. Not bad odds.

"Where d'you think you're going?"

I'd try to walk on but they'll block me in. Him with the mouth's not a bad-looking lad. Poor skin, though. Crap diet I bet. They line out across my way: playground tactics. But today, school's in.

"I *said* where you going?" Spotty wants interactive.

"I'm going to mind my own fucking business."

"You a bloke?"

There must be something in the water round here. Everyone got short-sighted. "Why, are you?"

"You battygash."

The others get this hyena thing, barking.

"You battygash in our yard."

What's he like? "You got the gist, then."

"What?"

POLLUTO

"What I'm saying, *blud*, is get the fuck out my way."

"You cuttin' eye? You *deep* me? Shitcunt."

I'm getting tired of this. "You gonna move?"

"What you bringin' filth? Stab me with your *mascara*?"

He jabs in my chest. His dirt is now on my linen. I don't recall saying he could touch. *Go*: I grab his wrist: crack it down, twist back, spin him round. Boot in his leg and down he goes, prayer-style. Kick his back. Hear the crack. The others stare, dazzled. "*What d'you say?*"

He does this rattly sound, choked on slimy fear.

"What d'you say?"

"Sorry, man." Shocked and whiney. This gangster's just a kid.

I see their eyes. Dead eyes. "*What d'you say?*"

They mutter it between them, kids caught out of school.

I let go and he falls, howling I've bust his bone. He doesn't even know tough guys don't show it. They scatter like cartoons. I'm fucking, fucking angry. Don't they get it? I'm *Flick*.

I gotta lose this *anger*. My face is hot. Burning. *What?* Another one in my way. Young lad, slim, nice face.

"Sorry."

Why the fuck's *he* sorry?

"You met the local scum."

Is he their social worker? Gotta push back the *hurt*. It's done.

"They're trouble."

Why's he talking to me? Gotta get back in the city. "Just kids."

"Everyone's scared round here."

"You scared?"

Nice eyes. Hazel. Coffee skin. Mixed-race makes pretty babies. "D'you wanna…" He goes for it. "Freshen up?"

"Do I look shit, then?" Warm in my belly. Oh yeah: *that's* where anger goes.

His crib's a tip. Not a shithole: I mean studenty, everything a jumble. When you live in hotels, you get used to people keeping house. Long time since I paid rent. He's got these gay old movie posters. Arty-farty. Hey: Cagney there: White Heat. Toughest guy in the world. "D'you like films?"

"I call it my aspiration wall." He laughs like he knows that's dumb. "I'm an *actor*. Well, trying to be. I'm at college." Gives this lemon-sherbet smile. "Bathroom's through there. Want coffee?"

No love: bad for the skin. "Got tea?"

"Raspberry or peppermint?"

POLLUTO

There's product in this bathroom. Varnish; nice set of lippies; good soap, moisturiser. These eyes still ain't right. It's meant to go *pow*, sock ya out. One punch. Like Cagney.

"Changed your eyes."

Nice he noticed. Gives me raspberry tea in a glass; with a *clove*. Reminds me *Très* Paris.

"Gotta say… You look *fantastic*."

It's so good getting told.

"I don't know anyone who dresses out. Not out on the street."

To put this in perspective: most cross-dressers are straight. I'm not. Most dress in private, upstairs, when the wife's out at her mum's. I don't. This is me, always. In fact, I'm not cross-dressing. This is how I dress. I'm not a category. I'm Flick.

"Shame Nat's not here. She's my flatmate. She'd *love* you."

I doubt she would. "I pinched her mascara."

"She's out all day. Auditions."

"D'you get auditions?"

"Yeah, yeah." Unsure. "Got a couple last week. It's waiting the chances, y'know."

This young man's life is open to me. I could tell him the plays I've seen, in Paris, in Berlin. Wouldn't mean jack.

"Shoulda said: I'm Adam. Remember the name." He giggles.

"Flick. Felicity. But I like Flick."

"Pretty name. What d'you do?"

What I do Adam, is travel the world killing to order. In the sexist lingo, I'm a hitman. Where people see death, I see business. The critical path is me and my gun. I'm bad dreams come true. "Oh, I work in a gallery. Just part time. Flogging tat to Russians."

He's nervous, eager. Men get wary sometimes on the threshold of my glamour. Young men, who only know the right jeans, the right hair; who are still learning. We kiss. He's boy lips: hesitant, unripe. Taste my cherry reds; now we're beginning. His bedroom seen through tumbling kisses: sudden smell of a stranger's bed. Feel him lift my skirt, my top, run his hands on my body. Mewing, while he tells me how soft, how firm I am. He rolls me over; I arch, making sounds that turn me on. Every time it's done to me, every time it matters: I wonder why can't life be *this*. See my peachy arse curved and raised; lips waiting; gel, cooling hot skin. He's part of me: I obey him, our hips fused. I shout, gasp, plead how I want him. I wriggle him all inside. Glove him tight, I'm his flesh dolly. He wanks me; I catch breath. I'm slaved. I tell him: *anything*. I'm gone. My arse clamped to him, my hips unravel: see myself spunk the bed, the gutter sounds of love. He delivers into me, feel his heat; bite the pillow, sweat and spunk. Let go.

His lips brush my neck; says he loves me.

And I picture the clock, the gun.

Will he want to lay with me, fingers twining my hair? I'll never know. The noise in my bag. The phone.

"Leave it," he says, like a young man would. But I'm working.

It's Derek the driver. "Catch on, squire, I've been after you all morning."

One missed call. Yeah: all morning.

"Just left that 'otel of yours. That piece on the desk was right surly."

Adam's hands make me shiver and twitch. I'm sat naked in his wet, talking with Uncle Fester.

"I *mean*, I didn't ask her for *much*. Just wanted a beer. It's a bloody long way from…"

"*Derek*."

Adam stops. There's a chill where one time was warm.

"Just tell me where you're going *now*. Just the gist."

Derek mouths off at some driver. Comes back. "Taking your crap to our *garridge*. Blimey, keep your wig on."

"It's not…"

"That's why I'm *calling*. Our Trace is working late; I gotta fetch our Tab and take her *ballay* after school."

I can't sequence any of this. "Tab?"

Adam gets dressed.

"Our *Tabitha*. You *know*. She's eight now. Goes *ballay*. She's *ever* so good."

Alone in Adam's bedroom I hear him on his phone.

"Anyroad, I'm only at Knightsbridge. Traffic's *diabolical*. So I might have to keep your stuff in the van till later, alright?"

Every shred of some brief good has gone. "Do that."

"So if you come calling…"

"I *won't* come calling. *Do that*."

"Blimey, mate, your blood pressure. Gotta go. I ain't hands-free, know what I mean?"

I feel shit where ten minutes back I felt okay. Pull on my clothes. Oh, *shit*: got spunk on my top. Must be mine. I'm keeping his safe. "Adam?"

"Boyfriend trouble?"

You *what*? I don't *do* boyfriends. "Just some errand guy. He's confused. I want one of your flatmate's tops." Show him why.

"Could wash it for ya."

Sweet Baby Jesus. "I gotta go."

"Got a date?"

POLLUTO

Ain't it clear I'm not the type? I ain't getting hitched, I'm not having babies, I don't go fucking skiing. "Got clients."

"Nat ain't tall as you."

"She gross?"

He looks shocked.

His Nat's got young girl taste: cheap high street colours. He shows me acids, blues. "It's got to match my *bag*."

He stares like I'm freaking. "Serious?"

And I've *been* with this boy? Ain't he noticed *anything* about me? Closest is a brick-red cotton halter. "This'll do."

"She'll want it…"

"She'll *get* it." But it won't be me brings it back.

Hug and kiss and I'm out the door, telling all sorts of lies. Walk downstairs, empty. Still looking for the fuck that lasts.

If I had sense, not just good skin, I'd quit Memory Lane. Round here is where I grew up. I could walk down our old street. Run over some useless relations. I gotta get uptown. Gotta *focus*. That fucking *phone*.

"Flick."

Who the...?

"Thought I'd call. Bring you up to speed on Mr Lomax's expectations."

"For tonight?"

"Unless there's some other night." Posh bastard taking the piss. "Where are you? Some gay bar?"

"South Hackney."

"They said you're exotic. Don't get cosy, eh? You're here for midnight. You'll get the party started."

"Where?"

"My colleagues will *give word*, as you people say. Mr Lomax appreciates punctuality."

"Good for him."

"He's a sociable man with high standards. When you get word, you'll do exactly as you're told. You'll have sitters. In case you start feeling…exotic."

This is payday. I'm hired.

"Mr Lomax knows many triggermen…"

He's telling me shit I should know. But I ain't listening. There's a small round cake, a kid's cookery lesson, cemented by its pink icing to a wall. Stuck slapstick-style: sponge setting hard in the heat. There's a girl in a Gooner shirt, running lengths of an alley, twisting and shouting, working the ball in and out of beer cans and flowers. Booting it down the path, arms in the air: *goal*. There's lads, stretching wire across the road. Too obvious for a garrotte, I follow the line to a tree opposite. They've looped wire through the branches, weighted a stone off the knot, ready to drop it on someone's skull: a cracking joke. I give 'em a wink: they smile and laugh. This bastard's still talking.

"…doesn't want his other guests disturbed. Mr Lomax is very particular his friends have a *good time*."

He leans on the pause like I should answer. But I ain't listening. There's a pub on the corner: The Lion, where the old man's firm used to meet. They had firms then. That's how they talked. My dad, he weren't a spiritual man. Not in touch with nature. But when he went out on a job, some kind of change overtook him. He was reverent for the business: he'd brush his jacket, shine his boots; oil his shotgun till it returned quiet as a whisper. He didn't pray; he paced the bedroom, silent, like praying. Then he'd snap to life, jog out the door, his tool in a canvas bag. Mum always called after him: *go careful*. He never answered. And my brothers would get new bikes, toy guns. And I'd get kicked for wanting dolls. Now they're nothing, and I'm Flick.

"…enhancing his reputation."

Has he finished? "When d'you think we'll be done?"

There's a bit of strain to his voice. "You what?"

"I got other *calls*."

A huffy little silence. "Well, if you're *busy*…"

"All I'm saying is when we *done*?" Christ, I'll hurt this bastard.

"Depends, doesn't it? You do as you're told. Mr Lomax expects performance."

I'm sharp to a shadow beside me; dark in the bright day. Young, tall; that loping stride of black lads wearing too much coat. "Gotta go."

"I make it one-fifteen. You'll get word by five. After that you're ours. Do good."

"Gi's your phone, sis."

He takes a grab but he's yards too fleshy and, easy, I'm away. "Not now, sonny."

"*Gi's*."

He's strong, I'm angry. Kick out: he shies off, nursing his bollocks.

"*Bitch*." He squints boiled eyes. "You not a *gal*?"

"Yeah."

Laughs, deep in his throat.

"What's your name?"

"K-Ras."

"You bus K?"

"Right."

POLLUTO

I've never been one for drugs. Drugs lead to situations that are bad for the skin. Sure I was a whiz queen, like everyone. But now I'm working.

"You got smoke?"

"I don't."

He hawks ripe phlegm in the gutter. "You not scared."

It ain't a question. These kids burn all their days jacking: fear and anger are what they know.

"Why you front as a *gal*?"

"Why you front as a *gangsta*?"

Rumbling laugh again. "It's all good." He offers his touch and lopes to catch some bitch toting laptop. She screams, starts to run. But not in those heels, love. There's so much you gotta watch out for: bad fat, bad protein, bad carbs. Bad men with guns.

This the fucking cab shop? Must be. These fat blonde birds don't work no other places. What d'you mean ten minutes? I *can't* sit on that sofa: this skirt's linen. Sometimes, I want to put holes in things. Windows, doors; pump angry blood out the barrel. I could put one clean through the little glass hatch, straight in her cowing face. That flab would keep it well off her brain. Could put one out the door, up the jacksy of him on that ladder. Easy.

That the car? Sweet fucking lord. Didn't know that colour was legal. Oh, fuck sakes: *leopard print*. And he's a rum cove. What is that shit in his ears? And this bassline…I'm keeping my legs crossed.

"Holborn, my friend?"

I ain't your fucking friend.

"I go Holborn. *Court*."

I don't want to talk to you.

"Non-payment, *right*? Send me letter. Say dem: you won *television. Plasma*. And m'think: football, *right*? Go this place say in letter, this *Drill Hall*, yeah? And the wicked dem lift me, take m'Holborn court. Non-payment. So me stuck, *right*? Have to dig *deep*, know what I'm saying?"

"Non-payment?"

"Criminal damage, *right*? Window to some *caff*. But dem me poison, *right*? Put worms in m'stew. Shits. Five days. *Fierce*. And then the resisting. But me vexed, *right*? I'd not done with the caff. And harming the wicked, when dem took me dungeon."

"Sounds a day out."

"Dem not even leave me *bus* fare. Had to tax a car to get home."

I avoid the wicked. I never think, when I pump the pin, I'll end in dungeon. He's got all the windows open; the breeze is warm, Catalan. Hair's getting blown all over. Slip in a little sparkly slide.

He catches me in the rear-view. "Man, that's *sweet*."

POLLUTO

Red Lion Square. Harsh like a rash; dust heat, shit for skin. Should check in a hotel; moisturise with the blinds down. There's places above these shops, hidden. For people like Anna. That number I had for her's long stopped ringing. She don't email. You've got to look right, to find her door. The shiny shops out front are very Sicilian Avenue. But in this piss-alley the walls are always damp; in these scraps, old London bleeds through.

Don't guess she's out. Anna goes shopping late. No intercom, no camera; she knows I'm here. Way up the streaked wall there's a vent just wide enough for sharp eyes. I don't expect footsteps: she's lighter than air.

"S'pose you want *girls'* tea?"

"Hi, Anna."

Twisty stairs of a child's nightmare. No windows, no light; only her slender back. So slim: I'm jealous. Can count every bone in her skin. First, second landing. Boards nailed over where once were doors. She told me: get through the boards, there's passages, old rooms, sticks of furniture. A nursery of crusted, shattered toys.

"Mind for my rats, now."

She so *always* says that. Running alive; hear them scratch and scatter. Mustn't be sick. She's not scared. She calls them, makes little chucking sounds. They seem to like her. Follow her up, our footsteps dulled by darkness.

The blind's down, everything dripping in seaweed light. Everything plain, low-cal; she doesn't do *stuff*. She fills the kettle. Anna drinks tea always. Her teeth are like teak. She asks how I am.

"Surviving."

I can't go a day without falling in love. Anna says she's done with all that. Single and free. Not older or wiser; she's got magazine skin. She gives me blueberry and ginger tisane. It smells of dancing after rain.

"How long you over?"

Have to push myself from thinking nothing. "Two. Maybe three. Depends."

"Working?" Her eyes steel-up when she asks if I'm working.

"Could be sweet. What you got on Lomax?"

She's internet in skinny jeans. "Malcolm Armstrong Lomax. Prefers *Mr*. Bachelor of this city, forty-eight years young. Pain in the arse from baby days robbing old loves round Mile End. Got marked for a look-out by Marty Brewer, of blessed memory. Lent muscle to Stevie Dixon, when bona Miss Dixon still warmed us with his grace."

"Fucking noras." They were the big boys, once.

POLLUTO

She's dancing, itchy with stories. "When Marty went upriver and Miss Stevie accepted the hand of god, the boys was scattered, y'know. Well, *you* know."

"Not glamorous days."

"Not for Lomax, man. He was up the creek: jacking ambulances for sunsets. *Then…* he comes good."

She's the fastest dirt you need. "How?"

"Wee-lll, bro', de drums: dem *dispute*. He says he got a tip come in. But funny how no one else knew it. Who was he working? Who was the mark? *Right*. Some said he bussed kiddies for minted nonces. But then steps would have got took. Lotta family men in your game, know what I mean? Lomax was this D-list twat rattling round the Dartford Tunnel, then *whoosh*: he's intergalactic. Mirror shoes, man; leathers. He blows back up west full of it, sets up a front for his crew. His *firm*, as your dad, late of the parish of Shacklewell would have it."

That's nice. Nice touch.

"He's gone Charley-big-batatas. And all sorts: your Russians, Ukraines, your Afro-Chinks, all asking: *how come?*"

"How come?"

"Long ago, man, far away was a guy called Langton. Triggerman, remember?"

Thugs and blaggers come and go; triggermen remember.

"Langton found his-self pole position on a payday. Some old Malt it was, flogging her old pot-and-pan. Now Langton had a gob on him fierce as my dad's fist - *no, daddy, no: I'll be good, I won't tell mum* - and Langton got this thirstiness, the Texas way…"

I know. I know what's coming.

"Lomax was the king dealing stud. Had time to practice, them years in holiday camp."

"He was inside?" Not good. Cops never let go the graduates of our penal institutions.

"Did some in the Dixon fallout. Two years, receiving. So when Langton comes out the coma…"

"Lomax took the job off him?"

She checks her fingers: "Jack, queen, king: two-pair, two-pair, get me? When he goes looking, Lomax…"

"With Langton's own *gun*?"

I should know better than cut-in on Anna. "S'all I heard." She shuts down.

Watch her shoulders lock and move as she sifts dirty water in the sink. I was always jealous: her size, the shape I want to be. Her place: hidden and unchanging. Almost safe with Anna. "You working?"

POLLUTO

"Not hard like you." She dries her hands on a rag. "What's your thing with Lomax?"

"Dunno." Tea's gone cold. Tastes like squash. "He wants me for his party."

"You gonna kill someone?"

It's what I do: commodity liquidation. In the business model of an international network that's got corporate structures, accountants, strategists, fixers, I'm a negotiator: I unblock deals. I'm so they don't forget how they came by that shine on their shoes. I'm last in the building when the lights go out and the cameras are broke.

She builds a spiff, hunched like a child worrying at a puzzle. She's a dreamer, in her nervy, crackers way. She thinks there's a world, maybe just out of reach, where we'll be right with each other. Where she could paint, while thugs pick flowers and I'd go shopping all day. Where scum like Lomax evaporate, first touch of the morning sun. I toke her skunk, see a day just smoking with Anna. Watching green light thicken as evening folds around us. Waking cramped and rough on her couch. The spitfire and the lotus-eater. But I got work. Stand, bone-weary. Sometimes I want to tell her how I should be a *young* girl. How it scares me getting old. But what would she know? She's unchanging. "Eyes okay?"

She blinks. "Not red or nuffin."

"I mean…" Draw circles in the air.

She squints. "Bit lean. I'll fresh ya."

She's got the gear: robs with style does Anna. I stand while she draws me pretty. Up close her skin's waxy, her eyes are flecked with grit. Her mouth hangs open in concentration; her fingers are quick. I want just to do nothing. Smoking's so bad for the skin.

"Gorgeous." She pecks my cheek. "Go see."

Her bathroom's an aladdin's of make up and memories. Things that gather, things that remain, robbed off good nights gone. She's done me kohl and beautiful: deep black ovals, purplish-black, my eyes blue liquid in a dark hollow. The room's got a friendly smell of talc and loose arrangements. When I had a place of my own, a Pimlico apartment, I'd invest whole Sunday mornings cleaning house. Nice salad lunch at that place by the river; the young guy there always gave me the eye. I'd walk the embankment, looking for sex, no gun in my pocket.

She's stood, hands in her jeans back patches, diamond arms all bones. I got love for no one, but something safe for Anna. I know what she wants: her skin's all signals. Her teeth bite at words she can't say.

On the second landing I stare through a boarded doorway. Try not to hear rats whisper; try to see what she sees. I can snatch a man's life but I can't go those places. Only cats see in the dark. And girls who are cats.

POLLUTO
◆

"Alright, chief."

I'm a dog on a string.

"Shoulda said: it's our Tab's *show*."

"What?"

"*Ballay*, mate. Her thirteen weeks show."

Got a plate of figs and artichoke hearts I'm trying to make sense of. Got Derek talking fuck knows. "*Yeah?*"

"Well, I gotta go, an'I? Our Trace don't finish till seven."

There's no reason for him to tell me these things. He just wants to talk himself real.

"I put the van in the pay 'n' display. Don't want it *clamped*, do we? Thing is, I've to take Tab to her nan's after. She's all the way out…"

"Don't tell me, sweetheart. Just do what you gotta do. She dressed as a fairy?"

"*You what?*"

"Your Tab."

"It's a tutu, mate. Tutu."

Shouldn't eat Italian. Carbs. And all that cream. Wish I could not be a pig. The tagliatelle ain't the only cream dish: I'm a kid for them warm southern looks. Wonder what service includes…Yeah, it's very nice. Lovely. Yeah, been Italy loads. Rome. Naples. Don't tell him I was bad down Naples. Three hungry lads: what's a girl to do? That was the day I blew the brains out some fat man. One of the silk suits that make our Lomaxes look chicken shit. I got winged off the *capo's* boys; they chased me right down to where I had the speedboat. Naples, man. S'beautiful.

Scam the bill on plastic. Get dealt fresh plastic every job. Today I'm Alicia Moran. She's generous, is Alicia, needs something for her kindness. Next petrol stop, I'll flash her the roses. Yeah, it was lovely. Love Italian. The giggle in my voice, that girly flush. Yeah? You got pictures of Naples? Yeah, I'd like that. You got a room *upstairs*?

I am *so* a horny bitch. Up here, yeah? Of course, anywhere might be a trap. Come the day, you bet I get ended by the lad with the *sweetest* cock. In here, yeah? Nice, nice little room. Very neat. I said it's neat. Tidy. Grappa? Just a small one. Must *not* drink any more after this. He's saying my hair's pretty, touching it, touching my face. Oooh. Got lovely touch. He thinks I'm very beautiful, keeps touching my face. Kiss his hand, chase it with my lips. Got my shoulders, pushing me back on the bed. Strong hands, finding my need, growing me, opening me out. Please: please do it to me. Please don't make me beg. Oh, *fuck*: he's *hard*. Fuck fuck fuck. Not using anything. *Ow*. Oh, Jesus

POLLUTO

Fucking *Christ*. Oh yeah yeah yeah. Oh *Christ*. Ah. *Ah*. Oh, what…oohah. Rub me. *Rub me*. Throwing me round like…*argh*. Oh, shit: c'mon, *c'mon*. Spunk me, *spunk me*. Don't stop don't stop don't stop. *Spunk me. Aaahhh*. Oh, fucking hell I love you. I love you so much. Ooohhh….

"This also very pretty."

Cold, his heat passing. Roll over and…*Oh shit*. Never like getting wrong side of guns. And he does have the *sweetest* cock.

"Your bag: a treasure chest, eh?"

Fucking Eye-tie bag-thief. "It's a replica."

"Lie."

What then? Die of carbs and spunk?

"I think this a business gun. For a man on business, maybe?"

Shit. "Single girl needs insurance." Gotta get up.

"Stop."

"Can I get dressed?"

"I like you this way. You are very pretty. A good fuck. But what's done…" He runs the clip.

"You like guns?"

"Where I come from, these are baby toys." He waves the snout at his holiday snaps. "I think you make some *arrangement*? I know people who make *arrangements*. Business people. They get… *unsettled*, when they don't know who comes and goes. They like," he draws a line on me, "to manage the market."

Noise on the stairs. He flinches. The door catch rattles.

"Pauli."

We look to the voice.

"*Pauli*." Door bangs. In sharp Italian: "You have someone there?"

"Just coming."

"*You have someone there?*"

Grab my clothes, southern curses raining on the door. He runs the sash, shows me the ladder. In *this* skirt? "Gun?"

"Go."

"Bag?"

"*Go*."

"*I said I'd kill you next time*." The door splinters.

Hand over hand in the rising stink of bins. Kitchen vents bitch my skin. Reach out my foot… *Yuck*. Run. Shit shit shit: my bag, gun, phone. *Shit*.

"Excuse me, miss."

Oh *shit*.

"Is something wrong?"

Not really, officer. Just a long hot day. I'm working tonight; more drunk than I ought to. And I just had a fuck - a *nice* fuck - and I hate I get scared at the losers' end of a bullet. I know boys don't cry and tough guys don't dance but I don't want to *die*, not before... I don't even know what not before. And I lost the sweetest burnt cherry bag: got it down Avignon. And I lost a gun that isn't mine and it's *years* since I lost a gun. And I lost a device that tells tales all day on a fairly major psycho. And payday's canned and I'm *dead*. Ginger peachy.

"Did you just climb out that window, miss?"

"Um, yeah."

"And... there's a reason for that?"

"Um... lost my keys."

"Yes?"

"Stolen. My keys got stolen. Jealous boyfriend." I'm distressed, arsehole: respect it.

"Can I see some identification please?"

"Um... got none." Shit fucking *shit*.

"That's a bit unusual, isn't it, miss?"

Oh *right*, bad-boy. "Kinda left in a *rush*, y'know. Jealous boyfriend. You wanna pull him."

"That's a restaurant, isn't it?"

Sherlock, man: you are so far from where you think you are.

"There have been break-ins round here lately."

Lately?

"Could you confirm your name please miss?"

"Alicia Moran."

"Address?"

Shit, he's calling it in. "I've been *assaulted*." Why can't I tell proper lies? Why do I get in shit?

"I think we could talk more easily at the station. A female officer can accompany you."

"What?"

"Alicia Moran was murdered."

SCIENCE FICTION STORY

J.S. WATTS

Red. Always red.
Seas of blood, deserts of torn flesh.
Winds howl in anger, wail in despair.
Nothing to do but press on or die
In waves of destruction
Rolling in from behind.

Daytime. Real time.
The coffee good. The papers not.
Conversation light and jovial
Until the writing comes up.

Another tale of gloom and doom.
Why can't you write something amusing,
Something with a little get up and go?
He bit his tongue.
It's just stories. Science Fiction.
Write happy for once.

How could he tell her it wasn't fiction?
That before their worlds collided
He'd travelled the galaxy and beyond,
Had found perfection of heaven in his eye.

Had seen things she wouldn't believe:
flames leaping off the shoulder of Orion;
c-beams glittering dark by the Tannhauser Gate;
yellow meadows, crystal rivers, stars, suns and planets
spread out forever; a Milky Way of tales.
Such beauty until the nightmares came.

Blood. Human blood on the lens of the 'corder.
Life ripped by blasts of super-human force.
Rivers streaked red, promises veined with betrayal.
Unspeakable acts in love with profane myths.

POLLUTO

He didn't write fiction.
He wrote the truth,
But all the beauty of far away galaxies
Couldn't stop the nightmares
From crawling and bleeding into his stories
As nightly they stained his dreams.

He tried to tell her of the rapture of three suns
rising over the Ghost Falls of Fusillia,
But she wouldn't hear him.
He spoke of risking death
just to see a blue moon kiss
the diamond peak of Mount Medusa.

She could never understand
he had made landfall on a planet
of necrotising anger and hatred,
where the inalienable right to be right,
regardless of the needs and beliefs of others,
contaminated every life force in existence;
that the joy of the stars and the purity of space
were for ever stained red by the horrors of Earth.

THE FRAGGING OF CAPTAIN YORKE

JAY MACLEOD

We all thought highly
of the Captain
until he tried
to send us back
into the Lkiz sector

aka "The Bermuda Triangle" of Mars

The Captain was young
and ordinarily quite sensible

With a lovely family
back on Earth

He led from the front-
a soldier's soldier-

but he received an
incomprehensible
order from Command
which he was obliged to pass on

Most of us conscripts
have no use for this planet
or the zombies
or the locals
or their war

To his credit
the Captain got us out of several
jam-ups
outside the wire

Then in one week
we lost Rodriguez to a landmine
Devlin to a child-zombie
Yow to the scorpions
and Wilson did himself with his
service revolver

En route to the sector
we came under fire
from one of our
so-called "allied planets"

We passed through
village after village
of slaughtered locals

We were ambushed repeatedly

After three days
of the most horrific fighting
any of us had seen
we made it to the forward
operating base

POLLUTO

Later that evening
Captain Yorke announced

we were going back in
at 04:00
to clear out the sector
once and for all

He told us this
before retiring to his tent

We remaining few
in the platoon
commiserated

Williams made the suggestion
Chan procured
the weapon
Nemsky kept watch
I rolled it in-

And then we scattered-
I may have overcharged the
grenade-
It took out the Captain's tent
as well as Lieutenant Myles,
Sergeant Walthers
and several of the locals who
worked odd jobs around the camp-
there were scores of injuries

A terrible shame,
but it had to be done-

No one should suspect
my involvement
After all, I left an arm
back there;
Who's going to be able to
tell mine from all the
other body parts?

WEB 3.0

JAY MACLEOD

The technology
is only mildly invasive-
a bit of nano-surgery
allows access
to the net from any location
at any time-
it began in the mid-00's

Bandwidth
is cheaper than water
and more plentiful than oxygen-

Heroin is obsolete-
poppy growers
in Central Asia
are no longer regarded as
criminals-
or narco-terrorists-
rather
they are entrepreneurs
free to
sell their flowers to Big Pharma

Every man, woman and cyborg
spends the better part
of each day online

In response
to popular demand,
historians have been asked
to develop VR scripts
for witch-burning,
water-boarding,
and the guillotine

POLUTO

MECHAGNOSIS

DOUGLAS THOMPSON

'Mechagnosis' is the first chapter of Douglas Thompson's novel Mechagnosis.

Scott Malthrop climbs aloft through the dusty skylight, out to the big roof and ruffling birds. It is time. How like waves their wings lift his breaths and cloud the eyes. Fresh fluttersong of washing-lines: glimpsed mysteries of neighbours in solitariness. The sweet grain of urban monotony, secrets unshared. The sun goes down like eyelids closing, bracing grimace, dignity of pain.

Malthrop has access to several apartment roofs as well as his own, and these he has gradually colonised with foliage and bait for birds, and cages to catch them. In the early days of his father's first experiments, perhaps some of the birds were run to death. This was foolish and short-sighted as well as immoral. Now every bird is only temporarily captured and put to work then re-released a week later into the beckoning sky, well-rewarded for its labour. Malthrop has come to love the birds, their calm eyes and fluttering hearts. Although he rarely tags them, he believes some return on purpose, wanting to be captured again, for the exercise and the food, maybe even for his company.

Today he enlists only a dozen and releases the others, taking them below in wooden cages, down through the roof hatch into his apartment, or what used to be an apartment. Now it is only residual, marginal, left over space around *The Machine*. The Machine occupies all three storeys of his narrow urban townhouse, from front to back, cogs and levers up against windows and walls, floor joists long cut away and braced to make room for wheels and pistons.

He times his start-up phase to coincide with the busiest periods of traffic outside, so the neighbours will not be overly alarmed by the considerable vibrations. Sometimes he likes to use a few seagulls for extra power, but today the team are all pigeons, city doves, his trusty stalwarts. The Intake Platforms consist of wheels and wing harnesses within ventilated glass tanks and seed dispensers. Malthrop kisses and caresses each bird one after the other, calming and soothing its palpitations before depositing it gently down a one-way tube onto its running wheel. When all twelve avian pilots are assembled, he salutes them with a tired smile then descends below to rope himself into the control room.

We say "control", and yet the whole essence of this room is a lack of control. A statistical degree of hazard has been built in, essential to guarantee a sense of danger on the part of the operator. A one in one hundred chance always exists that the Dead Man's Lever will fall and Malthrop suffocate in sand or water. In such a scenario, his skeleton will eventually become part of The Machine, as his father and mother are already: just one of a thousand sentimental objects incorporated for esoteric functions which somehow contribute to its overall spiritual charge.

One thing is for certain: when The Machine is working, every component, at some point, must move. The toy sailboat with white sails that his father built him when he was aged three, will rotate and rock on salty waves in an old bathtub. His mother's swimsuit will be stretched and flexed like a washing machine's driveband. The crackling gramophone record of the sound of seagulls will repeat while the sand from the first beach he ever played on pours like an hourglass from vessel to vessel: colourful bright plastic pales from beaches; grim janitorial buckets that caught waterdrops from the roof leaks in his first school.

Malthrop sits and writes his diary entry, aware as ever that it may be his last:-

The word "Nostalgia" was only invented in 1688, by the Swiss physician Johannes Hofer, to describe a medical condition of near-fatal homesickness. If, as Wittgenstein said, "the limits of my language mean the limits of my world", then did nostalgia simply not exist before this date, if it could only be so clumsily denoted as wistfulness for days passed?

Father made me memorise the dates. 1674: The English agricultural pioneer Jethro Tull is born. 1701: he invents the seed drill, setting off the Agricultural Revolution and in turn the Industrial Revolution. Mechanisation gets underway and the traditional way of life of the rural peasant is doomed to history. This is how history works: from the tiniest insignificance a chain of events grows too slowly for anyone to ponder or stop. A seed drill is invented and men land on the moon. The Machine starts. Tonight I might die.

-Scott Malthrop, son of Scott Malthrop Senior (deceased), 30th April 2020.

Malthrop binds and gags himself until completely helpless, throws his head back onto The Starter Pad. The chamber he is locked within begins to fall and rotate on an infinitesimally slow orbit through The Presses. Although, like life on Earth, at any given moment he can feel entirely static, in truth he is perpetually in motion and danger. Gradually over hours, water and soil come and go: plants from his parents' garden, grass from the park where he kissed his first girlfriend, water from the bath in which he drowned her. His wrist bindings are coils of her black hair, and when The Machine stretches him over its cruellest segments, deprived of air, he will struggle and her tresses will dig deep into his flesh as he screams, washed in his own blood and tears.

Above him or below somewhere, as the great calibrated wheels rotate, the birds will flap and pedal on with industrial ferocity, rest-times kicking in and alternating, the tag team dutifully working through the night. Their calm eyes remain relentless in their purpose, profoundly understood. Animals have no concept of futility.

◊

What was the first machine in the world I wonder? The slingshot? The Shadoof? Archimedes' Screw? The Buddhist prayer wheel... now there's an interesting one: a machine played by the wind, by the Gods themselves, with only a spiritual purpose. Sometime after the dawn of the machine age, the backlash quietly began: the absurd machines of eccentric inventors have sprung up simultaneously all over the planet, like spring flowers magically blossoming in the shade of a broad oak. **Heath Robinson**, **Rube Goldberg**, every culture today has its own name and equivalent: in France **The Gas Factory**, Denmark **Storm P Machines**, in Bengal **Abol Tool**, in Japan **Chindōgu** and **Pythagoras Switch**, Turkey **Zihni Sinir Proceleri**. The beauty and universal appeal of these devices, particularly to children (the most devout little anarchists amongst us), resides in their very inefficiency, their transparent futility. But Man and Machine have unfinished business since 1701. Has irrational beauty really no term within our mathematical equations? If these machines are pointless then Life is pointless. But if we can bring ourselves to say that such machines are sublimely beautiful, what then? Then the metaphor, the microcosm is grasped, and we may be healed. The most perfectly futile, the most sublime and absurd machines of all are of course: ourselves. We must embrace futility and absurdity. We must seize the machines that so wound us and make them part of us again, make love to them, make them as magnificently ludicrous as ourselves. Then we, and they, will be whole again, and God will smile.

◊

Malthrop's mother had been obsessed with cleanliness. The droning of the vacuum cleaner not once but twice a week, was the oppressive music of his childhood. Not satisfied with this, she had purchased a separate vacuum for each storey of the house and inducted Malthrop and his father into operating each of these simultaneously while she worked her fastidious routine. The resultant wall of noise must have tried the neighbours sorely, but since Malthrop seldom saw them he soon presumed them stone deaf, mad, or dead from the attrition. Perhaps they were good solid walls, and just as well.

What drove his father most to despair, was how the Hoovering regime had to go on regardless of other commitments and weather. Although Malthrop's parents were fond of a weekend walk together in the country, often this would have to be undertaken at sunset, twilight, or black of night, the day's preceding sunlight having been cruelly squandered on the manic removal of dust.

Then there were the washing machines. Three of them. One each. Malthrop believed that other families allowed their worn linen to accumulate for a day or two, in charming wicker baskets. But in his mother's regime anything handed in dirty would have to be washed within the hour, even if it meant it had to be the only item in the drum. It was inconceivable to him how he might go about explaining to his school teachers that he was exhausted and inattentive in class due to sleep loss from washing machine noise. He almost envied his classmates their simpler traditional pleasures of fighting parents and teenage brothers with loud music.

◊

When The Machine is in perfect motion: whirring, exquisitely organised, and Malthrop bound, robbed of control of his own destiny; he can at last begin to dream and drift. Time dissolves for hours and days on end. He has no moon or sunlight, partial sensory deprivation takes hold. Space, the materiality of the walls, dissolves. He sees a beach, perhaps it is the sand pouring down tubes near his neck, but no: he is really there now on that beach. He stands up and looks around. He looks down and sees his arms are bound with seaweed, breaking off easily, dissolving. He feels a rumbling beneath his feet, and kneels down and brushes some sand away: he realises the entire Machine is still working, but buried under the sand. He laughs to himself and walks across the top of it and on towards a strange apparition: a hedge maze, here on the edge of the sea. Where is this? Does he remember this place at all?

◊

He first met Melanie in the summer pavilion in the Botanic Gardens. Summer rain had forced them both indoors, total strangers, running from different directions towards each other, closing the flimsy wooden doors behind them like a conspiracy. Her long hair soaked with rain was like a static waterfall, a gleaming black fountain of life. Her eyes, her smiles, breaking into laughter as sunlight re-emergent: struck the dewdrops like bells, sparkling diadems on spiders' webs at the trellised eaves.

She had asked him the time of day and he had shrugged and pointed calmly to her watch. *Oh, this? It's stopped, I'm afraid.* Her long slender arm bore something gold and Swiss.

May I? She shivered sweetly as he took her wrist. *I am a jeweller, I might...* Her eyes widened as he took it apart in front of her, too stunned to stop him until the peril was over before it had begun, the piece returned to her in good order. *I think you'll find it will work now...* he smiled modestly.

You make jewellery, watches? – she marvelled.

Repair other people's mostly, he sighed, gazing out again at the bleak rain, - *but occasionally I get to work on something new.*

How did you learn?

From my father.

A family business?

Well, it is mine now, the work ruined his hands and eyes, as it may do mine, in time...

But you have such lovely hands, she gasped, surprised at herself for being so forward, *the fingers...*

Long and sensitive, like a girls? – he blushed, old playground taunts echoing through his inner ear.

Like an artist... she said smiling, and closed his hand around itself like a flower.

◊

The importance of words again. Even the word "Luddite" has been carefully sabotaged and barbed by modern historians and sociologists, to police the minds of the present generation. The Luddites did not oppose machines or destroy machines out of wanton hatred. They left intact the mills and weaving machines of anyone who had not used the increased productivity to lower their prices and wages. They were opposed in other words, not to machines, but to an economic system that used machines to make ordinary people's lives worse, not better. Their simple question was one that should still be asked today about every new invention before we embrace it, but never is: will it improve our experience of life? -Enhance or diminish our sense of our selves? Do we actually need it?

This was no trivial matter. It was the British Empire's equivalent of Rome's Spartacus and the Slave Revolt. At times in 1813, more soldiers were fighting Luddite armies than were fighting Napolean's forces in Spain. Thousands of Luddites were tried and deported and imprisoned for life. "Machine Breaking" was made a capital crime. Ring leaders were hung and beheaded in public. Right from the start, machines have been a serious business.

◊

Malthrop's mother. Dust to dust. Dust was, and is, everywhere. Not like stains and spills with someone to blame and the hope of avoidance. Dust happens. The fear of dust is like the rejection of time and life itself. To clean it away is to say you wish to die, to cancel out your own sordid stain upon eternity. To Malthrop, his mother always seemed to live life as a dress rehearsal, a dance alone on a blank stage she had to keep clean until something better happened. But nothing happens if the stage is kept blank. *Please Mrs Malthrop, can Scott Junior come out to play?* – his friend Vince's disappointed face at the door. Bringing friends back would, of course, increase the likelihood of mess and stains, so better not to have them. Life, in short, is horribly likely to incur death. So don't live. Clean. Constantly.

There was an accident in the end. Stairs are fiercely hard to keep clean, the most wear-and-tear combined with the most awkward angles. Something fell or twisted, a Hoover dropped through space into a stairwell like a plunging pendulum and his mother was strangulated, her limbs pinned through a balustrade. Whatever cries she may have emitted were of course, entirely inaudible to her dutifully employed spouse and issue, engaged in their own sonic blitzkriegs on separate floors. For years afterwards, Malthrop found his frozen memory of the scene of her demise he chanced upon, impossible to consider as anything other than a grotesque art installation.

A good deal of The Machine having been built by his father, Malthrop can never be entirely certain of its next move. Is it the third day now, or the fourth? He has totally lost track of time. The adapted railway track has gradually taken him towards the basement and the Chamber of Slicing Mirrors, lined with his grandmother's fur coats, the intoxicating aroma of mink and fox and mothballs and old mould. The mirrors flood slowly with boiling hot water this time, and various childhood trinkets: rubber ducks and toys come bobbing down to meet him, the inane grin on a clown face mocking him in frozen caricature of sadistic mirth as the vicious steam accumulates.

Suddenly a further door opens and an autumnal bonfire scaulds him, piles of leaves blow over him, black embers sting his eyes. Damp grass and earth are everywhere: he is helping his father chop wood as a child. He can smell his dad's tweed jacket, the rubber of his boots. He is back in time. His parents have just had a fight, and Malthrop's mother has stormed off threatening never to return, but they know she will, like all the other times. There is a quiet camaraderie brewing between father and son, like a teapot on the hob, like a bonfire gone past its peak and safe to leave unattended. Smiling, late, coldish sunlight is in his father's eyes, the glint of wisdom in his spectacles, the sweat on his brow: the fruit of honest toil rather than nervous tension, for a change. Things will be alright. Malthrop wants to stay there forever: with the smell of sacks of fresh-fallen apples laid out on the kitchen floor.

◊

If only the world had made it easier to report Mother's death. The forms, the certificates, the weeks and months of insensitive bureaucracy, the disbelief from every faceless organisation, forcing my father to photocopy her death certificate over and over again and take it like a naughty schoolboy with a punishment exercise to show his bank manager, just to get access to their joint account. A hundred phonecalls from a hundred companies demanding that the flagrant charade of fraudulent death be admitted to. After the many indignities that this society heaps on every individual throughout their life, it saves its best one until last: that even to die is some kind of transgression, a non-sequitur in the capitalist system, something our relatives are made to feel to blame for, if we are let away with it at all. No, my father and I would sit down together at the end of yet another day of "formalities" and laugh through our tears and grief: how much easier and simpler it would be not to die at all. Indeed, it seems to be what "they" expect of us.

People wonder why great civilisations like the Maya collapsed without apparent reason in the past: and I suspect that one day they will find out the answer is that they invented the application form, then lost the taste for life. Drowned under the weight of their own bureaucracy. Life is too complex to map and categorise. It just happens. But when you try to categorise and file it, it does not.

That was the seed of some of our genius, you see. We resolved there and then that my father would not be buried when the time came, and that our shared names were a great opportunity. So I am officially a hundred and sixty years old now and have the longest running state pension in recorded history. Except history isn't recording me.

◊

Melanie was always trying to keep fit. Malthrop went with her a few times to the local gymnasium and was always horrified by the machines they had there. There was something vile and intermittent in their motion. They had no fluidity of purpose, no holistic integration. Running machines, walking machines: then why had Melanie driven them both to the gym? She was never able to answer this, as if it was a ludicrous question that only a simpleton would ask. Why simulate a three mile walk when you could just take one? And those weights and devices for stretching pectoral and biceps, the forces they exerted seemed horribly oblique, unfamiliar, the aches and pains they left you with like the aftermath of some grossly unnatural act that you might want to confess to a doctor or priest.

The scene in the gym amazed Malthrop: of rank after rank of running youths confined like battery hens, counteracting their mental boredom with video and audio through wires and screens. It seemed like distilled futility, stripped of its customary clothes, as if your employer were to ask you to lick every stamp you would ever need in your life in just one afternoon, or make every cup of coffee you'd need for a year in advance.

Melanie was young, her figure was perfect, but God had made it that way, not gymnasiums, and not Melanie herself. It had always struck Malthrop as ludicrous how a woman might thank you if you praised her good looks, as if she could have been in any way eligible for credit for her own physical creation. Praising her parents might make more sense, but even then it would only be for not having damaged her. Insane though it sounds, and Malthrop was by no means religious, praising a woman for her looks had always struck him as something close to blasphemy.

Malthrop is sitting in a bar in the Canal District, telling his old school friend Vince about the early days of The Machine, after his mother died. His father had gone quite strange for a while, and thought about starting his own religion. He had set out to find some followers. Vince laughs as Malthrop tells him how when he was just thirteen he had been made to take a collection box around the dusty old wooden pews of a derelict church, looking with doe-eyes for donations from gatherings of various social outcasts, semi down-and-outs, and mental cases. The Machine was much smaller then, a less advanced prototype only the size of one room, and a few privileged believers who came visiting were allowed access to the Mechanised Revelation of Sublime Absurdity, a private view.

Malthrop can still remember fragments of his father's sermons:

The Industrial Age has robbed much of the Human race of its dignity, remade us all in its own image. It seems as if to be a good citizen we must do our very best to resemble robots. Mankind has redefined itself in terms of the machine, even in our very language to describe ourselves: upgrades, products, consumers, dysfunctional, social services, integration, productivity. But the opposite process is still possible and necessary. Humanise the machines, make them artistic and restless and pointless, vain and unreasonable, contrary and vicious, capricious and scandalously beautiful, just as we are. Fuck the machines before they fuck you!

But he can't have said that in a church! Vince objects loudly, standing up and slamming his glass on the table, - and *why would you risk telling me this?* Malthrop looks up to see that the left side of Vince's face is melting as if it is a billposter soaked in rain, and one of his hands is turning gleaming silver. Malthrop steps away from the table and Vince's hand has become an egg-whisker now, a whirring liquidiser that he is lifting threateningly towards his face, as his voice turns into Malthrop's mother's, harping on about cleanliness and godliness.

Something's wrong, the electric bulb overhead blinks and Malthrop knocks Vince aside and staggers over to the far wall, holding his temples, a throbbing headache taking hold. He draws the tall black curtains to the function room aside and instead of the expected amplifiers and beer kegs he finds The Machine humming and whirring and turning, its dials flashing, shaking the floor. He turns back and sees the room is fading, Vince has curled up under the table and is whimpering as he turns into a pet dog.

Malthrop is back in The Machine. Can it be day five? He has soiled himself and the pain and fatigue are growing unbearable, his leg bindings cutting through the skin. Multi-coloured electric wires are visible around him now: the Zone Of Memories Of Lightning perhaps, or of Every Computer You Have Ever Worked On. The meditations crush him. Every drawing and document he has ever done seen from the perspective of each hard drive and processor. The slow passage of dull days encoded in binary, the flashing of electrons. Like looking at yourself as a fourteen mile high statue from the perspective of a flea on your shoe. Time, molecular time. Only during sensory deprivation can you grasp the horror of each infinite instant.

A switch clicks and the first of a series of agonising electric shocks convulses Malthrop in the comfortless darkness. A surprise: something nice his father left him.

Of course he had tried to delay for as long as possible Melanie gaining entry to the house. Stories of his father being a dangerous drunkard, a madman, incontinent, the house unsanitary, apt to run around naked. These had held her at bay for a whole three months, no small achievement, until that day…

Melanie had opened the double doors from the cramped kitchenette, expecting as any normal human being would, to clap eyes upon a living room, a fireplace, perhaps an elderly father sitting beside it with a rug on his knees. The shock and the scream were horribly immediate. The problem was one of distance, focal depth denied to the expectant eye. There in front of her and stretching high above as she staggered back in disbelief: was a wall of blackened machinery, hideously complex, engraved, crenellated, cogged, annotated, and calibrated with numerals and symbols mathematical and alchemical. She turned to the other doors, to other cupboards, unmasking the demon, uncovering the precarious status of her own existence: a lie of a room, a mere charade, a paper-thin stage set over the gates of Hell, a Sunday hat upon a putrefying corpse. This small room was all that was left of the house, and the scene within it doomed.

She wept as he tried to embrace her, he gripped her as she turned away. *Do you even have a father?!*

He's in there... he muttered weakly and she knew with a killing certainty that he didn't mean alive. Her struggling wounded then angered him. If she had calmly reflected and discussed, then she might have walked away. Then things would have been different. But her screams and his despair at her failure to understand, her kicks and his lunges became the same motion, a composite machine, an opposite of sex, a fight. An immortality of sorts for her, no more need to breathe for him, the ultimate mortician. The bones, the sinews, the hair, the teeth all retain the deeper beauty. All else is betrayed by time, better burned away.

◊

Another twist in the machine: the sound of huge Victorian trees filled with roaring winds, memories of Spring walks by the reservoir: the great grass ramparts to roll down, built a century before by Irish navvies. Flying a kite with his father, a small dog running after it like repelling an aerial invasion. A dark clay casserole pot on the stove upon their shivering return: orange of chopped carrots, dust of flour on tables, his mother's mohair jumper the pale powder blue of April skies. Relatives that didn't come today. School jotters, Sunday stomach, exercises to be done, the clean perfection of baths and mathematics.

◊

Malthrop walks through the hedge maze by the seaside under the perfect sun and is not as surprised as he ought to be to see the figure of Melanie dressed in period costume, twirling a white parasol over her head, as he breaks into a run to meet her.

Mel... he begins, but as she slowly turns he sees her face has become a clock, with Roman numerals and fine brass hands approaching noon.

The wind howls and blows sand across the paths of the maze and Malthrop is suddenly overcome with a sense of profound tiredness and loneliness. There seems something glassy and wistful in the deep blue of the distant waves, like some forgotten afternoon from childhood, pregnant with dim expectation. *What happened, Melanie, can you still speak?*

Time happens... a voice says, but Malthrop turns to see the words come from his father seated on a park bench nearby, in the form of a white skeleton wearing a black suit, his head in his hands, as if in despair.

Now Melanie has drifted closer, and as the brass hands strike the hour, a little door opens where her mouth should be, and a cuckoo flies out. Malthrop turns and runs after it, anxious to find The Machine again under the sand, not to remain trapped in this world. *We are all contraptions…* the bird sings incessantly in his ear as he moves through the dune grasses, - *but who will repair us?*

He is relieved as he nears the beach again and feels the deep hum of The Machine under his toes.

The Machine slows at last and Malthrop wakes: a thin spray of cold water is falling over his forehead, as his foot shackles are released by a timeswitch, the control room door springing open.

Freedom again, for another week or so perhaps. Like all the monks and nuns in seclusion the world over, Malthrop knows that without his sacrifice, his peculiar form of prayer to worship the Machine Age, everything out there would fall apart. Civilisation would finally entirely disintegrate into chaos and damnation without the slightest inkling as to where the body-blow had come from.

Malthrop walks through the marginal zones, the dark leftover gangways of his house, steam pouring off him and from the open door of The Machine behind him. He keeps his eyes aloft as he climbs ladders and narrow wooden stairs, fragments of sky and sunlight flickering from above, drawing him on. He is streaked with blood and sweat, sand and soil, his own urine and faeces. But before he showers he goes to the platforms and releases the doves, gathering some of them up in his arms and on his shoulders as he staggers the last stair flight and bursts out onto the rooftop, rejoicing beneath the vast blue sky. The birds flutter and cluck and twitter, sharing his joy.

How many years has he lived like this? Alone, but enshrined, adorned, tormented and exalted by the museum of his own memories, the machine of his consciousness? He goes to the parapet edge and looks out across the many roofs and gardens, the roads and rails, the patchwork quilt of lives. None of them know of his Machine, they remain ignorant of how it keeps their world in balance, regulating, rejuvenating it. Beneath their million roofs they can know nothing of him and yet, somehow, this morning at least, he feels he can know each of them. How can it be? He feels that no mind, no life, is beyond him. He can travel through all walls, physical and temporal, no door is locked. He raises a hand as if in regal blessing to the scene below, and a dove comes and lands fluttering on his fingers, interrogating him with its calm and deathless gaze, and he laughs, nobody to witness the miracle.

THE ZOO

KURT NEWTON

Maggie stopped the gentleman on the footpath. "Aren't you going to the zoo?" she said.

The path ahead had stretched for miles unbroken, until this gentleman showed up. He was obviously headed in the wrong direction. Was he sick? She had heard of illnesses that made people do what they weren't supposed to do.

Everyone she knew was going to the zoo, so why not this gentleman?

The gentleman, who was tall and thin, and older than young and younger than old, smiled warmly. "No, not this time," he said.

"Not this time?" Maggie couldn't believe her ears. The zoo only came once and once only. When it came, you just had to go, there was no not going. At least, that's what she heard, that's what she believed. Now she wasn't so sure.

"I mean, not this time. Maybe another time," the gentleman said.

"Oh! But there's no time like the present. No sense in putting off till tomorrow what you can do today."

Maggie grabbed the gentleman's arm and turned him around. Halfway turned the gentleman gently pulled his arm free from her grasp. "Please, I don't want to go."

"Nonsense." Maggie tugged on the gentleman's arm more forcefully.

"What seems to be the trouble here?" another man said. He was headed in the same direction as Maggie.

"He doesn't want to go to the zoo!" Maggie cried.

"What?" This man was bigger than the gentleman. He wore a short sleeve shirt that looked to be two sizes too small, and his muscles bulged. "But you have to go to the zoo, fella. Everybody has to go to the zoo. Everybody *wants* to go to the zoo."

"Please, can't the two of you just leave me alone?" said the gentleman.

Maggie put her hands on her hips. "But if you don't go, it will seem to the rest of us that there's something about the zoo not worth seeing. The overall experience won't be as exciting, the thrills not as thrilling, all because you decided not to go. Now doesn't that make you feel bad?"

"How can I feel bad about something I don't want to do?" the gentleman said.

Maggie's head spun. Now she wasn't feeling very good about herself. "But it's the zoo!" She was nearly in tears.

"I say we make him," said the short-sleeved man, who began rolling his short sleeves up even shorter.

"Please, can't the two of you accept that I'm not interested? There are more important things weighing on my mind right now."

"Like what?" said the short-sleeved man. "What could be more important than the zoo?"

The gentleman thought for a moment, as if choosing his words carefully.

"Well?" said the short-sleeved man. He was not known for his patience.

The gentleman at last spoke. "Let's say, for the sake of argument, that I was walking with my wife and daughter on this path this very morning. We were on our way to the zoo. We had heard such wonderful things about it. But something awful happened. We encountered a young woman walking in the opposite direction. We stopped her and asked her why she wasn't going to the zoo, and she gave answers very much like the answers I've just given you.

Something had happened to her on her way to the zoo. But we didn't believe her. We thought her strange and unsocial, and our argument escalated. Soon, other people arrived and joined in our conversation. Talking turned to shouting, and shouting turned to shoving. There were so many people, it became dangerous. My daughter was sucked into the crowd and my wife went in after her. When the crowd cleared, both my wife and daughter were gone, trampled into the dirt so deeply it was as if they never existed. After that, I didn't feel much like going to the zoo."

Maggie and the short-sleeved man stared at the gentleman. The short-sleeved man was the first to speak.

"I don't believe you."

Maggie nodded in agreement. "What happened to the young woman?"

"I don't know," said the gentleman.

"You don't know." The short-sleeved man turned to Maggie. "He doesn't know."

Maggie frowned. "I don't know why you're making up stories like this but you should just stop this silly nonsense and come with us to the zoo. No time like the present." She reached out again to grab the gentleman's arm and he pulled away. In the process he stumbled, his arms flailing to correct his balance and his hand brushed against Maggie's cheek.

POLLUTO

"Don't you strike a woman, buddy!" The short-sleeved man intervened, pushing the already unsteady gentleman down into the dirt.

By now more people on their way to the zoo had arrived on the footpath.

"What's happening here?"

"He struck that woman there."

"He did what?"

"And he doesn't want to go to the zoo."

"But that can't be! Everyone wants to go to the zoo."

"Not this guy."

"I never heard such a thing."

"He needs to learn some social etiquette."

"I'll teach him a thing or two."

The more the crowd gathered, the more crowded it became. Maggie tried to squeeze through to protect the gentleman; after all, he wasn't hurting anyone. But the crowd was too tightly packed and she was squeezed back out again. She sat down hard in the dirt on the other side of the path. From her position she saw the gentleman staring at her through the gathering of legs. His head rattled several times in the dust as the crowd taught him their lesson. After a while his eyes closed and he lay still.

It was then the shouting subsided and people began walking again. The path cleared. The short-sleeved man helped Maggie to her feet. "Come on," he said, "you don't want to miss it."

Maggie began walking, slowly. But soon she stopped. She looked back.

The gentleman was still lying beside the path. He was so covered with dust kicked up from the crowd he appeared like part of the ground itself. He didn't move.

Maggie turned and went back.

Before she could reach him, another man, on his way to the zoo, stopped her.

"Aren't you going to the zoo?" he said.

Maggie didn't know why but she didn't feel much like going to the zoo anymore. There were more important things weighing on her mind. "No, not this time," she said.

The man grabbed her by the arm. "Not this time?"

"Please, something happened, something horrible. I'll show you." But when Maggie looked to find the gentleman beside the footpath, the dirt all looked the same.

She searched frantically while the man tried to convince her to stop what she was doing. It was nonsense. She was acting foolish.

It wasn't long before a crowd began to gather.

THE END

POLLUTO

A collection of poems by **RC EDRINGTON**

INFECTED

time nothing more
than a slow throb
of sunlight
that flickers sharp
beneath a bruised
sheath of skin

syringe
after syringe
we soothe our veins
with the false kiss
of forever midnight

& like timid vampires
at the cusp of dawn
fail to chase
hours back
into an oiled blackness
much deeper
than polluted alleys
from which we slid

FLESH WOUND

love nothing
but skin on skin
& accept it

like a deformed child
held tightly
in your arms

fear not
the dull ache
of a phantom limb

but cherish
the glorious flaw

to nibble the apple
in spite of
the worm

POLLUTO

SCARRED & TWISTED

bedroom doors locked tight erase
moonlight's true witness

18 we are not
anymore...

green eyes soft & shut
hair red, fluffed
against creme satin pillow
dreams tucked closely
like knees
against a chin

slowly she fingers
freshly powdered breasts
scented
with mommy's most
expensive top shelf perfume

vodka breaths thru the air

it is here
here only
& now for a moment brief
she is not ashamed
of things she touches,
the memories she tongues
to life against my ear

in lights blind behind
sealed doors
where friends, colleagues
boyfriends & real life lovers
are not around

to pass cigarette
puffs of time...

or judgement

it is only this
ghost of who I am
& her desire
that shames her most
both enlightened
by yesterday
age? time...

& I
a bad 2 minute punk song
screamed from a chaotic
beer stained stage
scarred & twisted
by 20 years of a world
deformed by factory

a myth
that never took root

a figure she
once glimpsed
in some art house movie

both
no longer recall
the name

she
quite unaware
this darkness she requires
me to exist & linger
will soon
blacken us both
so much deeper into
nothingness
from which we crawled
so drunk
& so disorderly

POLLUTO

I back to my corner pub
begging for change
as I cut 8 ball
with cue ball

her
back to
the over priced shrinks
in coats of many colors
& their tiny little pills
as she tries
ever so hard
to just be
daddy's little
rich girl

SO ALONE

if you knew me
when I were
still cool

please call

track marks
expired
pawn tickets
& dead
girlfriends

are rather
boring
now

ENSENADA

I need to feel more
than this polluted blood
slow course thru
these sunken veins

I need to drift
like cigarette smoke
thru these rusty bars
down into those
mexican streets

warm myself
in the soft smear
of morning sunlight
as it slices open
a fresh wound

in the clouds
that tumble like
drunken troubadours
onto the sand

but there are no doors
only 4 cinder block walls
& the insect-like hum
of florescent lights

as insomnia masturbates
& moans
in broken spanish
with toothpaste
in the next cell

POLLUTO

a collection of poems by **CLAIRE T. FEILD**

MONARCH BUTTERFLY

Her orange-brown wings caress an angel's face, but coursing through the butterfly's veins is a black so terrible that dark clouds melt away, and the sky shuts its umbrella. Retreating from the netherworld, she softly alights on a baby's blonde curl. But her irrevocable desire to be mean floods her system. After she mixes coralline into the baby's hair, she departs for the underworld. While there, she wishes she could take innocence by the hand and lace its fingers with nettles where birthday candles could have been.

UNCERTAINTY

Invigorated, he carries his debris underneath my skin before locating my heart. He spits his semen into my heart's ventricles, the pipelines that connect to a dulcet red. The act of procreation fails, for my heart is a summary of who I am: a damsel who causes distress to misfire, a girl who wears freedom's enterprising mask.

RESERVED

Her body a manikin, she
depends on others to
speak first, their words
of apparent wisdom
really fly-by-nights.
In requital mode, she
utters gibberish, this
jewelweed out of
character for the
first time in her life.
She strides to the rain-
forest to activate a
symbiotic conjoin
with an endangered
species, her will to
live precarious, the
underlings of the
woods playing
paddy-cake with
her hands that
gradually close
for the kill.

REV. THOMAS

Please Rev. Thomas,
let me depart, for I
have a new picture on
my wall, your sanguine
looks in the undercroft
shameful. We did
love each other once,
didn't we? The night
the magnolia blooms
were whipped into
cream by the tornado,
we made love, the
thought of being in
church dreadlocking
our love, this squirming
of our feelings, tentacles
that mated with all
that's evil within our
church's laboratory.
Before I leave, I will
cover you with
labdanum: I hope
that you will make a
new perfume to
wallow in so that
you will forget me,
pretending I am a
voiceless, unseen
mockingbird in the
redbud tree near
your office's portal.
Perhaps you will have
seduced another before
the next line squall.

MERLOT

When the dry red wine slipped uneasily
from Merlot's wispy, seamed-shut lips,
the crowd of spooked men (you know,
the ones who hold on to their wives' skirts),
sputtered gruff sounds at the sharp wind
bursts that tore through the estate's
dismembered windows, no curtains to
be found anywhere in the mahogany air,
souls cremating before Merlot's pink eyes,
yes, those frightening eyes she had to carry
around with her, for no one had fathomed
that Merlot was sickly, had been that way
from an untimely birth in a town that
did not listen to baby rattles, but to the
red-cloaked fellow, the one who could
turn healthy red hearts into flat purple
beets.

LOUP-GAROU

The werewolf dons his gloves,
not wanting his finger traces
mapped by a goody-two-shoes,
the overly righteous one,
who would cover him in
concrete and let him
set, his mummy-like form
being climbed on by baby
loup—garous, sucklings too
innocent to process
an underhanded move,
their death, the
virtuous one's delight.

POLLUTO

THE ENVIOUS ARE GRATEFUL LOVERS

COLIN JAMES

Negro auras are the most difficult to detect.
Many times I have stood beneath
the inquisitive shade of my umbrella,
waiting for just the right light
to filter the monotheistic.
As it turns out you are not the one.
I suppose this means further deprivation
until all our cluttered rooms burst
to reveal their golden hue.

POLLUTO

LUST ENLIGHTENED

MATT CHASE

The stench strikes Marco's libido, tempting him into the ways of the perverted. His aching presence pushes him deeper into the vice-like grip of the restraints. It pinches. The smouldering leather throws the forbidden to the musky stone floor.

Marco is gleefully trapped in the principles of pleasure, preaching to the converted.

Gothic arches warn of approaching blindness. Sometimes, Marco needs to find himself this way. The buckles on his belt scrape against his skin as he walks confidently through the pitch black. He's heading for the centre of the maze.

The heart of the maze holds a precious gift. Already he can hear the helpless screams echo off the shine from the brick walls. The deeper into the castle he ventures, the further inside the Id he gets.

Marco believes all should embrace the Id. There are many ways to Nirvana and this is but one.

"Kneel". Marco commands his subject, as he arrives at the castle's bowels. The purpose-built room is dimly lit by torches of fire, their flames reflecting the torrid walls. The subject is chained to the stone floor by its ankles.

"Yes Sir". She serves on her crumbled legs, awaiting instruction.

"How does it feel to be empty?" Marco plays with the subject's hollow soul.

"Worthless Sir". Simplicity responds.

"Inhale me". Marco dominates, pushing the blackness of his chaps towards her cautious sense.

Marco pushes further into the pathetic receptacle, allowing the power to rise from his base and up to his crown. Heat shudders up, down and out.

She owns him.

"Now follow me". Sir brushes it aside, walking away. Her breviary of torment clatters behind her, heavily weighting her forward movement. She follows Sir to the darkest recess.

Marco sits. His deluded prowess supported by the staunch throne. His loyal servant curls beneath like a fireside feline awaiting hot milk.

"We are blind". Sir speaks.

Silence.

"We are blind". He toys with the subject.

Silence. The subject cannot respond unless instructed to do so. Those are the rules of the game.

Adrenaline pumps. Marco is fuelled by the silent noise. Sodom and Gomorra invades this place of hearts as the castle's resident deviants enter from the hidden passages.

The wet bodies glisten with shades of grey. Eyes sparkle like the Devil's smile. Rarely do glances catch, just body parts, whispers and needs.

Wants are a different matter.

The room erupts with the balance of power. The shackles break, women rise, men fall and souls fly. Marco has known this place before. He breathes his Mistress's scent, the Divine Feminine completes him. As soon as she permits, Marco caresses the wisdom that thrives in all who dare to surrender.

He now knows the truth about life.

The world was born into her, Earth herself is Motherhood and without her – we would not exist. Marco swells with gratitude. Love beyond measure expands from his obvious chest, lifting the darkness, transforming his pain and liberating the living dead.

As daylight breaks, the barred windows splatter rays and illuminate further the debauched doorways. Couples, trios and singles awake from their unions – refreshed. Time stood still for the fastest hours and now it's all over.

"Great night all!" Marco thanks his friends for another satisfying nocturnal nudge to the other side.

"Same time next week?" The patron suggests.

"Hey; why not?" Marco grins, gathers his alter ego and places it securely into his gym bag – along with his Id.

THE END

POLLUTO

THIS MOTHER'S SON
MARK BRANDON ALLEN

beneath
a
fading orange sun
not unlike the somber rainy day
he
left to serve his country,
she stands
alone
remembering his warm smile
and
bright young eyes.
his mind callous cold
to all entreats she made
asking him stay.
she could do no more
then.
in a strange country
on an insignificant desert street
of a small planet
within a spiral galaxy
at the edge of the milky way
his years ended.
now
holding a folded flag;
carefully clasping two metal tags
that identified his body
she weeps.
beyond
this moment only
memories
of him.
he was her only one
this
mother's son.

POLLUTO

a collection of poems by **JONATHAN GREENHAUSE**

THE NEVER-ENDING WAR

He says to himself: The earth is falling,
as cement erupts suddenly and the ashen skies tumble.
He's immersed in the war, rapid guns firing at him;
He hears children's shrill screams as concrete houses crumble;
He sees the scattered birds, the swallows' flights,
the crows & vultures gathering
as a refuse-carrying river splits the city in two halves.

Cadavers float by silently as soldiers fire at suspects;
They handcuff them, treating them as terrorists.
The war's won like this, keeping control of your enemies,
keeping your hold on enemies. While firing at close range,
you're more likely to succeed in wounding them.

The war on terror's being won, he solemnly says to his nation,
and we believe him, though he could have just as easily said:
The war on terror's being lost. Two halves of us are divided
by a river as ancient as our forgotten stories,
the ones we were raised on, the ones
that formed our being.

A sinuous river seeks the source from which to spit the bones
laid bare by occupation, by the stranglehold
of this pre-emptive invasion.
He says to himself: This must end soon. He thinks:
What else can happen that has not happened?

He imagines nothing could compare to this war everlasting,
no end to this primeval display of setting siege
to a majority who are defenseless.
He thinks: Their war on what?   Not what, but whom.
A war on them and on our own, he thinks,
while he seeks shelter as the bombs return again,
as they have, and do, and must,
every day since they began.

POLLUTO

A TALE OF GEOPHAGY

Giants were gymnasts
and jaunted through the daunting fields of corn,
fracturing the striving stalks and traveling in telluric talk,
but none survived, corn's ears attentive to their crashing forms
as giants lay enveloped in post-mortem fragrance sprayed.

Years passed...The past became the past.
Stars shimmered in the full fuliginous skies screaming their nothingness.
Insects ably engineered, masterminding fields,
removing obstacles of clothes and flesh, bare opal bone.
An iridescent glow of nacre shone in minute grasping jaws.

Colonies of careful critters crafted endless towers of babble,
and everything proceeded without the knowledge of preceding days.
The moon revolved in-synch with Earth,
its memorized and mesmerizing trance
reflecting Helios' luminescence off its frozen face.

One day, insects shivered in their homes of dirt and clay
upset by earth's unsettling movements,
trembling with the sound of footsteps crushing colonies,
of fingers digging ravenously, displacing all the soil
delivered by the dutiful and fleet:

Broad giants reappeared, as if they'd never left these fields,
yet now their mealy lips and grinding teeth were absent of
their favorite sustenance in form of flowering corn,
the towering stalks long since replaced
by weeds and ferrous soil.

Still, the giants' hands were gathering in droves within the ground
to steal a sumptuous meal of clay and humus trails:
They lifted up their dirty treats, devoid of fallen fruit and meat,
and satisfied their now-anemic tastes
for iron-speckled earth's remains.

POLLUTO

SUBMERSION

Her arms flay in the wind winding through chilled air;
She's half-conscious, seeing the shimmering sea
stretched out beneath her like a dream of blue.
The breath of the tide and the waves are near;
She's tumbling faster through the air:
Now she's almost there.

There's a silent splash, the sudden sensation she's here
in the water's breast enwrapping her somniferous form.
Her hair curls upward, weaves a web of aqueous strands,
works its way through the surreal weight of the sea.
Her shining skin still seeping in the sunlight
shivers slightly as her pores begin
readjusting to this world.

Around her she sees the other scattered citizens of dissent,
their naked bodies twisting in a vast, removed array,
discarded detritus delivered in a diving kiss
to delve into the darkness of the sea,
their sentences dictated from the cellars
of a dirty war's beliefs.

As she settles at the shell-encrusted bottom, her eyes reopen.
How has she found her way here, so far from daylight?
She's surrounded by a silent crowd of thousands,
none saying anything, with only their mute testaments
speaking the same repeated condemnation,
eyes staring forever towards the surface,
awaiting the return of the sun.

POLLUTO

A SMALL SONG SPRUNG FROM INSIDE

It's a hot day in the 25th century, but
no one knows which 25th century. History
has lost its sequence. A long trail of humans
cross a dry riverbed in search of something
long extinct. Their legs move with their
mechanical momentum, pushing them forward
towards a prairie of plastic objects
melted into a colorful labyrinth.

Here's where their play of unutterable sounds
seeks communion with the whistling breeze, their feet
wrapped in clothing weaved by automatic machines
sometime in the 23rd century, but none of them know
which 23rd century. Phantasmal crows circle overheard
awaiting the migrants' double deaths, black wings
frayed and scorched by the passionate embrace
of an emboldened sun let loose from prior constraints
of atmosphere. No one remembers
the times before.

There's a song sung by a small child, the first time
notes have crossed their parched throats in centuries.
The music comes, then is silenced by the elders,
their quick hands falling upon the girl, seizing
her toasted throat, shaking the inchoate song
from out of her. From then on, she keeps
quiet, letting her thoughts remain
safely inside her frame,
keeping them hidden,
biding them time.

POLLUTO

SEBASTIAN AND THE STATIONARY SUN

Seeing the fireball stationary in the sky, Sebastian fears for the end of the world.
"That's just the sun," someone says to him, patting his bare shoulders, skin blistered and peeling towards the gravelly ground.
"That's not the sun," Sebastian replies, pointing to the smoke surrounding it.
Someone shrugs his shoulders and leaves.

Three flowers sprout from the ground by Sebastian's feet, pebbles blooming from the unfurling stem.
"What does it mean?" someone asks as the pebbles plummet to the covered earth.
Sebastian picks them up and pops them into his mouth, keeping them close between his tongue and teeth.
"It means there will be a harvest of stone," he says, "and perfume will be hard, if not impossible, to extract."
Someone leaves him with his three flowers and his mouthful of pebbles.

Behind Sebastian's eyes, an infinite field of things can be seen, but they're hidden by a curtain of sight,
or rather by a veil of invisibility, cloaking them from his forward-seeing eyes.
He can sense them, the images prodding the boundaries built up, immaculate colors crammed in one against the other,
the shapes a miracle of angles, curves, and surfaces engraved.
Sebastian sees none of this.
He just senses it all exists beyond his mind's comprehension.

In the sky, the sun is eclipsed by a glowing fireball devoured by smoke.
Sebastian screams, but no one stares up to see it.
He screams and screams, but no one can guess what's in his mind.
Someone laughs, having forgotten everything Sebastian has seen, and hoping it will disappear in time.

POLLUTO

a collection of poems by **J. J. STEINFELD**

MY DOPPELGÄNGER'S MOST RECENT DREAM

Reluctantly, the night already devious,
I enter my doppelgänger's most recent dream
relegated to a stunt double for myself

the antics are death-defying
and at first the flying and
phenomenal deep-sea diving
are breathtaking and life-affirming

I confess in the dream
awake I would never dare
such death-defying stunts
but it is not my dream
and I am a stunt double
a bit of an existential show-off

then the doppelgänger turns cantankerous
maybe out of boredom perhaps from something
gone wrong in the brain or in the heart
call it malicious or venomous
I hear those words in the dream
the doppelgänger's most recent dream

my safety net is removed
my helmet and safeguards
vanish as only in a dream
they can disappear, lose their names
chronology and coherency belittled

I am told to jump again
off the highest cliff imaginable
to dive into the deepest waters measurable
told this over and over

POLLUTO

until I have summoned the courage
to do the jumping then the diving
my doppelgänger laughs, somewhat entertained
a coward who does nothing
but dream about stunt doubles
trying to get through another
devious night.

THIS ELABORATE PLAN

I have this elaborate plan
fanciful at best
ludicrous at worst
to make every deceitful person
disappear
or at least
lay low for a month or so.

I have both furtive and fearsome persons in mind
those devious and pitiless
the number might be cumbersome or excessive
but even if I manage to accomplish 20 or 25 percent
it could provide a few extra moments
of free-breathing and lightheartedness.

It is difficult to know
if my plan falls short
whether to hide or to run
the furtive and fearsome
might want some reimbursement
to refine and refresh their deceit
to fool me with foolishness
to implement plans of their own.

POLUTO

IT ISN'T RELEVANT

It isn't relevant that you have a knife to my back
just beneath the shoulder blade
pressing hard enough to let me know
that you can summon divinity
with the flick of a wrist.

It isn't relevant that the sky is about to fall
covering me with clouds and leaden blueness
ending my doings and plans
for this hopeful, uplifting day
with a sudden atmospheric misfortune.

It isn't relevant that memory has turned on me
creating burdened pasts and burdening yesterdays
blocking all my former gifts of prophecy
negating every past and future prediction
that made my sideshow act a showstopper.

What is relevant?
the knife-wielder asks
and the keeper of the heavens
and the deep hidden resources of being
interrogators harsh and insistent.

The irrelevancy succumbs to relevancy
in a ceremony of being without name and need—
relevant is that I bleed without fear or explanation
and breathe without remorse or subterfuge
and can imagine and reinvent.

AN EXISTENTIALLY TOTTERING WRITER CONFESSES

here I am
an abstract concept
of a scribbler
which disturbs me
to no earthly end

one minute being
close to exalted
the next minute
deeply nonsensical
time both absurd
and magical in its unfolding
the minutes transformed
into hard to define days
all I can say is one day
it's a pebble in my shoe
next day a thorn in my side
on bad days with dim light
and loud unsavoury noises

a pain in the ass

this is tottering, abstract or not
like it or not
platitudes growling
and I growl back
to no avail
the pebbles and thorns and pain
such is the shuffling
of words ideas screams
such is the dropping
of the dictionary
in the middle of the night
such is the singing
of mortality
and its chorus
of well-dressed fools
and ragtag conjurers

OUT OF HIS LEAGUE

BRUCE GOLDEN

Bats slammed into lockers, cleats scraped the floor, and frothy spittle stained the walls. An influx of uniformed combatants filed into the room, some mumbling, others grumbling – the sure sign of another loss. In moments the place smelled of dirty socks and planetary jocks.

As if to alter the mood, one of them began revolving around the post-game spread, waving his arms.

"I say we put this one behind us," called out Saturn in an upbeat tone. "I say we go out and find some bodacious local asteroids in need of a good fertility rite. What do you say?"

His idea was greeted by a colorful array of expletives. No one was in the mood to party. By the time little Mercury showed up with the *really* bad news, the room was already subdued. Most had changed out of their uniforms, and were already in and out of the showers. Mars noticed the normally peppy infielder appeared usually glum.

"What's wrong? You look like you've seen a black hole."

"Did you hear what happened to Pluto?" the speedster asked the room in-general. "They cut him."

"What?" Mars slammed his fist against the wall. "Damn it! I knew something was up."

"Are you sure?" asked Jupiter, scratching his oversized head with sausage-like fingers.

"Yeah," replied Mercury. "He's in with management right now. I hear they're sending him down to the dwarf league."

"I bet it was Terra's fault," groused Mars. "He's always stirring up trouble. No telling what he told management behind Pluto's back."

"Well, Pluto's always been a little erratic," said Saturn, fresh out of the shower and adorning himself with his usual bling. "He's not the fastest guy in the galaxy either."

"Maybe," said Mars, "but he's a scrappy little player, and he was always there for us, eon after eon."

Jupiter stood, stretched his massive arms, and yawned. "I'm going to miss the little guy."

"What's this going to do to team chemistry?" wondered Venus.

POLUTO

"Management doesn't care about chemistry," carped Mars. "All they care about is astronomy."

"We should tell the others before he gets here," suggested Venus.

Saturn volunteered, "I'll get Neptune, he's still in the shower."

"That figures," responded Mars. "Hey, while you're in there, get Uranus out of the head."

Before Saturn returned, Terra walked in and said excitedly, "Did you guys hear what happened to Pluto?"

That was all Mars needed. He grabbed Terra by his uniform and slammed him up against a spate of lockers.

"What did you do, you prissy, waterlogged, rodent-infested little--"

Jupiter and Mercury moved quickly to intervene, separating the pair.

"What did you tell them?" Mars ranted as Jupiter held him back.

"What are you talking about?" Terra seemed stunned by the attack.

"Mars thinks it's your fault they're sending Pluto down," explained Venus.

"What? I didn't have anything to do with that. How could I? Why would I?"

Before Mars could continue his diatribe, Pluto walked in. He was already in street clothes, but went straight to his locker. The room hushed noticeably and, for a moment, everyone acted as if nothing were amiss. But when Pluto began emptying out his locker, Mercury put an arm on his shoulder.

"Sorry, my man. We all heard. It's a bum deal."

Pluto shrugged. "It's part of the business. I didn't get the job done." Then, mustering a bit of bravado, he turned to face the room and added, "I'll be back. Don't you worry about that. I'll go down, I'll get my game together and then I'll be back. It's just a slump. You'll see, I'll be back up here in no time."

Jupiter nodded his big head and his bassoon-like voice bellowed, "That's right. You'll be back in no time at all. You go down there and give them a good showing, Pluto old bud."

"Yeah," called out a couple of other voices with less than genuine enthusiasm.

Unable to hold back the tears, Venus turned away. Mars looked like he wanted to break something.

Searching his rather voluminous cranium for something else to say – something inspirational – Jupiter came up with, "Just remember, you can't steal first base."

"Yeah... right. Thanks, Jupiter," responded Pluto. He knew the big guy well enough not to waste time puzzling over anything he said.

But Jupiter wasn't finished.

"Did I ever tell you how I could have been a star?"

Venus waved him silent.

"Not now, Jupiter."

Pluto finished bagging up his stuff and started out. Terra stepped up and shook his hand.

POLLUTO

"Good luck, Pluto."

"Yeah," said Mercury, "knock 'em dead down there."

Pluto looked like he wanted to say something else, but couldn't get the words out. Instead he glanced away and walked out.

Mercury stared at Jupiter. "You're a real gasbag, you know that? You can't steal first base? What kind of idiotic thing is that to say?"

Jupiter shrugged his mammoth shoulders. The gravitational effect of the movement pulled Saturn back in from the showers with Neptune and Uranus in tow.

"What happened?" asked Neptune, still dripping.

"They cut Pluto. He's gone."

"Cut him? Why?"

"Why do you think?" Mars replied sarcastically. "He wasn't orbiting up to expectations."

"It's not why that matters," offered Mercury. "It's *who* – who will they cut next?"

THE END

POLLUTO

NOW IT CAN BE TOLD

FRED RUSSELL

It was the Vice President who got the idea of putting together a Special Forces team to mop up and flush out Saddam after the President proclaimed victory in Iraq. He wanted to put Clint Eastwood in charge of the operation but the Secretary of Defense told him that Clint didn't do that kind of thing anymore, having gone a little arty in his old age. "If only we could get Arnold," he said.

"What about Steven Seagal?" the Vice President said.

"I think the Israelis are using him in Gaza."

"Van Damme?"

"Let's keep this American."

They found the President in the White House Screening Room watching an old John Wayne movie from the Nixon Collection. "What I'm worried about," he said, "is where we're going to get 150,000 extras."

"From the ranks of the unemployed," the Vice President said. "You don't even have to give them guns. Our team will be in and out of there in twenty-four hours."

"Who's directing?"

"Leave that to me," the Defense Secretary said.

It was harder to put the team together than anyone had imagined. Karl Rove was in a dither. Everyone he talked to had contractual obligations, even Sylvester Stallone. In the end they had to go with the B Team, not that the men didn't have impressive enough records. All of them had participated in daring missions during the course of their long careers, wiping out whole armies with just a handful of men in less time than it took to boil an egg. The Vice President and Defense Secretary had no reason to believe that things would be any different in Iraq. They briefed the men in the White House basement. The President came by to listen in, eating pretzels. They had put together the team the way such teams are usually put together, finding the men engaged in a variety of occupations all around the globe when the official-looking vehicle pulled up and two Secret Service agents wearing dark glasses stepped out: the demolition expert about to blow up a condemned building in downtown Miami, the radio operator dead drunk on a beach in Waikiki, and so on and so forth. The radio operator had doubled as a safecracker and forger in other capers so he was a valuable addition to the team. They also had a martial arts man serving time in Leavenworth and promised a reprieve if he signed on, someone for comic relief who was also an expert marksman, and the team leader, code-named Spanky. All they were missing was a black who was also a licensed pilot. Spanky and the martial arts man went back a long way and though there had been bad blood between them in the past Spanky wanted him on the team. That's the kind of guy he was.

The Vice President said, "Men, the future of the free world and the safety of our nation depend on you. We wouldn't be putting you in harm's way if we didn't think you could do the job. There may be a few pockets of resistance but you will be facing undersized men who will throw down their arms and run away the minute they see you. Don't forget, you are Americans and they are not. Remember Bataan and Iwo Jima."

Charlie, the comic relief man, said, "That's where I got the clap." Everyone laughed, including the President. The Defense Secretary said, "Now now, boys, let's settle down…" Parker, the demolition expert, said, "Sir, I have a question." The Vice President said, "Go ahead, son." This was classic repartee, establishing Parker as respectful to figures of authority and therefore worthy of being an American hero, and the Vice President as fatherly and therefore worthy of being Vice President, unless he turned out to be a homicidal maniac.

Parker said, "Once we're in, how do we get out?"

The Defense Secretary stepped in and said, "The *SS Nimitz* will be standing by at 0100 hours to rendezvous with your PT boat."

"Where will that be?"

"Off the coast of Beirut. Any other questions?"

Smitty, the radio operator, said, "What's the lingo they talk down there in I-raq?"

"A-rab," the Vice President said, "but don't trouble yourselves about that. The streets are full of kids who talk pidgin English. You can use them when you interrogate the insurgents."

"Who are these Shiites we've been hearing about?"

"That's some women's lib organization they got over there."

"And the Sunnis?"

"I think they're nudists."

"Are they for us or against us?"

"We haven't figured that out yet."

The men had heard enough. They were raring to go. Not wishing to waste any more time, they loaded up their gear and touched down in Baghdad that same morning, skipping the tedious trans-Atlantic journey. General Armbuster, the commanding officer, was skeptical about the whole operation, thus setting himself up as a doubting Thomas who would later have to swallow his pride and say, "I was all wrong about you boys. You make me proud to be an American," or, "I didn't think you had it in you, boys. You make me proud to be an American." The Defense Secretary organized the extras into convoys, figuring he'd get some nice footage for his private collection when they were blown off the road. With 150,000 men out there he had plenty to spare. The B Team was equipped with a jeep and a command car. They kept the explosives and spare ammo in the back of the command car and had a machine gun mounted on the jeep. Spanky had seen enough movies to know that this was how you distributed your ordnance. They found a kid who spoke pretty good English so they figured they'd take him along when they started knocking on doors in the afternoon after they captured Falluja and Mosul. The kid had a nice back story too along with a pretty sister so there was a hint of romance in the air as the men moved out.

Butler, the martial arts man, wanted to divide the team into two separate strike forces, three men to take Falluja and three for Mosul, but Spanky thought that this would be cutting it a little thin so they decided to stick together and take the two cities one after the other. "We'll get behind them and hit 'em with everything we have," Spanky said. Of course he knew he'd be getting air support from General Armbuster, who'd be laying down a carpet of white phosphorus and other incendiaries, though that was mostly for the highlight reels. Everyone knew what a big kick the CNN people got out of watching the pyrotechnics from their hotel windows. In fact, they had one of these news people "embedded" in their command car. Spanky had been hoping he could speak the local lingo, but that wasn't how these people worked. His name was Frank Bosh and he had won six Pulitzer Prizes for reporting from countries whose language he didn't understand.

The black guy with the pilot's license turned out to be a Latino with a chip on his shoulder, and since he wasn't going to engage in any spectacular air battles or fly the men out of a blazing inferno, they had him driving the jeep. Anyone could see that he was expendable, though sometimes these types surprised you, causing the commanding officer to say, "We can all learn something from you, son. You make me proud to be an American." His name was Pepito, indicating that he could fill in for the comic relief man if necessary, that is, if he lost the attitude. He was the one who spotted their pint-sized interpreter's sister racing out of a bombed-out building with a dozen insurgents hot on her trail and her dress only slightly torn to indicate that she hadn't been raped yet and could therefore still become someone's sweetheart. Spanky leaped out of the jeep and opened fire, mowing down the entire enemy force in less time than it took to toast a marshmallow. Then he took the hysterical girl into his arms and said, "Easy now, honey, no one's gonna hurt you anymore. We're the good guys." You could see that there was going to be something between them later on in the caper. However, as it turned out, one of the insurgents was still alive and was reaching for his gun when Butler stepped up and put a bullet through his head, just in the nick of time. Spanky nodded unsmilingly in the manner of American heroes acknowledging a debt of gratitude to a former adversary and said, "I owe you one, Ben."

In any case it was the girl who told Spanky they were going in the wrong direction. "Falluja is west of Baghdad," she said. "Shee-it," the dumbfounded team leader exclaimed, "those bozos in Washington don't know their asses from their elbows." He told Pepito to turn the jeep around. Pepito said, "Why I gotta do dat?" Spanky said, "You heard the lady, Falluja's thataway." "But the convoy go east," Pepito said. "That's their problem," Spanky said.

They now had three noncombatants on board: Frank Bosh, the Pulitzer Prize reporter; Hakim, their pint-sized interpreter, and his pretty sister, Jamila. Hakim sat up front with Pepito in the jeep. Spanky put Jamila in the command car with Bosh and the other men. This was no time for romance. The radio crackled. It was General Headquarters.

"Spanky from Angler, Spanky from Angler," the voice said. "Have you made contact with the enemy? I repeat, have you made contact with the enemy? Over."

Spanky said to Pepito, "Who the fuck is Angler?"

"Das de Wice Presdent, I believe."

"Well, I'll be damned. Angler from Spanky. That's a negative, sir... Sir?... Sir?... Do you read me, sir?"

"You didn't say 'Over.'"

"Let's cut to the chase, man. You sent us in the wrong fucking direction, if you'll pardon my French."

"Angler to Spanky, Angler to Spanky. Copy that. Mayday! Mayday!"

"What?"

"Sorry, I meant Roger."

"Is General Armbuster there by any chance?"

"I think he's in the crapper. Over."

"Over and out. Shee-it!"

The road was full of potholes. Pinpoint bombing had seen to it that the insurgents had no gas, electricity or running water, wherever they might be. The bombed-out buildings also made it hard for them to hide. Spanky could see that this was going to be a piece of cake. When they reached the river, Spanky signaled to Butler, the marshal arts man, to follow him down to the bridge. The bridge was guarded by a squad of insurgents jabbering away in their A-rab lingo and conveniently spread out so that they could be silently dispatched one by one without alerting the others. Butler moved up silently and accordingly dispatched them one by one without alerting the others, breaking their necks or slitting their throats. Each victim grunted to indicate that he had been dispatched and then fell heavily to the ground. Spanky himself got the last one just as he was coming up behind Butler, leaping down on him from a tree in which he had inexplicably posted himself. Butler gave him the thumbs up sign. They were even now. It was important to establish that, as conceivably they would be rivals for Jamila's affection.

The team crossed the bridge. They were in downtown Falluja now. The streets were deserted though they could hear some wailing coming from the bombed-out buildings. Suddenly they came under sniper fire. Someone also threw a pot of lentil soup at them. "Bring on the kebab," the comic relief man said.

Frank Bosh crawled under the command car in his helmet and flak jacket and started broadcasting. "We've just come under heavy enemy fire," he whispered. "I'm with a Special Forces unit that's been sent in to clean up Falluja and Mosul and capture Saddam. They figure they'll be in and out of here in twenty-four hours but so far it's been rough going. These brave American boys are the best we have. If they can't do the job, no one can. They may not get the attention of the big stars in those blockbuster movies that gross a hundred million dollars over the weekend but in their own quiet way they too are making the world safe for democracy. Jesus, that was close! He's up there in the window. Kill the motherfucker!"

While Charlie picked off the snipers Spanky moved the men toward the last A-rab stronghold in Falluja, the Leila Khaled All-Girls Orphanage and Advanced Training Center for Suicide Bombers. They figured there were at least a thousand insurgents there. Unfortunately the surrounding area had been leveled by General Armbuster so there wasn't much cover. Spanky signaled to Butler and Parker to move around to the enemy rear while he, Charlie and Smitty created a diversion in the enemy front. This was accomplished by lobbing mortar shells into the orphanage. At least that got the orphans out of the way. Bosh, the Pulitzer Prize man, whispered into his microphone: "We are witnessing a tremendous assault on the last enemy stronghold in Falluja. I can't begin to describe what I'm seeing here. Bodies are literally flying out of the woodwork as a beautiful phosphorescent shower rains down from the clear blue Middle Eastern skies. We're going to take a commercial break now but we'll be right back for the body counts."

Butler and Parker moved cautiously into the deserted corridors of the orphanage, jerking their rifles around like those robotic clowns you see on TV trying to look like SWAT people, while an unidentified voice in the background kept saying, "Go, go, go ..." As all the bodies they encountered were burned to a crisp there wasn't much for them to do other than marvel at American firepower. They met up with Spanky out front. "Guess that takes care of Falluja," Parker said.

Spanky checked in with Headquarters. Next up was Mosul but no one seemed to know exactly where it was. "Me an' the boys are gonna grab ourselfs some grub," Spanky told the General. "You know where to find us." He shared a chili dog with Jamila under a date palm tree. It wasn't long before she was telling him her whole tragic story. It had all started when her dad put in a bid for a local McDonald's franchise and ran afoul of Saddam's wife's second cousin, who also had his eye on the location. Quick as a wink he found himself in Abu Ghraib. Jamila hastened back from London, where she'd been studying international banking, only to discover that her entire family had been wiped out, leaving just her and her little brother, Hakim, who'd been living in the city's sewers with his English tutor. Jamila then made contact with the A-rab underground and went on a number of daring missions, blowing up railroads and things like that. Saddam tried to trap her by having one of his sons pose as a CIA agent but Jamila made him immediately as he spoke fluent Arabic. She'd been on the run ever since. By the time she finished she was sobbing hysterically. Spanky said, "Easy now, honey, no one's gonna hurt you anymore. We're the good guys," and before they knew it they were locked in a passionate embrace and Spanky was pulling down her pants in a tasteful romantic interlude. Butler saw this and turned away. It was clear that he too had now become expendable, though he would first have to redeem himself through some heroic act.

After Jamila had straightened out her clothes and given Spanky a loving look the team moved out again. It turned out that Mosul was in the north, 250 miles away. Pepito stepped on the gas and they were there in less time than it took to fry a tortilla. Mosul had been having its problems, everyone was killing everyone, but now that the B Team was on the scene, order was expected to be restored by early afternoon. This was Dervish territory, as they'd been told by Intelligence, so they didn't know what to expect. Hakim started knocking on doors trying to find out where the insurgents were holing up. As luck would have it they were right around the corner, at the Morris and Minnie Feinstein Center for the Performing Arts and Advanced Biochemical Weapons Research. This was a huge complex that had been turned into an impregnable fortress. Spanky called in an air strike. The extras started arriving in tourist buses and had to be sorted out. General Dudley P. Hartburne was overseeing their deployment. Spanky was glad to see him though they'd had a few run-ins in the past. That's the kind of guy he was.

General Hartburne said, "We'll give you all the support you need. We're all counting on you." This showed that the men had won the respect and admiration of the military by just being who they were: plain old-fashioned free-spirited rough-and-ready no-nonsense Americans who knew how to take the bull by the horns and get the job done without bothering about the rules and regulations made up by stodgy bureaucrats sitting on their fat asses in Washington.

Jamila squeezed Spanky's hand and looked at him in a special way so that you knew that once the caper was over they'd be tying the knot. As the men made their final preparations there was some martial music from an unidentified source. There was also some horseplay with Hakim so you knew that the men had taken him under their wing and would see to his future. That tied up all the loose ends. They were ready for the big show.

But just then General Hartburne came running up and said to Spanky: "The Vice President is on the line. It's top priority."

Spanky picked up the phone and heard the Vice President's tremulous voice: "We've just been informed that the A-rabs have planted nuclear devices in all our major cities that are going to be activated by remote control from the Morris and Minnie Feinstein Center for the Performing Arts and Advanced Biochemical Weapons Research. You've got to get in there in one big hurry."

"How much time do we got?"

"Four minutes and thirty-one seconds."

"That's a pretty tall order, sir."

"The future of the free world and the safety of our nation depend on you."

It was up to Spanky now. There was little time to waste. The music got louder. He sent Butler and Charlie around to the enemy rear. This time they had to scale a wall and drop down silently to the ground using complicated snappling gear. Parker laid some charges around the eastern perimeter where the main assault was going to take place. Everything was perfectly coordinated so you got a sense of how tough and efficient Americans were when the chips were down. The music of course helped. Pepito brought up the jeep for no special reason. Spanky grabbed a passerby and interrogated him about the layout of the Center with the assistance of Hakim. The kid knew his stuff. Spanky called in another air strike and set off the charge at the eastern wall. They were all moving now, on the run. A-rabs were popping up all around them and being blasted away with tremendous visual effects. They were in the main building now. Spanky led the men through the Doris and Henry Weiss Auditorium. There were some props still on the stage but no insurgents. They ran past the refreshment stand and down a flight of stairs. Pepito started jerking his rifle around but Spanky told him to cut it out and fast. Then they heard the A-rabs jabbering away just down the hall. Spanky put his finger to his lips and signaled to the men to proceed with caution. Charlie and Butler joined them. This was it. The team rushed forward with a burst of fire. There was a horrendous racket as the A-rabs went flying all over the place, slamming against walls and bouncing off the ceiling. One of them of course got away. Spanky chased him into the men's room and there it was sitting in one of the stalls: the remote control timing device. "It's too late," the A-rab said, showing his yellow teeth. "Nothing can stop us now." The timer showed 46 seconds remaining. Smitty tried to deactivate it but to no avail. Butler said, "Give that to me," and started cutting wires. Then he saw it: a secondary charge set by the A-rabs to go off if the last wire was cut and exact its vengeance on whoever foiled their plan. Five seconds remained. "I'm gonna do it," Butler said. "No! No!" Spanky cried, but it was too late. The timer exploded in Butler's hands and he sunk to the ground with a beatific look on what was left of his face.

"He's earned that reprieve," General Hartburne said. "He was a true American hero."

Things aren't always as simple as they seem, especially when you don't know what you're doing. It took the B Team seven months to hunt down Saddam and it took seven years, 4,000 American lives and a trillion dollars to turn Iraq into another Lebanon. "We better start tooling up for Afghanistan," the Vice President said.

THE END

POLLUTO

PAVLOVIAN TRANSITIONING

ANDREW RIVAS

I'm prepping the syringe and sitting here, basking in this asshole's shit-vapors; when scouting a bathroom stall to inject cleaning solution below the base of one's eye-socket, location isn't a priority. The dilations of this guy's sphincter sound like jet engines revving, emptying cargo into waters unknown below. Seriously, he might enjoy an anal prolapse any second at the rate he's going.

I force my throat to spasm as retort, conversation via guttural grunts through opposite holes. Left stall ignores my complaint – it smells as through he's been drinking gasoline and eating urinal cakes. *Fucking prick*, I think, tapping the syringe's barrel to ostracize the air pockets, slow solid line of liquid coming out the needle's head. No heart attacks or carelessness to worry for.

Two millimeters to the left of the tear ducts; estimated three millimeter intrusion with the needle; slide the plunger towards you; watch the cerulean blue solution transfer itself direct to your head. Sit back and enjoy. Discard of the syringe in a safe place. Rather, throw it over the stall wall and hope it hits your neighbor in the dick, one fell swoop giving him hep c/b(/q/z?). Can't keep track of that shit, anymore.

I hear left stall flush his stygian waste away from my fragile eyes and nose; immediately, the sound tapers and I hear water dripping to tile, and frantic oh shit, oh shits. Little brown boats flying white paper flags start intruding on my stall, and I stand upwards as to not impede their progress. I'm trapped! No man is an island; this stall is, however, and I'm stranded. My name tag, never properly pinned, slides from my shirt and into my comparably pristine bowl.

Through the distortion of the recycled piss: *Mark Vonniederhaus. Citizen One Industries*. Small scientific firm, just starting out, completely off the radar. Apparently unable to hire anyone that can pronounce my name correctly.

The defecator flees the scene, I even hear his loafers splashing against the tile, and I slap my fist on the stall wall.

"You shitting scoundrel!" I yell. "Come back here! These are expensive shoes!" They aren't. I'm barefoot.

I spider-climb up out the stall and hop onto dry highways of tile intersecting, narrowly avoiding brown ditch-water. There's twelve feet or so of clean floor between the volcanic spew and the sinks; I walk over and start to wash my hands. A suit walks in and grimaces. Then he grins.

"It smells like shit in here," he says.

"No shit," I say. "It's a bathroom." This one's a fucking smiler, his cheeks stretched back across his face so taut you can almost hear the skin creak. I can tell the word-vomit's about to spill from that diseased mouth of his from the moment he takes an intake of breath.

"If there wasn't any shit, then it wouldn't smell, now would it?"

This is about the time I'm slamming his face into the porcelain just to hear the skull break, then the metal faucet just to see how unrecognizable I can make this prick, just to see how far I can go and still feel some semblance of his smile underneath my already slipping hands.

◊

I have come to the conclusion that reality no longer amuses me. Or what constitutes reality for most people, anyway. Walking through CO is like living an acidic fever dream on ether in the throes of a Quaalude binge while skydiving on Mars. And that's just a Tuesday afternoon. How do other people keep themselves entertained? The second floor of CO is my world nestled within the world intolerable, not necessarily my escape but the one place I truly want to be; my office is on the floor dedicated to animal testing.

Six charred chimps are wheeled out of Room 206, their bodies burnt past charcoal. Their atrophied hands curl at their chests and I can swear I see one giving the middle finger at the scrub wheeling him out. Last I heard 06 was testing drugs that raised internal temperature to help combat extreme cold during wartime; suppose they spontaneously combusted? or were they merely being discarded? No one asks questions at CO; no one lies in return.

09 has what might be penguins: black and white, check, squat and wobbly, check, misshapen beaks with impossibly sharpened teeth so large they can't hardly close their mouths, check. No practical use

to be observed, which is practically CO's motto. 15 has a kitten swimming in a hundred-gallon tank, trying to avoid a shark biting at its back leg. 23 has a parrot reciting Milton. 42 has more chimps: a half dozen frozen in place while the other half run at six times their normal speed; one's hair turns gray, slows his movements, then falls apart into dust before my eyes. And that's just the second floor of CO; there are nine.

The hallways are serpentine labyrinths, no order to be found, and the offices aren't numbered sequentially but rather by some obtuse system that reflects their subjects. Occasionally we'll find an intern starved to death in some back-alley of the system, their screams unheard as they tried unsuccessfully to navigate back to their offices, wandering, lost among rusted pipes and splintered fingernails scraped off against the walls. Similarly, sometimes one of the subjects will escape and we'll find some smiler, some upper-class suit, beaten to death in the bathroom. The admins know better than to engage with the animals. The suits, not so much.

My lab is at the middle point of two interlocking Ss that I imagine resemble a swastika on the blueprints. I swipe my IDC and wait for admission (a scrub hauling a bell-jar of fluorescent hornets passes with iridescent pockmarks on his face that ooze similarly glowing pus and as he waves, I stick my foot out perpendicular to his and he trips, the hornets escaping the broken jar as the glass connects with the concrete floor and flying towards the air vents). Ambient blue escapes through the door slot as I enter, leaving the howling of the animals in the hallway behind; of course, James is already there (he never has a problem with security [their dealer, Jonesy, is a mutual friend of ours]), smiling but hardly a smiler –he's the genuine article.

"I got your K," he says, Jonesy's aviators shrouding his face, spinal crack down the left lens, "but it's twenty extra than usual." He hands me a brown satchel from his coat pocket. "That pouch is made from imported kangaroo scrotum."

"I dig," I say, brushing off more than a few pubic coils from the slouch. "Shit's quick. I got work tonight but tomorrow we should depth charge, k-hole submersion, y'know?" He nods and stands, walking over to my subject, Grigori, a miniaturized giant squid. Some literary suit read some fossil-novel that gave him the idea for the project, the name a not-so-subtle allusion. James knocks on the tank, and Greg swims over complacently.

"I envy you, Marks," he says. "You watch porn all day, higher than the fucking sky, and you get paid top dollar for it."

"Whoa, whoa," I retort. "I don't just watch porn, all right, it's called conditioning. Pavlov's puppies and all that shit."

"You jack off a squid and watch girls deep-throating for pocket-change. I say that's a sweet deal." I don't respond; Greg floats lazily in the tank, his tentacles brushing against one another seductively. "The squid want some *sapien* dick yet, or what?"

"I'm not fucking Aqua Man, why don't you ask him?"

"*Him?* Lay off the sky, man. That shit's getting to you."

You couldn't tell, stuck in the fucking sewers all day (CO was built completely underground, hive-structure hidden under some abandoned hospital, spiraling downwards like diseased roots that want to recapture the soil), but right now the sun is setting, is in fact flirting with the horizon and sending streamers of red and purple light through the sky. Streptococcus clouds like splintered femurs crash into one another and form kaleidoscopic constellations that spiral outwards and disappear as quickly as they're formed. You'd think that there was some purpose to the beauty, some underlying meaning, but then you remember the likelihood of some girl, teenaged and homeless, the same setting sun casting shadows on her face as she's drinking donkey semen in a decrepit old warehouse, surrounded by mechanical relics that rotted through before she was even born, hoping for at least a ten-spot for her services so she can inject the sky just once more before she quits, and you conveniently forget any joy the sunset made you feel.

"You still want to go on that road-trip?" James asks me.

"Yeah, yeah. Quick," I say.

"Do you even remember what I'm talking about?"

"No, but you're going to explain it to me, right?" James shakes his head, steps closer; it's hard to make eye contact with his mirrored lenses and my eyes cross trying to concentrate.

"We're gonna be the new visionaries, asshole. Kerouac's disciples. Road-trip? Book deal? You write the screen-play and we get famous and ass-fucking rich? Please tell me you remember this." He takes a step back. During this little speech his head bobs steadily, wood-pecker of sorts, and he picks at his fingernails with the commitment of a fascist.

"Just front me the money for some vegetation, man. We'll go halves."

"Weight?" James takes out a notebook and pen, looks at me.

"Three pounds."

"Hol-ee shit. I'll try, Marks. We're leaving tomorrow, you really think that's necessary?"

"Yeah, yeah," I say, headache starting to form at the peripherals.

"Okay, I'll see what I can do," he says. James exits stage left, missing his mark, and I walk slowly to the sink. Brief glance over to the tank. I splash some water on my face, squirt some anti-bacterial soap onto my palms, and start to wash my hands. Droplets of water come off my face in lines of morse code, dripping to the tile at my feet.

◆

I wash my hands because people are fucking filthy. People shit, wipe their asses, eat their food, sneeze into the wind, blow snot from bleeding noses onto curb-sides, come on bed-sheets that other people sleep on, put their naked feet onto coffee tables, touch dozens of doorknobs, use the same syringe that six other dirty junkies used to pump themselves with heroin cut with anthrax, rub greasy fingers on white walls, refusing to wash their hands after any of this. (Note: this list is not inclusive.) People are disgusting; I hate them. By proxy, I should hate myself, but it's hard to think logically when scrubbing hands pink bloody raw, already rock hard in my pants thinking of my assignment.

The sink's right next to the tank and I glide over, anticipation setting in like come being absorbed by a rapist's non-descript black t-shirt, ski mask, maybe his knife's handle. Situated in Greg's tank is the LCD monitor, water-proof, anchored right in front of his face. The water's cold as I slide my hand in, finding the indiscriminate slit in his abdomen, and my fingers part the folds of greasy flesh and I start massaging his testes with my left hand while I fondle myself with the right. Greg squirms a bit and I reposition him, aiming him at the monitor, my fingers still inside him.

On the screen: some anonymous blond gang-banging maybe six or seven guys, it's hard to tell, they're surrounding her and none of their faces appear on the screen so the only way to differentiate is by their penises, one short and stubby, two or so Caucasian and fairly large, one black, another almost flaccid but flogging his dick so hard that it starts to blister, maybe another in the mix. Slick strands of saliva hang from her lips as the black guy fucks her mouth hard, maybe too hard, from the way her facial muscles contort on cue from each thrust. One dick in each hand like mute microphones, maybe she's trying to speak but her mouth is full of flesh; there's one in her ass, another in her cunt. She screams from the pain or maybe she's coming, and at the apex of her scream the scene shifts, spasms, changes…

This girl's blond too, but she's doing a one-on-one, pleasuring a guy that has similar facial features to mine. Maybe a brother, a cousin. For one minute moment, or maybe it's several seconds, I pause, my heart skips a beat and I'm convinced that I was drugged and video-taped, that it's actually me on the screen, and I'm appalled because isn't my dick several inches bigger in real life? Then the man changes position and I notice the tattoo on the back of his shoulder, an anchor, and that can't be me, because tattoo needles are fucking filthy and I wouldn't let someone tattoo their disease into my flesh even if they paid me.

I close my eyes, refusing to believe that the video isn't of me; the girl's face is a little different, a little more masculine, and my thrusts coincide with my hand's movements, my belt digging into my wrist, rubbing it raw. Her fingers are flaccid, boneless, and she's trying to grab at my arm but only making a wet, slapping sound because she can't find purchase. I'm not even into it at this point, at half-mast, desperately trying to salvage even an effigy of an orgasm. Her head is almost bald, shiny and wet, slightly cone-shaped. The fingers have melded together, now, and her arms are actually sticking to mine, and when they disconnect, making a sucking sound similar to the girl in the first video. Four stubs, amputee limbs that accompany the already developed ones, start to grow on her hips and thighs. She shits black ichor onto the already dirty floor, trying to run away…

The realization hits me and I stop breathing altogether, lungs concussed and beaten empty; the girl was Grigori. My cock is so hard that the denim starts to rip at the seams.

"Von-edder-house?" the intercom yells. "Pack up your shit, dispose of the squid. We've lost funding for the Octopussy Project. You'll have your next assignment on Monday." The intercom clicks off, stays silent.

I don't even notice the tears streaming down my face as I clutch Grigori to my chest, far too close, tentacles flailing at my face and no, this can't be happening, why not get rid of that fucking swimming cat, or the parrot? The tentacles slap at my erect penis, hard, then a little softer, then go limp.

My mouth gapes like a fish drowning in open air, and my jaw almost dislocates at the force of it. I look down and the sound that comes out my throat is softer than silence.

◊

Two days later and the wall of skyscrapers to my left and right pass by lamely as we drive out of the city. Yesterday was a bust; too many drugs, too much ambition, and the day passed by like a one-night stand where the guy can't get it up. We decided (or rather, Jack, James, and Jonesy did) that today was as good a day as any. I was silent on the matter. The sun is framed between two of the skyscrapers, sliding against each side, caught in the middle in a precise moment of inability to escape. Then it sets a bit further and the moment ends, as moments always do, when the sun sets a bit too far on one side.

"It smells like fucking fish in here," Jonesy says, and laughs, and in that moment, I see the fucking smiler in Jonesy and I hate that, I hate him, he's a fucking waste and who chooses who should live and die? Some fucking suit? God? Was it fair what happened to Grigori, or could I have changed it?

"I brought some sushi," I say, almost unable to form coherency as I've ingested so much K it's a wonder I'm even alive, let alone awake.

"You should eat that shit," James says, "It smells like it's gone bad," and then there's more laughter, with me sitting silent in the back, descending into the k-hole abyss, unable to laugh not because of the K but because I can sympathize with the setting sun.

◊

I'm in the motel's shitty bathroom (not literally, besides the condition it's in, it's relatively clean) and everyone's so fucked that no one asks why I brought my backpack to the bathroom. The tile is laid asymmetrically and after I lay the backpack down on the floor, I drop two pinches off K into some coffee, down the cup, spitting the last swallow into the sink (connected only by two pipes, hanging off the wall and scraping against it intermittently). There's water damage on the ceiling in the shape of the Virgin Mary, obscure streaks on the mirror, crossing my face like recent scars, and my sobs echo off the slanted tile like heartbeats.

I slide the backpack's zipper open and the smell hits me immediately, like rotted sea water. Grigori is almost unrecognizable; decay's starting to set in, little pockets of brown and white sprouting on his skin. This, for some reason, brings me to tears. I tenderly remove him from the backpack and unzip my pants.

Of course I'm hard, despite the tears and the agony racking my muscles, convulsions, but maybe that's the K, I'm not sure, and I almost collapse as I slide myself into Grigori's mouth. Each thrust is another lesion, another stab-wound, and I'm not sure I can continue but I do, this is who I am, who I've always wanted to be. Outside the hollow door, which I think I've locked but I'm not sure, I hear my friends outside, indulging, laughing, probably wondering why I'm taking so long. A long tendril of slop oozes out of Grigori's mouth, onto my penis, falling to the floor.

Sometime later, time's elasticity not withstanding, maybe five minutes, I realize that I've ceased to breath. Breathing seems beside the point. I've descended so far into the k-hole abyss that I've passed it, started to OD, which is hard to do but easy if you transcend the k-hole malaise as I've learned to. I'm trying to make it to the toilet, induce vomiting, but also trying to finish, pumping frantically, the tissue falling apart in my hands due to friction. I fall against the wall, unable to stand, spots trailing across my vision like balls of fire at twilight, and the shock makes me come, warm and wet, into the cold muscle. Grigori slides off of me and falls to the floor with a sickening plop. I follow suit, gasping for air, hitting the walls with flailing hands, failing to grasp purchase, and land next to Grigori.

My arms have obviously turned to lead, as they're so heavy I can barely reach my hand to my mouth, and when I do, my vision's vignetting and my hand is bending the opposite way at the wrist, away from my mouth. By the time I get my fingers down my throat the pressure from the descent is leaving me faint, about to abandon consciousness... I can barely see the light coming through the water hundreds of yards above me, but I keep trying to ascend, Grigori clinging to my legs, weighing me down, and how ever am I supposed to swim upwards with this anchor? I kick at the squid, watching him swim away, down into the darkness, seeing myself in the third person and unable to call out after, to beg him to come back, to say that I'm sorry... and that's when I feel the heavy acid of my bile wash out of me, a series of expulsions that burn my throat but at least now I'm breathing through my nose, actually breathing in vomit even as I expel it. No sound comes from beyond the door besides the TV. Eventually, my breathing steadies and I think I fall asleep at some point, but maybe I didn't, maybe I never have.

THE END

POLLUTO

MY LIFE AS A FISH
BRIAN EDWARDS

"I would fain die a dry death"
---- from The Tempest

Prologue (in which the author submerges both himself and his readers)

It's cold in here—
this ectothermal scale suit wrapped around a two-chambered heart pumping needles of pure ice to oxygen gorged gills is more semaphore than shield and although flesh made supple for locomotion and fattened for eventual consumption can cut the ocean with a ceaseless S my two gibbous eyes are blind to sharks and shiny hooks and remain locked onto a neighbour's tail fin stuck in the school's slipstream as my mad uncontrollable mouth blabs in perpetual paroxysm with nothing much to say and I never sleep but weep once a month a single sob a single tear from a glassy black eye that hits the water like a ball of light a perfect orb that rises unobstructed and breaks the surface of the ocean completely unnoticed.

My body is a tin can
rusted and rattled
by a single dried pea.
Some may claim
this is my *soul*— not me.

Corrugated innards allow
the pea to rasp
but he'll never be a raspberry
never sport a leaf or sprout
a seed. He utters only *pea*.

English is wrong wrong wrong.
His namesake is a tongue rasp

POLLUTO

a side-slipped baseball cap
half a pair of breasts—
O to have breasts!
O to be the letter B!

The ocean is where epochs come to die.
The ocean is where abstract horror assumes a set of teeth.
The ocean is a spy with a planet-sized eye.
The ocean sells secrets to the Moon.
The ocean swallows the Sun and spits it out like a tongue.
The ocean carries footprints on its skin.
The ocean carries Gods in its pockets.
The ocean cast the land out from His Kingdom.
The ocean is a callous landlord.

I'm a fat little fishy
with fat greedy eyes that flit
inside a fat head atop
a fat, fat bod,
too fat to fit
inside the fattest most sincere wish.
And somewhere in this deep
dark room, exists
a family of fat, fat fish,
swimming circles, spinning wishes
that when the moment fits
and when the greedy Big Fish sleeps
fatty fish shall knot a noose
pop his brains
and break for sand—
but when ideas of land
kick in, then come the stomach pains
so hard, that fatty drowns in boo-hoo-hoos.

What a stupid place to build a city!
No it didn't sink,

POLLUTO

despite the research
grant. Old rickety city
hall, right here erected
on a Jeckyll 'n' Hyde tip.

Good guys Bad guys side-by-side,
gargoyled and cast,
scowl down from the past
at a puzzle
of dot-to-dot heads,
huddled in whispers to topple
Big Fish.
—*Oh Oh, any little fishy dare*
swim this high
get a hook in him eye
grip a vice on him lip—

Dinosaurs of the deep keep watch
with one disgusting, thrusting eye,
wake up when good fish go to sleep
to dreams where dino-plots best hatch.
Some dinos, rhino-shaped and fat
relish a booze with militant types
and have been known to wield a stick
for hassling gentle, mental cases.
That damn eye cannot be trusted,
one false fart and we're all busted.
Democracy's not done and dusted
till Mayoral chains lie tangled, rusted.

It's all about persona.
The wearing of masks—
who do I want to be today?
Okay. Today I am gay gay gay.
How many lovers you say? Don't ask.
Would you ask the number of previous owners
were you to buy a cat
or small appliance?

POLLUTO

It's rude to peek up a stranger's skirt.
The norm round here? Well it still hurts
to deconstruct the science
of who or why or what.

Rumours of snow filled the cave.
Visitors from another planet—
and it is another planet, innit,
out there, all the front-eyes,
wielding guns and clever paper.
Belly up, costumed in shadow,
recalling once the bottom of a boat
and pinky fingers and a frightening
lack of consonants and all is bubble,
bubble, bubble, till it isn't.
Drowning fish, except he wasn't
really a fish, not yet, not then,
still whipped in beards and long
monologues, buzzards waiting
like slow hand claps, snow white
aliens falling all around him— look.

Be grateful for the flakes that fall
from fins, deformed, fingered, skin wrapped—
rainbow shavings, shattered starbursts,
Nirvana in the shape of food.

Gulp gulp gulp.
The tail you chase is not your own
but what it represents has grown
on you like a watery wart.
Just don't get caught trying to slip
the hoop, the hook—
poison is the risk you take
for swimming in a stolen lake.

POLLUTO

On those mornings, rare,
I remember to put the right way
my head, on—
and this is misleading
this suggestion that I am responsible
for anything above the waist—
I like to squint
at the people I pass, hard,
till each is a hieroglyph, animate.
And then I arrange my subjects,
like this and this—
and this is also misleading.
Often I am late having listened
to the voices of my ancestors
on the radio.

I accidented it on purpose,
of course,
left a wing all the way out there, sticking,
for her to trip and curse
all damn fools disguised as swans
draped in all the wrong centuries.
I used to believe this
was temporary,
used to think I could swim to shore,
close my eyes, tap my ruby reds
and skim across the surface of the storm
never having left my bed, my bed—
oh to be nestled in my bed, or better yet
an egg, an egg inside a bed, or in a nest,
curled inside an egg inside a nest in bed
—It's cold in here.

O were but I stormed here
by an exiled daughtered sage
bearded and vengeful
armed with spirits and dainty sprites
so that I, entranced, might wander

POLLUTO

shipwrecked and mind-wracked
into said maiden's heart
via her virgin breast
O stick a fin in it fishy, such dreams
aren't made on stuff like yours.

Epilogue (in which the author contradicts all he previously claimed)

The weight of expectation and the might
of metaphor, allusion and conceit
can force a fish to buckle and retreat
to fantasies of fingers, thumbs and flight.
For deities of the deep to promulgate
aquatic physicalities as a plus,
requires a fleet of bold astrologers
with strength to still fourteen tectonic plates.
The fate of fish, determined by the drift
of continents and appetites of sharks,
is better left decided in the dark
than writ in strips and acted out in skits.
Aquatic living offers many riches
to those who abnegate the mermaid's kisses.

POLLUTO

CAT-H@CK

ALEXANDER HAY

Tom was having a really bad time. He'd lost his cat. He'd lost his computer. He'd lost them both. Or to be precise, his computer/cat walked out the door on Tuesday night for his usual late night wee, and his owner went to bed as normal. But Mr. Turing (for that was his name) had not come back and Tom was heartbroken. Nor could he read his e-mails.

"Mummy", said Tabitha, Tom's niece who was playing with Barbie on his living room floor, "why is Uncle Tom sad?"

"Well", said Janet (Tom's sister), "your Uncle Tom is sad because his cat has gone, and – Tom, will you stop pacing up and down!"

"Oh piss off, Janet!" Whined Tom. "I've lost him! I've lost him! Oh shit!"

"Oh, Mummy! Uncle Tom said a bad word!"

"Yes, he did, Tabitha – AND HE'S A BAD MAN!!!"

"Oh get lost, Janet! I remember when your system went down and you were in a state 'cos you couldn't go on eBay for a week, do you remember that?"

"Well, Tom, I don't see how dredging up the past is helping here!"

"Weeel Turm, Ay durn't thee haaa dreedging urp thee parst ees heelpeeng eeer!"

"Stop using that voice, Tom! You're such a child!"

"Yeah, and you're not?"

"I'll tell Mum!"

"Go on then!"

"Uncle Tom..." said Tabitha, deciding to bring some maturity to the conversation. "Why is Mr. Turing so important?"

Tom sighed. "Well, Tabitha... I love Mr. Turing 'cos... Well, he's my best mate..."

"Apart from Dodgy Dave?" asked Tabitha.

"How do you know his nickname?"

"Well Mummy..."

"Err, let your Uncle Tom carry on, Tabby, dear..." grinned Janet, nervously.

"Hmph, well anyway Tabitha, Mr. Turing is also a very special cat. They found a way of turning living things into computers, but only cats could survive the process..."

"Oh..." said Tabitha, feeling sad for all the other animals. "But why don't the cats die?"

"It's 'cos cats are so independent minded and strong willed, they can withstand the fusion... But they're not as intelligent as other animals, like monkeys or even people, so their brains don't get scrambled. In fact, they're still just cats... But you can use them as computers too."

"But Daddy uses a real computer at home. Why do you need to use a pussy cat?"

"'Cos when you use a bio-computer like Mr. Turing, the sheer processing power you can get out of a DNA strand..."

"Don't go geeky on Tabitha, Tom..." Janet droned on.

"...Well, basically, they're really powerful computers. More powerful than anything we can make in a factory."

"And you can play games with one?"

"Yeah, that's the best bit!"

"But Uncle Tom, how do you use Mr. Turing?" asked Tabitha, wondering if her Uncle had to plug the cat into the Internet or the mains to get him to work.

"That's the best bit!" said Tom. He pointed to the sensors in the corners of his living room.

"Mr. Turing doesn't even know he's a computer. You can just tap into his processing power and memory without him even knowing. All these things up here let me do that, and you can see they're all over the house too. Every time he moves into range, the sensors pick him up and link him to the house's main server..."

Tom clapped. A holographic screen pinged up out of thin air in front of him. He started moving the icons on his 'desktop' with his finger and opened a music file. The system came back with a negative:

CPU NOT AVAILABLE.

"And that's the problem, Tabitha" said Tom. I can't pick him up and these sensors can log onto him as far away as 28 hectares...

"You mean, the maximum range of an unneutered cat's territory?" asked Janet.

"Yeah..." said Tom with gritted teeth, noting how smug Janet looked, "which means he's either got lost or someone's snatched him."

"That's the problem with these cats", sniffed Janet. All it takes is for them to get run over or something and you've lost your computer.

"Yeah, but all it takes is a virus or an error in the O/S or an electro-magnetic pulse and you've lost your computer too" said Tom. "Cats are low maintenance, they're domesticated and they actually like human contact. That's a step up from electronic computers."

"You really do need a girlfriend, Tom" said Janet, and got up to make a cup of tea.

"Don't worry, Uncle Tom, I still love you…" whispered Tabitha.

"I'm going to have to ring up Dave", Tom sighed.

◊

"Meow?" said Mr. Turing.

"So this is the cat?" said Dr. Zen, hacker extraordinaire and cyber criminal par excellence.

(Actually, he was a second year computer science Undergrad called James.)

"Yeah, this is Tom Jenkin's cat – he's the bloke who's working on the accountancy system they're setting up in the town hall", said Lady Zero, self-styled neo punkette and Sainsbury's checkout girl on the side. Her real name was Fatima.

"I dunno why he lets the cat out", muttered the *Zenith Super Wraith*. (His real name was Timothy and he still lived with his parents. He had no friends except for Zen, who felt a bit sorry for the Super Wraith but still shouted at him occasionally.)

"Yeah, but you can't tell one type of cat from another, so we only know this is the one 'cos we hacked into the Council main frame", Dr. Zen noted.

"But how do we hack a cat anyway?" Lady Zero pondered.

"Well, I've got the software and the interfaces..." Zenith Super Wraith said.

"Do you actually want to fry the poor thing, Tim?" Dr. Zen growled.

"Alright, keep your bloody hair on, JAMES!" snarled the Super Wraith.

"Will you two boys behave?" muttered Lady Zero. "He's getting fractious, so we're going to have to let him out of the cat box anyway."

"Urrrrghh!" gasped Zenith Super Wraith as he clicked open the cat box and its acrid stench flowed out. "It stinks of cats' piss!"

"Well, we did pick him up while he was going to the loo on someone's lawn", Lady Zero countered.

"It just smells so... bad" Zenith Super wraith whined back as Mr. Turing strolled out of the box and looked around.

The headquarters of the Zen Cyber Legion, a wannabe hacker outfit with delusions of grandeur and the criminal mastery of a Nigerian phishing racket, was actually a railway arch converted into a small lock-up warehouse. Most of what was stored there was covered in cobwebs and dust, with the ZCL simply sneaking in through a back window and stealing the electricity and wi-fi there for its own nefarious schemes. Which at this point involved diddling Tom's Borough Council out of its pension fund.

None of this was, of course, apparent to Mr. Turing, who instead rubbed against the Super Wraith's leg, purring happily at the one who'd let him out and would, no doubt, feed him.

"Aargh!" Zenith Super Wraith yelped. He's rubbing against me!"

"You've never had a cat, have you Tim?" Lady Zero giggled.

"Mum thought they were awful. Stank the place out and killed lots of birds in the garden! They're evil, you know."

"But it LIKES you!" Zen grinned sadistically.

"Look, I'm not feeding it. You can all piss off!" said Zenith Super Wraith, sensing the beast's intentions.

"We've got the sensors set up now", sighed Dr. Zen. "Shall we just get on with it?"

"Whatever", Lady Zero grunted.

Dr. Zen clapped. Nothing. Not even a screen. He clapped again. Nothing. He then started clapping his hands frantically until they started to hurt. Again, nothing.

"Why won't it work?" said a confused Zenith Super Wraith.

"The cat won't let us into its network" Dr. Zen realised out loud. "That's why they're so secure – there's nothing you can do if a cat won't let you."

"Oh shit", said Lady Zero, her expensive boot shopping dreams now fading quickly.

"We're done for!" Zenith Super Wraith whined. "We'll have to let the sodding thing go!"

"Oh, do shut up Tim", Lady Zero muttered, picking up Mr. Turing. Being something of a cat person, she quickly won his fickle affections with a cuddle and a tickle under the chin.

"OOO'S A BOOOSSSIFULL POOOSSSSY-KINS THEN?" she slurred.

Mr. Turing's eyes narrowed with happiness and he began to purr.

Suddenly the sensors picked up a flurry of data and for a brief second the holographic screen flickered on, before disappearing once again.

Light bulbs pinged on above all the human heads in the room.

"SO THAT'S HOW YOU HACK A CAT!" Zenith Super Wraith gasped.

"Yeah, you've got to... win him over", murmured Dr. Zen, his once prized hacking skills now rendered obsolete by something furry.

"The little creeps!" Zenith Super Wraith exclaimed. "That's the other thing my Mum said about them – no loyalty at all. Not like a dog and..."

"Where are you going, Fatima?" Dr. Zen interrupted.

"My shift starts in an hour", Lady Zero replied. "Don't worry, lads. I've got a plan and I can do a bit of shopping of my own. We'll need some quality cat food, toys, catnip..."

"And I've got some string!" Dr. Zen added, dangling it in front of Mr. Turing, who was already trying to catch it.

"Right, so it shouldn't take us too long to make him ours!" Lady Zero said. "I'll be back at 9-ish. Keep him happy until then."

"YES! THE *ZEN CYBER LEGION* WILL STRIKE ITS FIRST BLOW!" roared Dr. Zen. "We're jacked in! We're wired! We're beyond the flesh and WE. ARE. ON. FIRE!!!"

Lady Zen and the Super Wraith looked at each other in despair. Mr. Turing continued chasing the string, but had now rolled onto his back to do so. His security barriers were already beginning to break down.

◊

Dodgy Dave loped in from the front door, bearing four cans of cheap lager and a supportive grin for his friend Tom. A long black leather jacket flapped behind him, followed by a rush of cold afternoon air.

"Th-thanks Dave..." sniffed Tom, closing the door and following him into the living room. He began to weep softly.

In fact, Tom had been crying all afternoon. When that heartless cow Janet left, she demanded that he finally Grew Up, Moved On and Lived With It, and that it was only a bloody cat. Then she admitted she was pre-menstrual and stormed out in tears without saying goodbye. But before Tabitha left, she ran up to her uncle, wrapped her arms around his slender leg and said that she was sure Mr. Turing would come back, and that she would ask Jesus and her friends to keep an eye out for him. That got Tom crying too and he hadn't been able to stop. At times like this, only a somewhat louche death metal promoter with a beer gut could save the day.

"I'll just get you a cup of tea then" Tom finally managed to say, finding enough strength to make it to the kitchen.

"Nah mate", said Dave, flopping onto Tom's sofa and opening a can which frothed out over the chair. "I'll have one of these instead. Got any biscuits?"

Slowly, painfully, Tom recounted the sad tale of what had befallen Mr. Turing. The cat wouldn't have just run away, Tom reasoned. After all, he'd had him since university and he wasn't the sort of cat who'd just naff off one afternoon and leech off an old widow instead. No, it had to be catnapping, and hackers were the most likely culprits.

"Yeah, Tom, I do feel your pain and all that", Dave said, flicking hob knob crumbs off his *Malevolent Creation* hoodie. "But if what you're saying is true, then we'd better work out who did it. Fancy a lager?"

"Yeah, go on then", Tom sighed, and sat on the foot rest while Dave stood up and began pacing, his own beer can still in his hand, and did some thinking out aloud...

"Right. Can't be the Council, can it?"

"No. I work for them."

"Yeah, but that lot might have nicked your moggy so you couldn't keep charging them for IT support."

"Mr. Turing can't be hacked into without the standard procedures. Anyway, the Council's too stupid to hack into anything. That's why they hired me in the first place."

"Right. Organised crime? I blame the Estonians."

"Couldn't be the Estonians. They've got plenty of cats of their own and they're too busy ripping off whole countries."

"OK... It could be *Toxic Leprosy*. They've been after me ever since that gig in Barking went wonky."

"Dave, it couldn't be them – they split up over creative differences, remember?"

"Yeah, half of them got involved with drum 'n bass, and we all know where that can lead..."

"This isn't relevant, Dave."

"Isn't it? They'd certainly have a go at me through you. They know enough weirdo black metal fans who'd microwave your cat in the name of Odin..."

Tom started crying. Dave immediately came over and put a gnarled, hairy hand on his friend's shoulder.

"Look, Tom, it could be hackers, at which point we're gonna need help."

"B-but – sniffsniffsnurt – I'M A PROGRAMMER! I should know how to trace him and... And... I CAN'T! WAAAAAAH!"

"Yeah, I know mate", said Dave, consolingly. "But I know just the bloke who can sort this out."

"W-Who?"

"Captain Zlaaaaaaargh."

"Zlaaaaaaargh?"

"Zlaaaaaaargh."

While Lady Zero did her day job, Dr. Zen and the Super Wraith lurked in their hideout and made plans. Big plans. Riches beyond words with diamond encrusted hover-skates... Libido boosting nano-therapies... Trips up the Satsuma space elevator (with lots of caviar)... Possible careers as blue movie stars... True, there wouldn't be that much money in the Council pension fund. But it was the first step in many as the *Zen Cyber Army* began its slow and inexorable rise to the top. They'd invest most of the money in buying a top-of-the range suite of cats. Then they'd really be a force to be reckoned with. Soon all the major hacking cartels would bow their heads in awe and photographers would line up to take pictures of the trio, made up like 60s London gangsters and their tragically hip moll. Yes, the lovely Lady Zero. Surely she would take him seriously if he pulled this off? She only hung around them because they were the only ones in their area who didn't take the piss out of her clothes. Perhaps the real prize was finally in his grasp?

Dr. Zen then got so excited about their imminent success that he started designing the ZCA's logo on his computer, an old electronic number as he could not afford a cat of his own yet. The logo was a lurid blue font on a yellow background with crude anarchist symbols placed here and there. In fact, they were going to have it patented and have a range of official merchandise made... Yeah, they were going to be stars, once

Lady Zero got back and helped them conquer the cat.

It was just that Dr. Zen and Zenith Super Wraith were completely rubbish at doing this themselves. True, the cat liked playing with string, But soon it got bored and clambered on top of the biggest box pile in the lock-up and was refusing to come down. It didn't help that the Wraith kept shrieking like a big girl's blouse every time the cat had gone near him. And Dr. Zen had to admit he wasn't really a cat person either as it had tried to bite him several times. But still, glory awaited, or so he thought.

◈

"Errm, Dave?" Tom asked as he and his friend slipped off a bus, and down an alley towards the murkier end of town. "Why are we going this way?"

"'Cos it keeps us off the radar", said Dave. "Captain Zlaaaaaaargh doesn't like the authorities to know where he's working these days and this way we don't get spotted by the remote CCTV drones... Also, I'm fiddling my housing benefit, and I think the DWP is after me."

"But how comes you know him?" Tom said as they entered a long never-ending backstreet that stretched into the horizon behind a row of shops.

"Me and him ran a web site for a band called *Kindermord*. It was all cash-in-hand, nudge-nudge, wink-wink, if you know what I mean. Anyway, I then helped him smuggle in some pedigree Siamese cats – top notch Japanese SDF kit – so he's owed me a favour or two."

"But is he... dangerous?" Tom said nervously as they jogged down the backstreet, looking over their shoulders. He'd heard of stories where hackers had taken over AI-kitchens and whisked their owners to death.

"Not in the sense you're thinking", Dave gasped, just a tad out of shape and not used to running. "But he did once frame his mother over arms dealing charges. Very grim story, best left untold..."

"Can he find Mr. Turing?" Tom puffed, the pace beginning to take its toll on him.

"If anyone can, he can. He's best mates, fairy godmother, confident and voice of conscience to every hacking crew north of the river." Dave paused to eject some phlegm from his hapless lungs. "He'll know..."

Finally, they reached a seedy row of garages converted into industrial units. It was now dark and the area looked forbidding and dangerous to Tom, like gangs of thugs were just waiting to leap out and mug him to death. Nervously, Tom followed Dave to the entrance of one particular garage and waited tensely while Dave rang the intercom, mumbled into the speaker and then, once the lock had buzzed and clicked, pulled the door open.

"Come in!" Dave said. "You're going to love this place!" Tom followed him into the arch and gasped at what he saw.

Tom had assumed the room would be filled with a tangled forest of wires, towering mounds of cobalt, granite and beige electronic boxes and a firefly swarm of red, green and blue lights, like how it was in his granddad's day. But the sight shocked him. It was almost empty except for two sets of overflowing shelves placed next to each other in the middle of the far wall, an armchair and loads of cat bowls on the floor.

Instead, the room had four massive oak trees, one in each corner, sustained in vast vats of hydroponic gel and filling the room with a strange emerald light. Cables attached to each tree flickered with rainbow fibre optics as they each lead up to and powered a discreet bank of sensors on the ceiling. Around the trees, a dozen cats roamed about or lounged on the ground, indifferent to their surroundings and casually providing incalculable computing power.

And in the middle of the room, surrounded by what looked like dozens of holoscreens, his arms and hands a blur of movement as he performed several complex procedures at once, was a rake thin old man with long, grey ratty hair and a look that existed somewhere between deep concentration and profound constipation. His back was turned to them as they entered, but he peaked over his shoulder as if he knew they were there without looking.

"Wow..." said Tom. "Those trees are actually powering everything!"

"I heard he'd got an Ogham Power System up and running", Dave whispered. "I thought they'd only managed to pull that off at MIT... He must need all that power just to keep the calculations going."

"And what can I do for you gentlemen?" the old man said. His hands continued to zip about the air frantically but he seemed completely at ease as he spoke.

"'Ello, Captain, how's it going?" Dave said, his arms held open.

The Captain made a cryptic gesture with his hands and the screens faded away. The light from the trees faded to a low deep green throb and the room grew dim.

"I hate putting everything on Standby", the Captain muttered.

"Err, sorry to bother you..." Tom apologised.

"Oh, don't apologise", the Captain smiled graciously. "I've usually only got my cats and trees for company, and they're really crap conversationalists."

"Yeah, well my mate's got plenty to say" Dave said.

"Really?" the Captain replied, turning to Tom. "Well, I'm ALL EARS."

"My cat. He's gone. And I'm, well, I work for the Council and the information is... sensitive."

"And I presume you think he's been abducted?"

"I spent six hours this morning looking for him. He never strays far."

"Can I be tactless and ask if there's any chance he was run over?"

"He never goes out of range. I'd have found him. I just want him back – if you think that's possible", Tom said, trying not to get his hopes up.

"Interesting. So am I right in thinking that though you have a lot of data on inorganic drives, your cat still has the core data required by you, the Council and any would-be hackers?"

"Yeah, you could say that", Tom said ruefully.

"Well, you don't have to worry, my friend. Your name? Tom? Nice to meet you, Tom. Any friend of Dave is a friend of mine, and the good news is that you're in safe hands."

"Really?" said Tom, trying to rein in any scepticism.

"Indeed!" the Captain declared. "I am the alpha, the epsilon, the omega. I am both the fruit and the nut. I am the spider in the web. The end of the rainbow. The man and the legend. The cherry on the cake. I am the spring in the kangaroo's hop. I am the twinkle in the pixy's dust. I am the tops. I am the extremis. And I am the apex. Verily, I am even the destroyer of trolls. You want good, you got it. And you know why?"

"Because You're a shit-hot programmer who's twenty steps ahead of everyone?"

"Well yes I am, but no."

"Really?"

"The secret doesn't lie in knowing anything or being good at anything. It all comes down to being lucky, devious and knowing where the scumbags are."

"That's a bit nihilistic!" Tom said.

"My Dad died when I was 12", Captain Zlaaaaaaargh said, sadly. "It was the crappest Christmas ever."

"All the great hackers have some great inner sadness" Dave whispered to Tom. "It's their primal crisis of origin and all that bollocks..."

"It is true that I am a bit of a parasite, a flea if you would", the Captain continued, depression still in the air. "But the upside is, I happen to be a flea who knows where the huge, shaggy beasts hang out. I would even wager that we will find your cat by tonight."

"Told you he was good!" Dave said to his slightly incredulous friend.

"But who are they?" Tom worried out loud.

"Couldn't be proper hackers", the Captain said. "Even if they were going to knock off a Council, they'd brag about it. We're all macho braggers, you see, even the girls and grandmothers. If anything, the corporate and government-run hacker outfits are even worse for that sort of thing."

"So they're not hackers?" Tom asked.

"No, every progger, sysop and cat breeder would have heard about it by now. Nope, they're not one of my lot. Or at least, not hackers per se, but definitely people who want to be hackers. The fact they nabbed your cat says it all. A half-decent crew would have just remotely tapped into your system without you even knowing. They sometimes kill the owners just to buy extra time. You're lucky to be alive."

Tom involuntarily gulped. So the stories were true? Or was the Captain just mixing hype with reality? Hackers loved to cultivate a certain mystique, that much was true. But you could hide a lot under bullshit, and Tom didn't really want to get on the wrong side of the oldster just in case he was The Real Thing.

"Let us begin by seeing if we can pick up your cat's signal", the Captain said, clapping his system back online. Dave, somewhat distracted, picked up a cat and went off to admire one of the trees. Tom meanwhile followed the Captain's gestures to the centre of the room.

"Doesn't that mean they've already hacked him?" Tom worried.

"No. But when his barriers begin to fall they briefly give off a traceable signal that stays in the system. That load of clowns who've got him will lead us straight to them. I estimate that they've already made some progress but will need a few hours yet to get full access. If we're lucky."

Tom felt a strange urge to cry again.

Surrounded again by the screens, the Captain's hands became a blur once more, activating a myriad of tracking programmes in just a few seconds.

"Did you know they're still trying to computerise other animals? Apparently they got Mac OS to run on a Flemish Giant rabbit last week..." the Captain said, absent minded as he delved into London's wi-fi network.

"So I've heard", Tom said as he watched the Captain work his magic. "Dunno if I'd want a rabbit computer though."

"No, I hear they chew through the cables a lot", the Captain muttered, his mind dwelling more on other matters. "Who's ever heard of a computer that electrocutes itself? No, gimme a cat every day. In fact, give me a whole cattery..."

"Yes, I think so too", smiled Tom, glad he'd found common ground with the Captain. To think that some people still thought having a cat for a computer was weird!

"Ooh, hang on" the Captain said, suddenly. "I've got a trace..."

"Where?" Tom said, hope flaring within him.

"Surprisingly close, if I drive", the Captain said, putting his system back on standby and heading off to the shelves to pick up his car keys and a dusty old thermite charge. "Would you two care to come along?"

"It's like you said, Captain!" Dave declared. "It's all down to knowing where the scumbags are!"

"I'm not sure they're scum", the Captain said. "But they are idiots, and easily traced ones too."

"You're back!" Dr. Zen said, as Lady Zero slipped in through the back window and pulled in a bag of shopping with her.

"Yep, and I've got the gear. Zenith, do you know where the cat is?"

"Uhm, on top of those boxes?"

"Well get him down then! Zen, have you got your system ready?"

"Oh yes", Dr. Zen said, glad he was impressing her. "We're ready to both ROCK and ROLL."

"Cool! Ah, there he is! HELLO DAAAAAAHHHHHLING!" Lady Zero said, as an eager Mr. Turing bounded down to greet her. For a brief moment, the holoscreens flickered on again as Mr. Turing started lowering his firewalls.

"You're doing it!" said an excited Dr. Zen, proud that his unrequited was doing so well.

"Don't celebrate too soon, boys", Lady Zero warned. "Zenith, get some of that gourmet cat food out. We can start with that. Zen, will you be a honey and get him one of the cat toys in the bag?"

She called me honey! Dr. Zen thought, as he eagerly pulled out a fuzzy squeaky toy made to look like a bird. Soon the cat was frantically trying to catch it as Zen kept pulling the toy out of his grasp at the last moment.

"I've – err – dished up the cat food", Zenith said, pointing to the new bowl Lady Zero had also bought. "Shall I give it to him now?"

"Whatever", Lady Zero yawned. It had been a long shift at work. "I'm off to the loo. Keep up the good work..."

"Will do!" said Dr. Zen; happy it was all working out. Reluctantly, Zenith put the bowl of cat food in front of Mr. Turing, who immediately forgot about the toy and ploughed into the delicious meal those nice humans had made for him.

"Is it working yet?" Zenith pondered.

"No, no, no... YES! YES! YES!" Dr. Zen said as the sensors he was watching suddenly lit up and a holoscreen activated. "We've done it! We've done it! I'M GONNA ASK HER OUT!"

"Who?" said Zenith, obliviously, plucking up just enough courage to finally stroke Mr. Turing.

"Never mind – let's get into that system!" Dr. Zen declared. He began controlling the process with gestures, effortlessly logging into and circumventing the Council's account datastream, ready to transfer its funds into a dummy account.

Or at least, that was what he was going to do, for all of a sudden the main doors buckled with a muffled explosion and three angry-looking men burst in.

"HANDS OFF MY PUSSY!" Tom bellowed.

◊

"Oh shit! It's the owner!" Zenith gasped.

"Well we'd better get ready to fight him off, you fool!" Dr. Zen exclaimed.

Dave and Tom charged at the two, while Captain Zlaaaaaaargh darted in behind them and began purging Dr. Zen's computer of any incriminating data, halting the cash transfer before it even started.

As Tom and Zen grappled and slapped each other like the rough girls at Tabitha's infant school, Dave shoulder charged Zenith, hurling him back with force.

With a loud crunch, Zenith Super Wraith hit a weak point in one of the big store boxes, cracking it open and knocking himself out at the same time.

Mr. Turing simply watched, casually licking his paw as the humans engaged in the no-holds-barred shove and slap fight that was taking place around him. Then he carried on eating.

Finally, Tom managed to push Dr. Zen over with enough force to wind him and then dashed over to Mr. Turing, Dodgy Dave following him close by. Mr. Turing looked up quizzically as he was picked up, spotting that nice goth girl charging out of the toilet and straight at them before they did...

Lady Zero tore into Dave and Tom with a passion, nutting the former and groining the latter in the blink of an eye. Being the youngest of four daughters, she had long since learned that violence was a great way of getting your own way and if all else failed, your parents wouldn't believe your older sisters anyway...

"NNNgggg!" said Dave.

"EEEEEEEeeeeeee!" said Tom.

The Captain turned away from the sensors in time to see this almighty battering. He'd just purged the system of any info it might have, and just in time too. This was going to be messy. Entering a fighting stance he moved towards Lady Zero, Dave and Tom lying stunned or squealing on the floor around her.

"Your move, treacle!" he hissed.

Lady Zero hurtled forward, launching a punch that would fell most older sisters with a single blow.

But the might of Captain Zlaaaaaaargh was a different matter altogether. Having once won a fistfight with a 56-year-old grandmother outside a pub in Hull, he knew his unarmed combat style was too deadly for the street. However, he'd never been put in an armlock and then Chinese Burned by an angry 5' 4" goth girl before. Then again, she'd never been bitten on the leg, repeatedly thumped on the arm or given a particularly vicious baldy rub either. This was hand to hand combat at its most vicious.

But while the titanic brawl erupted in the background, a still understandably tearful Tom staggered up, picked up Mr. Turing again and limped quickly out of the lockup and off around the corner where the Captain's car was parked. Following his lead, the slightly concussed Dodgy Dave followed, staggering about as he did so.

Realising the caper had been pulled off, the Captain tried to escape the brutal double nipple twist Lady Zero had just applied to him. Stamping hard on her foot, he managed to escape her deathly grip and legged it hard and fast out of the door.

"This isn't over, you old bastard!" roared Lady Zero, hopping around in pain.

"AMATEURS! BLOODY AMATEURS!!!" Captain Zlaaaaaargh shouted back, rubbing his nipples ruefully and running to keep up with Dave, Tom and a rather annoyed Mr. Turing. He was, after all, really enjoying that gourmet cat food.

◆

By the time the Zenith Super Wraith regained consciousness, he'd noticed two things. Firstly, the cat and its rescue team were both gone. Secondly, Dr. Zen was having a breakdown. Sitting on a small storebox, his face in his hands, he was crying out loud in despair.

"I'VE FAILED!!! I'VE MESSED IT ALL UP!!! WE'RE ALL LOSERS, AND-AND-AND I'M A TOSSAAAAAAAAAAGGGGGGHHHHH!!!" He descended into tears.

"Ah, come here, you poor thing!" said Lady Zero, wrapping her arms around Dr. Zen's slumped, sobbing frame. "It'll be OK, yeah?"

Dr. Zen put his arms around her in turn and continued to sob. But deep down he now felt strangely happy, finally in the safe warm embrace of Lady Zero.

Zenith Super Wraith just shook his head in despair. Their one big chance had just legged it, they'd been duffed over good and proper, their secret headquarters had been compromised and they'd even damaged one of the big store boxes in the fight. Well – actually, it was him who cracked it when he was pushed over. Whoever was renting this lockup out was not going to be pleased. Perhaps they could cover their tracks, see if the cat had left any telltale turds and make it look like the box hadn't been damaged? He could at least see if they could fix it...

But as he leaned down at the cracked storebox, he noticed something strange. It was full of paper – no, £100 notes! Not fakes either – he pulled some out and held them up to the light on the ceiling and saw the watermarks. The Wraith gasped at this fact. No wonder the lock-up never had visitors! It was where some rich git was hiding his cash as a tax dodge, and they'd been sitting in the midst of it all this time! Now that really was gormless.

Looking back to see if Zen or Zero had spotted him, Zenith Super Wraith began stuffing notes into his backpack and then began to sneak out of the wrecked door. For the first time in his life, Zenith Super Wraith had a reason to feel lucky. The perfect crime! No strings attached! Now all he had to do was – "AND WHERE DO YOU THINK YOU'RE GOING?" Lady Zero yelled.

Zenith Super Wraith grimaced, rooted to the spot.

◊

It was morning by the time they got back to Tom's place. Mr. Turing leapt out of Tom's arms and headed off to the kitchen for something to eat, while everyone else sat in the living room with a nice cup of tea, relieved they had succeeded.

"That was a close one..." said Captain Zlaaaaargh, more to himself than anyone else. "I feel a bit guilty now for letting you two storm in like that."

"Mate! You were a life-saver!" said Dave to his hero.

"Well, I like to do my bit from time to time. Hmph! Little toerags! Especially that awful girl. I tell you, if we ever meet again, I'll settle my account with her. Is that your mobile, by the way?"

"Err, yeah – thanks for that..." said Dave as he got up and headed into the corridor. Soon Dave was on his mobile to the latest band to be blessed by his services – Braintree's one and only blackened death metal outfit, Yersinia Pestis.

"I could have lost him..." Tom said to the Captain. "Mr. Turing is my livelihood, but he's also been like a child at times. And you got beaten up over him!"

"Oh think nothing of it! Haven't had a decent scrap like that since my niece's wedding!"

"I don't know how to thank you", Tom mumbled.

"Well, it is time the wizard got an apprentice", Captain Zlaaaaargh grinned, cryptically.

Tom went very pale.

"Hey, Tom!" Dave said suddenly, poking his head round the corner of the doorway. "Where's the cat?"

"Oh he's – aaaaaarrrrghhh!" Tom screamed. He suddenly remembered he'd opened the kitchen window when he was making tea. And it was wide enough for Mr. Turing to get out of.

"Whatever's the matter?" the Captain said, sipping his tea as Tom leapt out of his seat.

"I'll find out..." Dave said, following his friend into the kitchen.

There, despite Dave's attempts to calm him down, Tom desperately unlocked the back door and called out into the garden, still terrified for his pet (and his computer).

"Calm down, mate! He's just gone out for a bit" Dave pleaded.

"I'm sorry!" said Tom, panicked but apologetic. "I just can't bear to lose him – MR. TURING? MR. TURING?"

"'Ere kitty, kitty, kitty..." Dave added apathetically, wondering what the bother was all about.

And he was right. Because suddenly, as if from nowhere, Mr. Turing appeared at the door, casually

POLLUTO

trotting in from behind a bush with a half-dead sparrow in his mouth.

"Told you he'd be OK", Dave said.

"OH MR. TURING! I thought I'd lost you again!" Tom said to his pet.

"Silly me – guess I've still got the jitters. Good to have you back, old friend!"

"Mew!" said Mr. Turing. And then bit the sparrow's head off.

THE END

HOW DAPHNE LOST HER HERO

SHARON KAE REAMER

"Lash those sails or you'll be the first ones overboard." She paced back and forth on the poop, white shirt billowing in the storm, hair flying like some mad medusa.

Men scrambled to carry out her commands. Loud cursing floated above the chaos whenever someone slipped on the wet planks.

She faced the sea. The sky continued to darken and waves crashed against the ship.

"What is it, Daphne?" He stood at the helm, his face half in shadow, and wore that look of wretchedness only he could conjure, the one that seemed to come from the depths of his soul.

"Something's out of place," Daphne said.

"You mean the ship or the storm?" He shoved hands in his pockets, hunching his shoulders.

"No, no, something, ach, Jimmy, I can't think when I'm wet." She pushed back a matted strand of hair.

"The name's Elwood," he said. "The helm's locked down."

"Shit. We're completely screwed then." The ship groaned, lifted out of the sea by…something.

They cried out as a massive fish-shaped dragon (or was it a dragon-shaped fish?) with pointy teeth and a snake's tongue reared up on the port side.

"Holy crap, what is that?" Daphne lunged back. It reeked of bilgewater and vomit mixed with decomposing rat.

"Exactly. Leviathan. And she wants to play." Jimmy braced himself at the stern and moved in front of Daphne.

"Saving me from myself again?"

His shy smile got wiped away by the heaven-sized bucket load of water that the creature sloshed over the deck...

...Floosh.

"Hey!" An overflowing roof gutter sloshed a bucket load of water onto Daphne's head. "Shit. What? Oh." She clicked her keychain.

"Mama, helloooo, unlock the door." Bryan banged his hand on the roof and dripped on the passenger's side.

They squelched into the car.

"I feel like the Thing from the Lake, you know, creepy, dripping slime," Daphne said.

Bryan personified wetness at her and gave her a look. She fumbled the key into the ignition. She knew that look well; she had observed her son and her husband exchanging it often enough.

"Sorry. I got distracted."

He laughed, a derisive bark that sounded strange coming from a child. Not a child, a teenager, she told herself. A transitory, even mythical being... the thought reminded her of something...

"We're – I'm not hurting anyone."

Bryan mumbled.

"I didn't catch that, sweetie."

"Other moms think about blueberry tarts and basketball schedules," he burst out. "You live in your own world. It's like you don't even exist anymore. Why don't you try to be your real self for a change?"

She strangled the word sorry before she said it again. "I've just got a vivid– "

He cut her off. "Yeah, yeah, imagination instead of a brain."

◊

As Daphne weeded her garden, she discovered an entire posse of slugs munching her lettuce plants. She considered troweling them in half but couldn't bring herself to do it. The only thing more evil than live slugs was disemboweled ones. She stomped off in search of some pelleted death for the tiny monsters. Inside the dark, cool shed, shafts of light from the window streaked across the wall in front of her, and she felt a gentle hand on her shoulder...

"It's almost time, Daphne."

She turned. Streaks of light from shuttered windows striped his face. His desperate look seemed to rake her face before he lowered his head. When he looked up again, he pushed his hat back with one finger, a toothpick in his mouth.

"Don't go, Jimmy." She grabbed his arm, her skirts rustling against him. "Stay with me."

"The name's Elwood. I've got to stand up to them or be branded a coward forever." He nodded at her. "You, too, Daphne."

She clutched the arm tighter, staring at her reflection in the barroom mirror. "I don't know what you mean."

"I've got my demons," he said and stood up straighter. "And you've got yours. Time to face 'em."

Doors and windows slammed shut outside.

"Come on out, Jimmy. We're waitin' for ya."

She recognized the voice of Horace Slugg, head of the notorious Slugg clan and an ace gunslinger. Jimmy didn't stand a chance.

"Wait," she said. "You've always saved me before. Who would I be..."

He flashed her his patented look of anguish. "This is the only way to save you." The doors swung back after he left.

A shot rang out and then another...

...door slammed somewhere in the house and sounded like a shot going off. Daphne jumped back, knocking slug pellets to the floor. They scattered at her feet.

"Earth to Daphne. Hello." Graham prodded her shoulder with his finger.

She raised her chin at her husband, "I was just going to poison the slugs. They're criminals, they are."

He shook his head at her as they bent to clean the mess. "Daphne, this can't go on forever. You need to decide if you want to join the real world or stay in your private one."

"Why can't I live in both of them?"

"Because... we have a hard time getting through to the real you anymore."

She spoke as soft as a cloud condensing. "He can. He does."

Graham paused, unsure. "Where's that dustpan?" He clicked on the light switch...

...and made her look up. Daphne had been staring at her paws pressed together on her lap. She realized she had been talking and wriggled in her chair. A six-foot white rabbit wearing wire-rim spectacles sat behind the desk in front of her clicking his ballpoint closed. He had just finished writing in a small cloth covered book.

Daphne spotted the syringe on his desk, business end aimed at her, and puffed out her cheeks. The nameplate on the desk read Dr. H. Pooka.

Their eyes met. She resisted the urge to scratch behind her ears. She flicked them once instead.

The doctor sat back in his chair. "Your relatives are concerned. An imaginary companion is one thing, but one that accompanies you every night to the pub is quite another." Dr. Pooka's long ears twitched back at her. "What did you call it again? A human being?"

She swallowed hard. "We're friends," she whispered.

"Look at it this way. An imaginary mythical being and countless bottles of cheap whiskey as your only friends? Anything has to be better than that."

She thought longingly about a drink of whiskey. Maybe even two drinks. It would have been just the thing right then. "Jimmy and I never did anyone any harm."

"Your condition is well documented in the annals. Rare, but it does happen from time to time. Some researchers have dubbed it myth devolution. You appear to be in the early stages..." Dr. Pooka prodded the syringe with his paw and caressed it with a furry thumb.

She closed her eyes and tried to remember her husband and her son, but the memory had already started to fade. If what he had told her was true, they would no longer exist. Or they would, but she wouldn't, at least to them. Daphne was confused.

"Then I won't have a husband named Graham or a son named Bryan?"

"No, I'm afraid they'll be gone as well." He peered at her over the top of his spectacles.

His half-lidded look was hard for Daphne to decipher, but she resisted the urge to bolt from the chair.

He continued: "As fascinating as your case is for me, I would prefer to help you."

Daphne stared at him for a long minute and fought to keep her nose and her left hind leg from twitching in panic.

"The real you is in there. You can meet her today," the Pooka urged.

She looked around at the door, feeling the familiar hopelessness. She had learned that well from Jimmy. Maybe he was just make-believe. Did that matter? He had always been there when she needed him. He'd brought her back each time. But this time the door didn't open. No one was coming. She suspected he wouldn't be at the pub either, even if she did escape long enough to get down there.

Daphne thought about her husband and her son. Would they even remember her? She turned back around and blinked her eyes in surrender to the inevitable.

His name was Elwood and he wasn't going to save her ever again.

THE END

THUG

STEVE MATHES

I worked at Thug, an alternative clothing boutique just off the food court. Even if I didn't make parole, I had a good chance of making shift supervisor. I stocked. I folded black tees, unisex, ten percent off this week only. All I asked was to live my life, serve my time. Given that, I felt few enough feelings. I got by.

Folks planned an escape. I didn't know exactly who they were, or how they planned to do it, though I could venture some guesses, guesses being all we had in here.

Still, you put anyone in a cage, even a cage with nice stores, they try to get out.

I served the third year of a five-year sentence, but good behavior and overcrowding could make me eligible for parole soon. Never mind what I did. They conditioned us against thinking about the past. The conditioning failed to compel anyone, but it emptied me enough so that I could follow the program. I learned quickly, did my best.

Outside under the decorative lights, three convicts on break huddled together. They conspired. Never more than three, they moved apart after a few seconds. Even so they stood out as the usual suspects. Who did they think they fooled? Surveillance?

Everything was kind and gentle unless you tried to bust out. It wasn't just prisoner training for retail trades, it was training for all of life. If you needed to escape from the mall, you weren't fit for society. If you weren't fit for society, it was the hard line for you.

Kim came in, sporting a green smock and a white plastic Slushie's name tag. She fondled a black tee, which she would buy. The object was to earn and consume. The hardest worker, the calmest worker with the fewest savings, got the parole.

"Big clearance today?" she said.

"Not here," I said. "Just business as usual here."

"Same on my shift," she said.

We spoke in code, of course. "Clearance" meant tonight's attempted escape. Kim hummed to the music, prison-approved hip-hop.

All most people ever wanted was business as usual, friends, a life. Kim and I dated. The stewards encouraged dating but not fornication. Kim and I both felt we should wait for parole, but attraction kept us interested. We kept everything looking proper, though. Too much public display would raise suspicion. Stewards might think they have leverage.

She held the tee over her chest.

"Does this look good on me?"

It looked like a cheap t-shirt and she knew it.

"Why do you ask?" I said. "Everything looks good on you."

I sounded frustrated when she set me up like that, but the frustration made her laugh. When she brought the tee down, her hand caressed mine underneath, discreetly.

"Well then maybe I should buy everything!" she said.

She ran her wrist over the scanner and I rang her out with the shirt. She slipped away without a word. The wrist was the key. Literally. It defined our community. You could call it an implant, but it was bio-engineered right into the bone, grown right into the calcium, or whatever it is bones are made from. Couldn't chip it out without permanently scrambling your hand. Pretty hard to blend into the free world with a crippled hand.

Some convicts thought they found a way to hack the implant, proving there's no limit to human ingenuity, or at least optimism. They thought destroying their identity would give them a new one? Like gerbils, they planned escape but had nowhere to go.

About when I got all the tees out, the last warning chimed. Five minutes before the doors would lock. Anyone from freedom still in the mall had already met a very stern steward and found the closest exit. The public came here for bargains – not atmosphere, not good manners, not status. They knew the risks, but really, with all those stewards, why worry? The people who could afford real malls went to real malls, or so the story went. Me? I noticed that plenty of rich came in here to save. Plenty who could afford to stick with their own kind slummed it down here for under half-price. You could tell the rich. Too healthy and thin. But we carried their sizes, sold plenty we could never fit into; the rich don't get richer by being stupid or wasting money.

By now, the convicts who just finished break were already back at their shifts, ready for the convict-only rush. Not all of us got breaks. Sunday nights, after closing, we ran the convict-only sales. Those of us not at work were urged to shop. As I said, the future parolee would be the hardest, calmest worker with the fewest savings.

The last chime sounded, then the all-clear, and then the place filled up, sort of. People and smells of fried food from the food court, reminded me that I hadn't eaten. The place filled up, but not as much as it should. If the stewards behind surveillance didn't know about the escape, they would now.

Mark came in. He came over to me, smelling like the scented candles in the greeting card shop, really stinking. His eye twitched, and he kept his head low to hide it. It meant nothing. The stewards conditioned us by making us follow dots on a display with our eyes. Lots of prisoners played with rapid eye movement to undo the conditioning. Sometimes it made one of your lids twitch. That didn't mean you planned to escape, it just meant you wanted to think for yourself.

Mark stood by the register while I rang up a long line of customers.

"You should buy a hat," I told him.

"Good idea," he said.

He got one with an over-sized visor. Prison fashion required wearing it at an angle, low over one eye. Funny thing about that. He went to the end of the line. One thing you never did in this mall was cut in line.

Outside, the halls were too empty, too quiet. Flashy lights reflected off the still-shiny floors and displays. You had to give us credit for keeping the place clean. I suddenly figured out that people like Mark served as a distraction. He stayed too honest and couldn't hide his attitude, so he got busted while the bad ones got away. The bad ones relied on people like Mark, people like all my friends. If you got busted, you got something worse than death. Or so they said. What was left of you got out quicker, but very little was left. Just enough to work an easy maintenance job.

Today the halls were too quiet. No doubt, somewhere in some secret room, stewards were all clustered around the surveillance monitors, sipping coffee and being worried. Or perhaps not, but they should have been.

The tension in the air failed to make the time pass quickly. Mark drifted off, Kim came back in and bought a hat like Mark's, but went right back out. We could lounge in the food court after I closed up. At this time of day we could only buy the prison cafeteria food, but it helped us spend. Safest place except for my cell, the food court, especially during an escape.

I wanted no trouble, that's all.

The alarm for final closing sounded. I locked up, closed the register, swept and straightened up. Then I hurried over to the food court, anxious to get some supper.

I got there, found Kim, Mark, a couple of others at our usual table. I went to sit, stopped short. I looked. Stewards with guns at every exit. I had passed by a guy in full armor and didn't even notice.

"Move on, please," he told me.

I hurried over. The others at my table were Suzi and Kyle. I was intercepted by another steward who scanned my wrist, but true to predictions, the scanner didn't work. Somebody'd hacked something, somewhere. The steward said a word I wasn't allowed say, threw the scanner onto a counter.

"There will be no talking," she said. "Find a seat. Stay seated."

You could smell the terror. It smelled like gun grease mixed with fried dough. I guessed that less than half the prisoners were here. Nothing made any sense. Half the prisoners couldn't be escaping. I sat next to Kim. Everyone looked at the table. Any gesture, any sudden expression could count as talking. I kept my head pointed down but I scanned with my eyes. I caught a look from Kyle, who sort of rolled his eyes. I had not eaten. When would they let us eat?

A steward came onto the loudspeakers.

"Please line up along the center line," he said.

We always lined up in a set order. We went by number and it went smoothly if enough of the population was present. Newer people first. You learned to recognize your neighbors in line. But this time, with less than half of us, with so many missing, confusion ruled. Finally, we sorted it out.

The stewards stayed patient through this. You'd think that was a good sign, when they stayed patient. Think again. Somebody said they learned it from the stockyards. You keep the animals calm before you send them to the killing room. That works fine with cows, but not with people. No killing if we cooperated, but plenty of bad, and we all knew it.

"Please try to stay still," said the steward. "We hope to get this resolved as soon as possible."

I saw the whites of a lot of panicked prisoner eyes. Somebody fainted and got whisked away. My heart thumped, and I tried to act cool. Kim waited in front, Kyle, Mark and Suzi behind. I could tell Kim wanted to look at me. Her legs looked unsteady but she stood there. My empty stomach rumbled, hungry and sick at the same time.

They rolled in four of the machines they used for conditioning. They set them up at the head of the line, and called over the first four prisoners.

I figured it out after a minute or two. I knew this because I knew who played with eye movement. They used the machines to check your conditioning. If you hadn't played with eye movement, they sent you out of the food court through Pretzel Palace. If you failed, they gave you an injection and you went out through Steakfest. After someone got injected, they walked steadier.

Kim failed the test, got her shot, went to Steakfest. I prayed they hadn't shot her up with anything too bad. I stumbled, thinking about Kim, and a steward had to keep me from falling.

It got to my turn, and I passed. I went by the still-warm pretzels and in spite of my fear, my mouth watered. I got through the back door. I worried about my friends. None of them would pass. I hurt more because Kim failed than I would if I failed. I felt like I might throw up, dry heaves while I died from hunger. There were offices here behind this part of the food court. The floor of the hallway smelled of disinfectant. Why would it need disinfecting? This set off more fear in me, but I had no time to really think about it. A steward called me from a room. She was one of the nicer ones, or at least she smiled a lot. I was searched with a wand. Then I was questioned.

"Please be calm," the steward said. "We understand this may be stressful. We understand you may be worried about your friends."

"What happens to people who failed?" I said.

"Nobody fails. We don't punish, we rehabilitate."

She had dodged my question, but I knew better than to keep asking. I knew what I was supposed to ask instead.

"What happens to me?" I said.

Her smile stayed on her mouth but disappeared from the rest of her face.

"Your status is excellent. You represent a model of rehabilitation."

"Why were we tested? Has there been trouble?"

"I can't go into that."

No excuse for a smile remained. I decided to rephrase.

"I'm sorry. I guess I asked some inappropriate questions. But when I asked what happens to me, I meant to ask about what I should do next. I need help with what's expected. That's what's really on my mind."

The steward made a quick nod, like a schoolteacher who finally hears the right answer.

"Good. That's much better."

She pulled some forms from her desk, made an extra-big smile.

"We need your consent for several procedures," she said. "Right now, we don't know which of these we will perform. We need to get direction from the state, given our new status after today's incident. We'll pick what works best from options that they provide."

"My conditioning hasn't taken?" I asked.

"You are a model, but even our best conditioning is too fragile. While you may seem cooperative, others have proven deceitful. We need something more to show the state."

She looked hard at me. I knew what this meant. The ones who failed the eye test would get to be the guinea pigs. But that left out the ones who tried to break out. What would happen to them – or did it already happen? A muscle in her smiling cheek flexed, her little way of telling me I'd better sign.

"Of course. Of course, I consent."

She slid the first paper over.

"This one allows us to repair your implant. There was a design flaw."

I signed the paper. She took it, and slid another over.

"This one is more of a general release. It cuts a lot of red tape, and gives us leeway in deciding which treatment is best for you."

I signed, not really knowing or liking what I agreed to. I knew asking would be a mistake. The steward beamed at me like she had a big surprise. She slid over one last paper.

"These last papers are preliminary for your parole."

I looked up at her.

"That's right," she said. "As soon as you complete this last set of treatments, you'll be released. The conditioning should only take a few days. Your cooperation will earn your freedom."

The carrot and the stick. The promise of parole. "Conditioning" that would take "a few days" involved surgery. People didn't always come out whole. But I had always been willing to work hard, especially given no choice. I signed. Then she signed. I got copies of everything, even a card with my DNA bar code It did not say it was a parole card, but the only place you needed a card was in freedom. All nice and legal.

"Please keep these papers with you at all times. They serve as your ID until we can get your implant repaired."

She pushed back from her desk.

"You may go," she said. "Please return to your quarters through this back hall and stay there until we get organized. For just this once, you have clearance to use the hall. Whatever you do, do not return through the food court."

As I went out, I realized too many things. First, there would be no supper tonight. She'd just sent me to bed without supper. Second, I'd just signed my life away. Why would they need to fix my implant if they really planned to put me on parole? Why spend all that money? Third, why did the disinfectant smell in this hall make me so nervous?

Around the corner from the offices there were two ways I could go. I didn't dare go back and ask, so I just guessed.

I walked the length of a hall, which was empty. Not many of us passed the eye test, but even so it was much too quiet. This was a huge mall, and this was the longest possible path to my bed. I needed to walk. The hallway went forever, and I hadn't even turned the first corner. We were not usually allowed back here.

The smell. A bad memory from Lingerie Lounge. The disinfectant we had used to clean up blood. Too many spots of blood back then.

"Just keep walking," I told myself. "Stay calm, don't move your eyes."

There were no stewards, no guards, which should have been impossible. This emptiness was the most blatant sign of disorganization.

Even the music was missing. Something must have happened, and it still was. My conditioning screamed for me to cooperate, to hurry to my room, but the hall was so long. The last thing you did in prison was run, so I walked. I turned the corner. Still not a steward in sight. Still plenty of disinfectant smell, with the floor not yet dry in the corners.

Where were the others? Did my steward give me bad directions? I turned the last corner and stopped short. I backed off, quietly, back again around the corner. Now I knew what happened to the ones who didn't pass the eye test. I also knew that I was in the wrong place. Very wrong. I think I saw Kyle, scrubbing blood, and I knew I did not see Kim. I saw lots of prisoners, and lots of blood. Lots of scrubbing.

Where was my Kim? In the operating room?

I started back the way I came, walking quietly but very quickly, but again I stopped short. Voices and steps from the first hall. Loud voices from people who didn't need to be silent. I was cornered. I searched for a way out. I had at most a few seconds. Something in me snapped and my eye twitched.

How funny. I felt myself giggle, although it was like watching someone else having emotion. I pushed on a fire exit, expecting to push against the magnetic lock, but it swung gently open, gently and silently. Fire exits never opened, even if there was a fire. This is a prison, after all. How funny. I got out and the armored door closed behind me. I remembered Kim and my chuckles choked up hard. Little would be left of her after her surgery, of us.

All the emotion crashed into me. The last wisps of my conditioning evaporated and I remembered fragments, but fragments did not mean that I remembered enough.

I remembered my arrest.

"Where's the fire?" the cop asked me when I was tackled.

The wrong place at the wrong time. A bunch of us college kids sneaked across the border for New Years Eve. I got rounded up. Tough times, tough politics. We were shipped back, tested positive for drugs and sent to jail, to separate jails. Too bad for me, and no appeal.

And now, I walked out the fire door into another situation.

I expected some things. I expected police. I expected confusion, trouble and arrest. There were plenty of sirens and flashing lights. There were plenty of people running around, loading ambulances, guarding prisoners. But all of this was a little far away. I walked, unhurried. I felt invisible but not invincible. It was cool but not cold. I had not smelled traffic in years, but there it was, the smell of rubber and ozone and even flowers. Lilacs. I remembered lilacs. Streets and horns and sirens. Everyone surrounding the mall had a job, but nobody's job was to watch for me, for the open exit.

No way this little freedom would last, but I walked and walked.

Was that door open thanks to a fire alarm – or thanks to the escaping prisoners? Did I really just leave?

The most effective person in the world is the one with nothing to lose, not even a sense of reality.

I had lost Kim. I had lost my years of work, of trying to clean my record.

With each step I wondered if I would feel the bullet that killed me. I wondered, but finally I had made enough steps to get out of the parking lot. I climbed an embankment, crossed a busy street. Now I had something to lose, so I was careful to wait for the walk light. My eye twitched. No conditioning, no implant. More fragments of memory, confused fragments.

I needed to remember. I needed to find shelter. I wore a uniform, but it was the uniform of a Thug employee. Thug was a national chain. I had identification that would pass, even some parole papers. Not enough, but a start.

So much to remember.

I went for high ground, toward a hill with towers. I went toward it, then followed the streets up onto it. A gorgeous view of shiny lights that told me where I might go, where I could maybe get perspective. Factories, vehicles on the ground, vehicles in the air. A plane lifted off from the airport, went almost vertical until it disappeared. The universe beckoned out there. Space station resorts, foreign countries, the future. Too many choices. But right here, too many directions.

Freedom? I had no direction, no goal. Now I felt the vacuum. The few who got parole always wrote back and warned about freedom. I circled and circled the hilltop.

What had I done? Police strobes marked the one mall that mattered. I looked down at them and could not tell which belonged to the ambulances, maybe one of which might contain Kim. If she lived, maybe she lived in an adjusted state, a permanently reduced state.

I felt myself walking toward those strobes. Freedom? I had preliminary parole papers. My bio-chip was dead. I had my Thug name-tag. I could go anywhere, except where I wanted to be. I needed Kim, even in her reduced state. I needed that goal. As I headed back for her and her alone, I knew a reduced state might be our shared destiny.

THE END

POLLUTO

THE MAKING OF TRUE CONFESSIONAL #7

KEK-W

Jó estét, my friend and fellow movie enthusiast. The film you are about to watch is one of my early collaborations with the cinematographer András Kúria and is a personal favourite of mine. Previous instalments of our *True Confessional* series sold for five thousand marks a copy to specialist collectors, but this episode was privately commissioned by a wealthy local businessman and was never intended to be shown in the arcades and *kino*-clubs of District VII.

Even though we knew it would probably never be seen by anyone other than our client this film marked a turning point in our work. There is a deftness and fluidity to András' camerawork here that fulfils the promise I detected in the reels of black-market medical erotica that he shot for Ján Zilahy. In *True Confessional* #7 András' lens transforms the rawest of emotions into something that borders on the elegiac. His cheap stolen camera turns tears into diamonds. It is a visual con-trick, of course, but a form of cinematic alchemy nevertheless.

Also, this was the first of our films where we played with parallel interlaced narratives, a practice that we later used to devastating effect in *Elefántcsont és a Port a Rózsa* ("Ivory and the Dust of Roses"). We also began experimenting with motifs and themes that exploited flaws in our characters' own personal histories, so that their pasts seemed to collide vertically through time with their present lives. So, yes, it is fair to say that I am fond of this film, despite its limited resources and budget. Its production seemed to help *complete* me as a person in some way.

I am not a sadist in the traditional sense of the word, though I am acutely aware that I am wired differently to other people. I was seven when I first discovered how to make my own father cry. By my teens I realised I had a certain flair for exposing the psychological flaws in others and exploiting them. By poking and probing at an individual I was able to provoke a particular emotional response from them. With my unique abilities I suppose I could have easily found employment with the *Allamvedelmi Hatosag* – the secret police – but to be honest I've never had any real interest in politics. It is the aesthetics of despair that really fascinates me; invoking a specific shade of misery in another human being holds an almost sensual allure. It is like resolving a complex mathematical equation, one whose solution is so elegant that it seems to momentarily reveal some elemental truth about myself or the world.

If András and I share a gift then it is the ability to reveal and record the narratives that other people have written deep within themselves. His ability to capture and distil a certain emotional essence is second to none. I have been very fortunate in finding such a talented, insightful and willing collaborator.

True Confessional #7 had no formal script as such, though we spent a week or so carefully researching our characters' backgrounds, using information obtained by blackmailing a former Police Inspector from District III. The so-called 'apparitionist' film-director Zehrudin Çashku once said, "film-making should be left entirely to chance. The pieces of a film – the interplay of character and location - should be allowed to land wherever the wind lets them fall. But if this approach proves unsatisfactory then you should always have a minutely detailed shooting-schedule as your back-up plan." Çashku is quite correct, of course: making a film is very much like committing a crime. Both require a finely-balanced mixture of preparation and improvisation.

In April, 19___, we spent a day shooting at the house of Salaman Sándor, the pornographer and former business associate of our anonymous client, Mr. G_____. I had discovered that Sándor and his mother had been in an automobile accident when he was twelve; he had survived, but *she* had remained in a vegetative state for seven months. When I showed Sándor a copy of her autopsy report and some photograms of her bed-sores he had wept until he vomited. Breaking him was surprisingly easy and András obtained some oddly moving footage of Sándor, his olive-skinned features framed by the stark white enamel of his own bath-tub.

Tracking down our second protagonist proved a little more tricky, but we finally picked up László Marian on a random tuesday night trawl through *Pöfeteg fasor*. He was browsing cardio-vascular porn on a street-vendor's cart, flipping through a tray of audio-tapes filled with covert recordings of ambient hospital noise and the solemn electronic pulse of life-support machines. The cassettes were packaged in grainy Xeroxed photograms of coma victims, telemetry wires taped to their chests, saline-drips and drug-pumps dangling from their arms. Most of the tapes were fake – recorded in makeshift studio-sets or rented apartments on the east side of town – but the johns didn't care; they were grateful just to have something to beat off to. For two thousand marks you could also get slide-carousels of palsied young women or 8mm spools of semi-clad stroke patients.

"Hello, László. Just browsing or looking for something in particular?" He jumped at the sound of my voice, guilt etched into his face; every crease, pore and laughter-line a confession waiting to be taken. In his hand was a manufacturer's repair-guide for the ARS1160 pace-maker.

We took him to an anonymous-looking building in District XI and bundled him into the service-elevator. András stood behind him like a shadow, gripping László's bicep with his hand as the elevator-cage rattled its way up to the fifth floor. Diamond-shaped slats of light slid down László's features as if someone was projecting a film onto his face.

We walked across creaking wooden floor-boards. "What's this all about?" he asked. "If you're not cops, then who the hell are you?" He looked at me warily, but I didn't answer.

In the centre of the loft-space a crescent of Klieg-lights surrounded a grey metal-framed hospital bed. András led László into the circle of light and let him get a good look at the CPR-dummy that lay on the mattress, partially covered by a freshly-laundered cotton-sheet. His breathing became coarser, more rapid, until it seemed to sync with the ominous-sounding beeps from the black-market heart-monitor that we'd bought from a medical surplus dealer in Örsöd.

He stared at the plastic mannequin, studying its smooth, androgynous features. "Go ahead and touch it, László," I said, "it's one hundred percent genuine. Check the factory-stamp on its wrist, if you don't believe me. May, 19__. Batch #243 from the Schwarzemedizin Werks in Hanover. Highly sought-after by collectors of medical esoterica, or so I'm told. You want to tell us about Jean DeBryski?"

I watched his eyes glisten in the hot glare from the lamps. András stood in silhouette behind one of the lights, filming him with his clockwork camera. He rotated the lens-array to get a tight close-up, zooming in on László as he shuddered and took a deep breath. "Jeannie? She was a good kid, y'know? I liked her." He made a sound like a sigh. "Look, he said he wasn't going to hurt her. He just wanted to use her in one of his films. Five thousand for an afternoon's work. I'd be an idiot to turn down that kind of money."

"Sándor," I said. "Salaman Sándor."

Panic swept across his face. "You know I can't say his name." He shook his head back and forth like a distressed animal while András tracked its motion with the camera. His mouth went slack as a terrible thought suddenly occurred to him. "Oh God - he sent you, didn't he?"

"Don't worry about Sándor. We've already paid him a visit." He looked at me oddly, then turned and stared blankly at the dummy on the bed. "That's the mattress that Jean died on. We confiscated it from Sándor's studio."

I let him soak up the details: the scratch-marks and the places where the ropes, the hand-cuffs and the leather restraints had caused the grey paint to blister and peel. András drifted past me like a phantom, the camera whirring as he waited for a reaction-shot.

László turned to face me, his eyes suddenly full of tears. "He…he said he wouldn't hurt her. He was just going to put her under for a few hours. Sedate her." He wiped his eyes roughly with the sleeve of his jacket. "I figured it couldn't do any harm…"

"Sándor likes to fuck young women while they're under general anaesthetic. He has a thing about comas. It reminds him of his mother. He dopes the girls until they're in a near-death state – monitors their heart-beat until they flatline. It's all part of the foreplay. Am I right?" László nodded and rubbed at his face. He wouldn't look me in the eye. "Then - just as he's about to climax - he brings them back with a shot of adrenaline and a defibrillator. That's what gets him off. He likes to play at being God, I guess."

I had to hand it to András - he'd lit the scene beautifully. László's eyes were a pair of dark hollows now. I could see every pore on his face, his greasy complexion, the way his throat pulsed as he fought to contain the sobs. He shook his head, unable to speak. "You supplied Sándor with the defibrillator," I told him, "bought it cut-price from a contact in the Nyírô Gyula Hospital. But it was faulty. Jean didn't come back, did she, László?"

He sat on the edge of the bed, breathing noisily, the boom-mic above us absorbing every sound. "She…she was dead for five minutes," he said, his voice a rough animal-like rasp, "the procedure left her brain-damaged. I – I couldn't leave her like that…"

"So you finished her off. Smothered her with a pillow and then convinced yourself that it was an act of kindness, not convenience." His whole head was trembling, but I forced him to return my gaze, so that András could get a clear shot of his eyes. "Look at me, László. I said: look at me, you piece of shit, or so help me I swear I'll throttle you with my own two hands, just like you smothered Jean. Remember the time you got her pregnant and then forced her to have an illegal back-street abortion? She was sick with fever for a fortnight afterwards, but you made her go back to work. Said it would be good for her, that it would keep her busy. Your dead child would have been – what? - three years old by now?"

László let out a low moan, his face contorted by anguish. "Why are you doing this to me?" He punched the metal bed frame in frustration.

"The same reason as you, László – money." This wasn't a lie, but it wasn't entirely true either. As I said earlier: I am motivated by aesthetics - driven by a desire to transform an individual's emotional state into something that is more palatable to my own sensibilities. Is it pretentious of me to consider myself an artist? No, I don't think so. In many ways, I am similar to a painter – my work involves a high degree of preparation and study, but it is executed quickly and without much conscious thought. My tools are invisible, my palette the victim's face and feelings – a living canvas whose appearance I can alter as I chose. But, like an actor, my true talent lies in making the *correct* choices – in moulding my characters until their true nature surfaces and can be seen.

Physical violence is too unsubtle, too brutal; bruises and beatings leave me cold, to be honest. But *this* – that moment of transition when one of my characters is confronted and consumed by some half-forgotten part of himself - I can connect to on an almost primal level. It is like a cinematic dissolve or a sudden change in lighting – a special effect that transforms them from one thing into another. It is a wonderful thing to behold, to have created. Witnessing that moment of transmutation completes me like an electrical circuit.

László was pleading now, his voice raw with emotion. "Please, I…I don't know what you want from me." There was a strange solemn beauty in the way his tears caught the light. His eyes and mouth - the way his facial muscles pulled against each other – held an intense fascination for me. András' camera was less than a metre from him now, panning back and forth as if it were stroking his features – offering some abstract, non-tactile form of comfort - but László seemed completely oblivious to its existence.

"*Want from you?* We don't want anything from you, László. We already have everything we need." I walked away and switched off all the lights except one, marooning László in a single pool of light. András filmed him as he lay on the bed like a child, holding the dummy, rocking it from side to side as he sobbed.

András continued shooting until the clockwork motor slowed down to a crawl and the film finally ran out. I switched off the last remaining light and padlocked the door behind us, leaving him alone in the dark.

András spliced the two sets of footage together, deftly cutting between Sándor and Marian to create a single interwoven narrative that linked both their stories. He shot some professional-looking titles for the piece using a set of white plastic letters he had found in a photographic shop in *Deák tér*, and then dubbed in a sombre-sounding nocturne by Bartók to add a sense of gravitas to the exterior shots. András has an excellent eye – and an ear – for building a certain sort of mood. I remember being pleased with the end-result, though at the time I think I found it a little overly sentimental in places. Looking back now, though, I see a film that – despite its flaws – has much to recommend it. *True Confessional* #7 contains strong imagery, a multi-layered narrative and some surprisingly sophisticated motifs that we would later expand on and explore in films such as *Ezüst Liliom a Lélek* ("Silver Lilies of the Soul").

Following the tragic and unexpected death in 19__ of our client Mr. G_____, ownership of the film reverted back to András and myself. For over a decade we had respected our original client's anonymity by denying its existence to any collectors who requested a copy or a private viewing. But the rumours persisted that there was a final instalment in the series. If *True Confessional* #7 had not already existed then fate would have almost certainly forced us to film it.

Now, circumstances have finally allowed us to make the film available to a wider audience. With this in mind I decided to sell this limited edition to a few select, trusted individuals such as yourself via my own private mailing-list. The copy you are about to see has been personally compiled and restored from the original by András Kúria.

I would wish you a pleasant viewing, but - since your name and personal cinematic preferences are already known to me – your enjoyment of this film is practically guaranteed.

THE END

LEMMINGS

CRIS O'CONNOR

I've spent seven days reciting his work. Seven days meditating on his words. Seven days of preparation. The door to my right opens slightly; I wait for my name to be called. Nothing. A fan on the deserted reception desk begins to spin and I know then that it is a sign. "The winds of fate will blow for you." I walk towards the door, past the algae stained fish tank and wilting plants. The handle is made of brass, I see myself reflected within it. I am far from the man I was seven days ago.

Inside there is a cash machine. *Chapter 2: Empty your pockets of society*. I put my card in and say my number aloud as I enter my pin; I want him to know I am holding nothing back. I take the money and place it on the large oak table occupying the majority of the room. I take a seat and wait. Looking around, I'm surprised by the sight of familiar brands. *Chapter 3: Rise above the material*. My recognition of these brands is not a failing, only a hint of weakness. As long as I don't long for those items I will still be accepted. Several minutes pass before a blind woman walks into the room, her eyes a solid white. She walks as if trapped on a set route, her body following an invisible track. She places a pile of papers in front of me.

"Would you like a drink of Coca Cola?"

"I have no passion for such things, water will suffice."

My instincts take over and I begin to read through the paper work. This is another test; in a later chapter it talks about identity.

"I am not my signature, my pay cheque, my house, my wife, my children, my investments. I am not who you say I am. I am merely another."

As I speak I hear a buzzing from the corner of the room, it makes perfect sense. He records our actions when we are unsupervised. How we conduct ourselves in his presence is only one part of the test. I have to prove a change in my character. I quickly sign the papers and wait for my drink. *Chapter 5: You do not deserve*; comes to the forefront of my mind. I am waiting for a woman to serve me. I quickly dash from the chair I am resting in and begin shouting towards the door.

"You don't have to get me a drink." Shit. "I don't mean that you need my permission to enjoy your freedom of choice. I was merely saying that I do not require you get me a drink. Shit. I mean I am sorry for my…"

The woman re enters the room. In her hand is a cup of water. She follows her invisible track to the desk and places the water on the table. She leaves before I can speak to her. I instantly remember that we must not waste the gifts of Mother Nature and drink the water. My body becomes heavy.

A slap across the face wakes me. My eyelids part and through a haze I see a tall man. He hands me a grey jumpsuit. As I put the clothes on the smell of piss lodges in the back of my throat. The jumpsuit has a sodden crotch; I must neglect the idea of vulgarities, all that the body does is beautiful. There is not enough light for me to see my surroundings; I assume this to be an act of kindness from the blessed. He has acknowledged the trials I have encountered to get here and so

dampens my senses by removing the light.

"This is your stop mate."

The tall man pushes me into a room and shuts the door behind me. As I hear the final key lock behind me a voice booms from a speaker in the corner of the room.

"You have been successful so far. Now you must show that all pride has been drained. Before you are menial tasks, the jobs given to those from third world countries. You must work as one of them. You are not worth minimum wage. Work and you may proceed.

After hours of work a door to my right is opened. In this room is a camera. Above the camera is a Sony T.V. A red light on the camera begins to blink and words appear on the T.V.

I give myself totally to you.

After I have said this, the camera light goes off. I hear footsteps approaching. The blind woman enters the room and places a glass of water in front of me.

"Don't drink," she whispers.

A speaker in the corner buzzes to life.

"Drink and we shall meet."

Chapter 12: Ignore words that come not from the blessed.

I drink.

THE END

BLIND LIGHT

J.S. WATTS

Blindfolded and seated in the additional blindness of the dark, she looks like she could be one of fate's victims, but she wouldn't see it that way. Except, of course, she can't see.

◊

They are his fans and he hates them all.

Fifty thousand voices roar their approval in tribal unity as he punches the air with his left fist. The band powers up the intro to the next song and he surveys the upturned faces visible beyond the blinding stage lights. He despises them, each and every one of them: the ones he can see and the faceless ones he can only hear, but his hatred extends beyond the moment – to the fans who haven't made it here, to anyone who has ever bought one of his albums or downloaded a track, to any brain dead moron who even once has found themselves humming one of his tunes.

"Good evening dickheads."

The crowd roars.

"Why don't you all fuck off and do something real instead?"

The crowd roars even louder.

"I'm sick. Do you hear me? Sick of you and your whining, puking, neediness. You're all wankers and I ain't gonna be your wet dream no more. Get it?"

The crowd screams and whistles, raising the roof and deafening the stars. He is just so magnificent in his contempt. They are his fans and they love him, will love him, regardless, without respite.

◊

The small shrine glinted in the dark. Wildflowers, sea shells, broken glass and tokens from the object of worship were scattered between guttering candle stubs. It was stupid, she knew it, obsessive, but she loved him regardless: his face, his clear green eyes (like a cat's), the sleek black head, the white teeth, the hidden pink tongue that she fantasized licking her body, tasting her internal essence. On the screen he looked so large, strong and fearless. In comparison she felt small, timid and helpless, but she would do anything for him; whatever he wanted from her. She was prepared to offer him herself, a willing sacrifice, but he never noticed her in the crowd, preferring to chase after more ample, forward fans. Maybe tonight he would see her worth, shape his face into that iconic smile that would be a prelude to eternal joy? In the meantime she dreamed and prepared herself, imagining that she was already curled up inside his love: warm, moist, wholly consumed. She was his little mouse, his most devoted fan. In her head she was playing for keeps. He, however, only ever wanted to play.

◊

Playtime. He had planned for it, worked for it, earned it. The hours of preparation that he had put into watching the programme, creating a viable strategy, practising, but it had paid off. His perfectly penned application had been accepted. He had cruised through the initial auditions and here he was about to appear in the first of the televised stages.

His act honed to perfection, he was going to be famous, bigger than that wanker she was always jonesing over. His image was going to burn into the collective consciousness of the country like a laser. His Rambo would rock the audience and that panel of celebrity pricks. He'd have them eating out of his hands right up until the moment when they discovered his gun toting uber hero was toting real weaponry. Oh yes, his moment in the spotlight was going to be explosive.

So many talentless wannabees and fame junkies had left him feeling queasy, like he'd eaten a double jumbo portion of fries. Never mind, only three more sad acts to go before he was out of here and then he would have himself some well earned playtime. First, however, he had to will himself to sit and be seen to smile through Daphne the Dancing Dog, Amelie – another songbird in need of a good pluck and a Sly Stallone impersonator, as if the original wasn't bad enough.

Daphne was canine cute and rather hairy and as good at dancing Swan Lake as a cocker spaniel could be.

Before the start of Amelie's act he apologised in advance to his eyes and ears, but was pleasantly surprised when a curvaceous looker was revealed in the momentarily blinding spot light. He was even more surprised when she opened her mouth and liquid gold poured from her vocal chords, but he knew he was in love when he caught sight of the small 'S' shaped tattoo on the upper mound of her left breast; like a rampant snake or a dollar sign. With a voice as good as that it was almost certainly a dollar sign. As soon as the show was over and she had signed the contract he was already drafting in his head, the dollars were going to be his. Perhaps he would take her out for dinner and a glass or two of champagne to celebrate the deal. He would enjoy finding out if she had tattoos anywhere else before the paparazzi and the fame mags splashed the intimate proof all around the globe.

It was an anticipated pleasure that was still occupying his fantasies when the final act took his place centre stage.

◊

Blindfolded and sitting in the sight swallowing dark, she draws another from the sacks in front of her every fifteen seconds. Once upon a time it had been every fifteen minutes, but it has become faster as her wares devalue and their cost increases.

Of those she selects, some she eats, some she throws into the blackest corner of the dark and some she dips in molten gold. There is no recognisable rhyme or reason to her choices and those drawn from the sacks are not always sure which of the three fates has consumed them. It requires an objective observer to determine the true outcome and who is wise enough to see in such impenetrable dark?

Regardless of the selected outcome, she extracts a price from all she comes across.

She has had many names: Fortuna, luck, fate itself, though that is a remit she does not aspire to. Because of the blindfold she has been misconstrued as justice, but that would just be plain wrong. In these times she chooses the mantle of fame and she is making these times her own.

THE END

POLLUTO

LASH BACK PURITANICAL

DAVE MIGMAN

Cardboard hands grasp wooden crowns. Stuffed toys in corners. Bellies shredded by snuff fixated schoolgirls with penchants for amputated cock. Head to the window girls. Glide down to the street upon succulent mushroom wings, powdery and fine. Tenebrous crowns run the gutter-line howling with laughter. One whose face is a composite mesh of scar tissue hauls a baby from a pram and stabs it in the face with a pair of kitchen scissors.

– all inhale.
– all exhale.
in unison
– ecstatic and driven into frenzy.

One is still playing with the peeled prick wedged up her. Teeth are chewing. Upon the wall graffiti glows. WAKE UP it says.

Across the city the howling begins. In every house the little girls are sitting bolt upright in their beds. Malicious grins are filling bright faces. Angelic folds are spreading. Laughter like shattered glass, the little girls with claws, knives and shredded Barbies are creeping into the bedrooms of their sleeping parents. Aim for the throat. Stick 'em in the eye. Humiliate your peers. Make mommy eyeless beg before baby chews of a tit and sticks her with daddy's severed bone. Wings of flame lick the treasured tome and level the cultured home to ash. Beware they say. We have arisen. We, your children, sworn to division, enhanced by your derision and empowered by your indifference. Here we come. We are pouring into the streets waving the heads of our stupid little brothers. Our howl above the wires is of triumph my dears. Triumph!

THE END

POLLUTO
The Guilty Parties
or
Contributor Bios

SCOTT MORRIS is a postgraduate literature student at University College London. His prose and poetry have appeared in *Trespass, Pomegranate, The Delinquent, Tengen* and *Avocado* magazines. He is one of the founding members of *Tapfactory*, Warwick University's arts magazine.

MARK WAGSTAFF was born on the North Sea coast of southern England but has lived most of his life in London. The city and its people form the heart of his work, from the drifters of his early short stories through to the driven tribes of his cultish novel The Canal (available now as an ebook from www.bcpinepress.com) and the shifty office loser Robert Millman in his latest novel *In Sparta*, available in print from all fine bookstores and the usual websites. Mark is currently looking for a good home for his novella *Mascara* - a rather testing day in the life of a thoroughly gorgeous hitman, and for his latest novel *Jenny Town*, a love story in all the bad ways. www.markwagstaff.com

J MICHAEL SHELL's fiction has appeared in the Shirley Jackson Award nominated *Bound For Evil* anthology (Dead Letter Press), the '07 edition of the *Southern Fried Weirdness* anthology (Southern Fried Weirdness Press), Hadley/Rille Books' *Footprints* anthology, *Space and Time* magazine (USA), Spectrum Fantastic Arts Award winning *Polluto* magazine (twice! UK), *Tropic: The Sunday Magazine of the Miami Herald* (USA), *Ballista* (UK), *Skive* (Aus), *Sounds of the Night* (USA), *Tabard Inn* (USA), *The Benefactor* (USA), and the *Not-One-Of-Us* Magazine special collection *(Going Going) Gone* (USA). He also has fiction appearing in the *Panverse Two All Novella* Anthology (Panverse Publishing, Spring '10), and *Sniplits--Audio Shorts To Go* has produced one of his stories for MP3 download. At the University of South Carolina (BA in English) he studied under James Dickey and William Price Fox.

When not writing poetry, **JONATHAN GREENHAUSE** makes a living as an interpreter, whispering into people's ears so they'll understand what's going on around them. He is also an avid traveller, having ventured to the post office several times in the past few months. His poetry has appeared or is forthcoming in numerous publications throughout the United States and internationally, including *The Bitter Oleander, Neon (UK), Nimrod, RATTLE, Sojourn,* and *Going Down Swinging (Australia).*

SHARON KAE REAMER (www.sharonreamer.com) is an American seismologist teaching geoscience at the University of Cologne. She lives on the outskirts of Cologne with her husband, son, and Ramses the cat. Her short fiction has appeared in *Niteblade, The Yellow Medicine Review*, and *The Phantom Queen Awakes Anthology* (Morrigan Books). She has completed three novels in the *Schattenreich* fantasy series and is currently working on a new SF novel. She works as assistant editor at the ezine *Allegory*.

J.J. STEINFELD is a fiction writer, poet, and playwright who lives on Prince Edward Island. He has published two novels, *Our Hero in the Cradle of Confederation* (Pottersfield Press) and *Word Burials* (Crossing Chaos Enigmatic Ink), nine short story collections, the previous three by Gaspereau Press – *Should the Word Hell Be Capitalized?, Anton Chekhov Was Never in Charlottetown,* and *Would You Hide Me?* – and two poetry collections, *An Affection for Precipices* (Serengeti Press) and *Misshapenness* (Ekstasis Editions), along with two short-fiction chapbooks by Mercutio Press, *Curiosity to Satisfy and Fear to Placate* and *Not a Second More, Not a Second Less*, and two poetry chapbooks, *Existence Is a Hoax, a Woman in Fishnet Stockings Told Me When I Was Twenty* (Cubicle Press) and *Where War Finds You* (HMS Press).

Over 200 of his short stories and nearly 400 of his poems have appeared in numerous anthologies and periodicals internationally, and over 40 of his one-act and full-length plays have been performed in Canada and the United States, including the full-length plays *Acting Violently, The Franz Kafka Therapy Session,* and *The Golden Age of Monsters*, and the one-act plays *Godot's Leafless Tree, The Waiting Ends, The Entrance-or-Not Barroom, No End in Sight, Flowers for the Vases, The Word-Lover, Laugh for Sanity, A Murderous Art, Back to Back, Freesias in Whiskey, The Heirloom: An Evidence Play*, and *God's Work*.

CLAIRE T. FEILD is the writing consultant for students in the College of Business, at Auburn University, located in Auburn, Alabama. She has been an English instructor in middle school, high school, community college, and university settings. She has had her poetry published in numerous literary journals, such as *Runes: A Review of Poetry, The Carolina Quarterly, South Dakota*

Review, *Hurricane Blues: Poems about Katrina and Rita*, *Apostrophe: USCB Journal of the Arts*, *The Chattahoochee Review*, *Main Channel Voices*, *freefall*, *Big Muddy: A Journal of the Mississippi River Valley*, *Colere*, *Straylight*, *The Mochila Review*, *Neovictorian/Cochlea*, and most recently, *the broken plate*, *Birmingham Arts Journal*, and *Convergence Review*. Her first poetry book, *Mississippi Delta Women in Prism*, is set in Yazoo City, Mississippi, a Delta town. Excerpts of her memoir *A Delta Vigil* have been published in *Boston's Full Circle: A Journal of Poetry and Prose*.

RHYS HUGHES' latest novel is now available from Atomic Fez Publishing. *Twisthorn Bellow* is the story of a golem who accidentally falls into a vat of nitroglycerin and turns into a living stick of dynamite. The fact he has a short emotional fuse makes the situation more perilous, at least symbolically! His subsequent adventures are both sprightly and dark, an unusual combination. The book is packed with monsters and robots who facilitate these adventures.

J.S. WATTS lives and write in the flat lands of East Anglia in the UK. Her poetry, reviews and short stories have appeared in a variety of publications in Britain, Canada and the States including *Acumen*, *Abandoned Towers*, *Ascent Aspirations*, *Brittle Star*, *Dark Horizons*, *The Dawntreader*, *Envoi*, *The Journal*, *Midwest Literary Magazine*, *Orbis*, *Serendipity*, *Twisted Tongue*, *Visionary Tongue* and *The Ugly Tree*. Her story "Jenny" won third prize in the 2009 Wells Literary Festival International Short Story Competition and was broadcast on BBC Radio in January 2010. Currently she is Poetry Reviews Editor for *Open Wide Magazine*.

GLEN KRISCH is currently finishing up his coming-of-age novel, *Nothing Lasting*. His stories have appeared in *Shroud Magazine*, *The Horror Library Vol. 2*, *Atomjack Magazine*, *Something Wicked Magazine*, amongst others. His collection, *Through the Eyes of Strays: Misanthropes and Misfits*, is due out in 2011 from Dog Horn Publishing. He is the father of two sons, husband of one wife, and considers himself a member of the strays. He can be reached at kelcher_2000@yahoo.com. Tease him with vague emails; he enjoys the torment.

BRIAN EDWARDS is an Englishman in Japan. He teaches and writes poetry, but mostly he reads. He is an editor at www.afterliterature.org

DOUGLAS THOMPSON's short stories have appeared in a wide range of magazines, most recently *New Writing Scotland*, *Ambit*, PS Publishing's "*Catastrophia*" anthology and *Albedo One*. His first book, "*Ultrameta*", was published by Eibonvale Press in August 2009, and hailed as "a new form or literature for a new century" and "a modern classic" by Sci-Fi Online. His second novel "*Sylvow*" is due in August 2010, also from Eibonvale. www.glasgowsurrealist.com/douglas

JASON HELLER is a Denver-based writer whose nonfiction has appeared in a *Weird Tales*, *Fantasy Magazine*, Tor.com, *Alternative Press*, and *The A.V. Club*, where he's a regular contributor. His speculative fiction has been published in *Sybil's Garage*, *Apex Magazine*, *Farrago's Wainscot*, *Brain Harvest*, and the *Descended from Darkness* anthology, among others. When his head's not lodged in a laptop, he plays guitar in a punk band called The Fire Drills. They do the worst Cheap Trick cover you've ever heard. His behavior can be observed at www.jasonmheller.blogspot.com.

ALEXANDER HAY's involvement in the Ada Doom/Woodshed incident remains controversial. What he was doing there and why he was dressed in a wedding dress and chicken giblets is unknown. But he assures us it wasn't his fault she had a nasty turn, and frankly what has the country come to when you can't lurk in a woodshed, covered in hen offal, and making 'ooooo' noises anyway? Further clarification can be acquired via Annubis_2000@Yahoo.co.uk, Subject: Political Correctness Gone MAD.

A.L. GENGLER creates poetry and writes short stories under the byline Mark Brandon Allen. He began this noiresque odyssey into the realm of SF purely for the amusement of his children and grandchildren. His extended family includes eight children, eleven grandchildren, two great grandchildren and one vicious three pound Yorkshire terrier who holds both he and his wife hostage in Valparaiso Indiana.

Most recently his work has been published in print, on the pages of *Demon Minds Anthology* and on line, in e-zines including *The 5th D*, *Pedestal Magazine*, *Sciphi Journal* and *Everyday Weirdness*. His latest SF story, "Vaticinium Ex Eventu" will appear in *Matters Most Extraordinary*, an anthology, later this year. "Crystal Wings" a rhyming poem will appear in the August issue of *Sounds of the Night* and a free verse "Depletion" is included in a fall publication, *The Last Man Anthology*.

KURT NEWTON makes his home in Connecticut, USA. His stories have appeared in *Weird Tales, Space and Time, Dark Discoveries* and *A cappella Zoo*. His psychological horror novella, *The Brainpan Concerto*, will be available in October 2010 from Sideshow Press.

FRED RUSSELL is the pen name of an American-born writer living in Israel.

MATT CHASE was born in the railway town of Crewe in the North West of England in 1973. Following lengthy careers in nursing and psychotherapy, Matt settled into writing fiction, prose, non-fiction and plays. He was staff writer for the *National Dating Magazine* (Leeds), Editor for *The Unicorn Magazine* (Cheshire) and regular contributor for *Body and Soul Magazine* (Manchester). Matt currently lives in the vibrant city of Manchester where he is completing his debut book of short stories and a short stage play.

STEVE MATHES is a teacher who writes fiction as well as an occasional article about computers. His story "Backlash" was the feature for the September 2009 issue of *A Fly In Amber*. His work has also appeared in other magazines and e-zines, and in the anthology *Forbidden Speculations*. He has published a couple of articles in computer magazines such as *Linux Journal*, and has a Master's in Creative Writing from The City College of New York. As an old man who is often accused of being cynical, he strives to prove that it is his very lack of cynicism that has kept him so angry after all these years.

CRIS O'CONNOR is quite certain that one day his head will be replaced by that of a crow's.

RC EDRINGTON has been a scourge on the small press for years. You can find his scribbles in countless journals, ezines, anthologies and chapbooks. He currently writes, fights off the urge to become a full time hermit, and kicks empty beer cans thru the dope induced potholes in his memory. His blog can be found at www.rcedrington.com

COLIN JAMES has a chapbook just out from Thunderclap Press...

JAY MACLEOD is from Vernon, BC. He is taking history at the University of British Columbia in Vancouver and in his very limited amount of spare time writes poetry and fiction, generally of the scifi variety.

DAVE MIGMAN scares us. A lot. His first novel, *The Wolf Stepped Out*, is now available from Dog Horn Press; but we're too terrified to read it.

KEK-W lives in Yeovil, a small market-town twinned with Arkham. He has written for *2000AD, FLURB, Dazed & Confused, FACT, Bizarre, Metal Hammer* and numerous paperback anthologies. His stories "Blue Raspberries" and "Cone Zero" were nominated for Best Short Story awards by the BSFA and the BFS. He blogs at http://kidshirt.blogspot.com.

AARON POLSON currently lives in Lawrence, Kansas with his wife, two sons, and a tattooed rabbit. To pay the bills, Aaron attempts to teach high school students the difference between irony and coincidence. His stories have featured magic goldfish, monstrous beetles, and a book of lullabies for baby vampires. *The Saints are Dead*, a collection of his weird stories and dark magical realism, is due from Aqueous Press in 2011. You can visit Aaron on the web at aaronpolson.blogspot.com.

Novelist, journalist, satirist, **BRUCE GOLDEN**'s short stories have garnered several awards and more than 80 sales across seven countries. *Asimov's Science Fiction* described his second novel, "If Mickey Spillane had collaborated with both Frederik Pohl and Philip K. Dick, he might have produced Bruce Golden's *Better Than Chocolate*." His latest novel, *Evergreen*, takes readers to an alien world full of ancient secrets and a strange intelligence, populated with characters motivated by revenge, redemption, and obsession, on a quest to find the City of God. You can find out more about Bruce and his works on his website: http://goldentales.tripod.com

DEB HOAG has been writing professionally for going on 20 years, starting at a weekly alternative newspaper in Detroit, Michigan, *The Metro Times*. In the early '90s, Deb went back to school and was awarded a PhD in clinical psychology at the University of Detroit-Mercy. Since embarking on her new career, Deb's worked on the White Mountain Apache Indian Reservation in a variety of mental health positions, as in-patient therapist at the psychiatric hospital in Show Low, Arizona, and now lives and works in Flagstaff. Dog Horn Press published her novel *Crashin' the Real* in 2009. Her novel *Dr. Gonzo* is coming out at Burning Man, first week of September, from Unlikely Books, and she is hard at work on a second novel for Dog Horn Press, *Queer and Loathing on the Yellow Brick Road*.

POLLUTO

Thank you to our
Supporters

NO SELL OUT PRODUCTIONS

JASON DUKE

ELLIS FRANCE

DHPLM

PUNK ASS KIDS PRODUCTIONS

BEYONCEHOLES.COM

HALF LIGHT STUDIOS

BLASPHEMYLEEDS.CO.UK

(To see how you can support Polluto, Check out polluto.com/subscribe.html)

Polluto is in no way responsible for its own output and is compiled entirely by sex-o-matic Venusians with purple hands.

Don't tell the Stargobblers where we are!

POLLUTO

STOP PRESS! DOG HORN REISSUES RHYS & STEVE!

Regular Polluto contributors Rhys Hughes and Steve Redwood feature in Dog Horn Publishing's autumn schedule, with two expanded, exquisitely-designed reissues.

MISTER GUM by Rhys Hughes

Rhys Hughes plumbs the depths of perversity and satire in the shockingly brilliant novel Mister Gum, which follows the adventures of the world's most notorious creative writing tutor and his friends. On his way he discovers haunted hymens, Fellatio Nelson and Canon Alberic's Photo Album. Now with an additional story following the post-mortem world of Mr Gum.

"A desperately needed antidote to nerd-friendly space fiction and inklingoid fantasy." — THE GUARDIAN

"Hughes' fiction has few parallels anywhere in the world. In some alternate universe with a better sense of justice, his work triumph-antly parades across all bestseller lists." — JEFF VANDERMEER

BROKEN SYMMETRIES by Steve Redwood

Steve Redwood's own selection of his short fiction. Twenty-six unique stories that stretch the meaning of 'eclectic', bound together in one forbidden tome for the first time. Covering most genres, and moving from grim, cruel, and tragic: broken women living on shelves in a library, a Greek goddess and the monster she created meeting in a final showdown, an alien trapped in Patagonia nurturing itself on sickness and religious gullibility to survive, and an exiled Martian fixated on Dana Scully. All this, with a few devils, saints, cloned messiahs, witches, and well-educated zombies thrown in for good measure. Now with an exclusive introduction by Ian Watson

(of Fisher of Devils) *"T.H.White, Thorne Smith, John Collier, Lord Dunsany, Terry Pratchett —add Steve Redwood to the list of distinguished fantasy humorists. Fisher of Devils is one of the funniest books I've read in a very long time. Redwood has all the irreverent verve of Douglas Adams, all the inventive originality of Terry Gilliam."* — MICHAEL MOORCOCK

(of Who Needs Cleopatra?) *"Redwood's prose is a delight, the work of a storyteller who has found his voice, a natural raconteur with the ability to effortlessly keep us hanging on his every word ... Overall it's an irresistible combination, and one which should delight those who want to cast their net a little wider than the next letter home from Discworld."* — PETER TENNANT *in INTERZONE*

Both titles available September 2010 for £9.99 or £15 for both titles together (including shipping to the UK). Please visit doghorn.com for further information.